DAKOTA KILL

SONOMA COUNTY
LIBRARY

DAKOTA KILL

PETER BRANDVOLD

A TOM DOHERTY ASSOCIATES BOOK
NEW YORK

This is a work of fiction. All the characters and events portrayed in this novel are either fictitious or are used fictitiously.

DAKOTA KILL

Book design by Jane Adele Regina

This book is printed on acid-free paper.

A Forge Book
Published by Tom Doherty Associates, LLC
175 Fifth Avenue
New York, NY 10010

www.tor.com

Library of Congress Cataloging-in-Publication Data

Brandvold, Peter.
Dakota kill / Peter Brandvold—1st ed.
p. cm.
"A Forge book"—T.p. verso.
ISBN 0-312-87212-7 (acid-free paper)
1. Frontier and pioneer life—Dakota Territory—Fiction. I. Title.
PS3552.R3236 D35 2000
813'.54—dc21 99-51785
CIP

Printed in the United States of America

0 9 8 7 6 5 4 3 2

For my father, Orbin Brandvold,
with love and gratitude

Oh roses for the flush of youth,
   And laurel for the perfect prime;
But pluck an ivy branch for me
   Grown old before my time.

—Christina Rossetti, “Song”

DAKOTA KILL

CHAPTER 1

SIXTY TONS OF Alaskan salmon freshly hauled from her gut, the schooner *Bat McCaffrey* lay at a long T-wharf in San Francisco Bay. The high masts groaned with the gentle teeter of the ship, and the stout hemp moorings complained against their stays. Occasionally the massive hull cracked and sighed when a shiver ran down her keel.

Mark Talbot sat in his bunk in the fo'c'sle, under a brass hurricane lantern that swung back and forth with the slow roll of the ship. The air smelled of seal oil, bear grease, rotten fish, piss, farts, and cheap alcohol.

If any of the half-dozen men remaining shipboard considered him at work in the shunting half shadows of his lower bunk, they no doubt would think him repairing an old shirt. At least, that's what he hoped they'd think while continuing to primp and preen in their shaving mirrors.

If they studied him, however, they would no doubt see the torn scraps of an old blue-and-white-striped sea jersey he was sewing together, quilt-like. Given time, even the dullest witted of his cabin mates would probably figure out he was fashioning a money belt for transporting a cache of greenbacks the size of which most of them had never seen before and probably never would again.

Thrifty, most seamen were not, Talbot had found. And

that's what kept them bound to cramped ships captained by mad loners and boisterous miscreants.

That's what separated them from him, Mark Talbot, the sailor home from the sea at last.

As of tonight, the twenty-seven-year-old Talbot was an ex-drifter who had come by most of his two thousand dollars honestly. At least as honestly as anyone else who'd spent seven years rousting about this country and Old Mexico and another year working his way up the western seaboard on a fishing vessel.

Now he plucked his booty from the crude compartment he'd carved in the planks beneath his bunk, and secured the cache in the belt. Stuffing the bills in the pockets and patting them flat, he smiled, imagining how thrilled his brother, Dave, was going to be when he saw the booty his long-lost brother was bringing home.

Talbot planned to hand over every penny of it to Dave, to help fortify his older brother against the creditors he knew were the bane of even the hardest-working frontier rancher. He figured it was the least he could do, having left his sibling to ranch alone in Dakota while Talbot went off to fight in the Apache Wars with General Crook in Arizona.

When he'd mustered out of the cavalry, the battle-weary veteran went down to Mexico looking for his fortune in gold but instead found himself hip-deep in another war, fighting on the side of a poorly organized band of peons against a small army of landed rogues.

It wasn't that he loved war, it was that meeting people here and there about the country had made him a sucker for the vanquished—the single man against many, the proud peon fighting the pampered nobleman for a small plot of ground on which to grow his peppers and beans and to raise his kids.

When the money appeared evenly distributed, Talbot wrapped the belt around his waist, then covered it with his two alpaca sweaters and wool-lined calfskin vest, a gift from a Mexican peon's daughter. He ran his hand over the vest, remembering the warmth of the girl's lips on his, the silky feel of her naked thighs under his work-roughened hands.

Pilar had been her name. Enough time had passed that he could think of her now, remember her almond eyes and her long black hair swinging across her back as she rode her dusty burro through a mesquite-lined arroyo—without feeling the rock in his stomach, the unbearable swelling in his throat.

She and her father, the widowed Don Luís, had nursed him back to health after he'd been ambushed in the Cerro Colorados by Yaqui bandits. Talbot had remained on their farm for two months, doing light field work while he recuperated, and falling in love with Pilar, his smoky-eyed Mexican peasant queen.

Then one morning while Talbot was off gathering firewood with a tired old mule, government soldiers raided the farm. Talbot saw the smoke and heard the gunfire, but when he'd managed to coax the mule back to the farm—his wounded left leg was still useless for running—the soldados were gone, and Don Luis lay bullet-shredded by the burning jacal.

Talbot found Pilar in the stable, beaten and raped, her skirt twisted around her waist, her lovely throat cut, her sightless eyes pinning him with a silent cry for help.

Well, maybe enough time *hadn't* passed, he thought now, appraising his garb through a veil of tears and trying to suppress the memory. Satisfied the money was well concealed, Talbot checked the time on his pocket watch. He had over three hours until his train left San Francisco. He knew the burgeoning California seaport was no place for a peace-seeking man alone at night, especially one with over two thousand dollars on his person. He considered pulling his army-issue gun out of his war bag but decided against it. He was tired of the damn things. Instead of preventing trouble, weapons often only attracted it.

Too antsy to remain aboard ship—he'd been anticipating this for too long—Talbot grabbed his war bag, bid farewell to his cabin mates, and headed up the companionway. On deck he strolled aft and gazed over the bulwarks.

It was a foggy, haunted night, and full dark. Somewhere in the surrounding hills, bells tolled in a steeple. It was a forlorn sound on a quiet winter's night. Not unpleasantly forlorn. It bespoke land. How long had he waited to set foot again on land? On American soil?

Without even glancing around to consider the ship and to bid farewell to the past seven years of wandering, the tall, broad-shouldered young man with a thick mass of curly brown hair snugged his watch cap onto his forehead, lowered himself lightly over the bulwarks, descended the long ramp, and stepped upon the freight-laden wharf with an involuntary sappy grin.

A landlubber once again and forever more!

He would have knelt and kissed the rough wooden dock but wasn't sure he'd be able to regain his feet; his sea legs gave him the precarious, slightly intoxicated feeling of treading water on land. Swinging the war bag over his shoulder, he picked his way down the wharf and through the dockyards.

He found the internationally famous Baldwin's Saloon a half hour later, sandwiched between a brewery and a closed market from which the noise of live geese and ducks issued.

Baldwin's was everything he'd heard it would be. Three front doors, several levels divided by mahogany rails, a half-mile long bar, and a clientele composed of everyone from doctors and lawyers to immigrant street workers and heavy-eyed night clerks on their supper breaks.

The Chinese market gardeners tended to seclude themselves in the shadows, but their conversations were no less boisterous than those of the Prussian-born bankers from Polk Street.

Talbot found a table and stowed his war bag beneath his chair. When one of the half-dozen shiny-faced, impeccably dressed waiters appeared, he ordered a long-anticipated meal and a stein of the beer brewed next door. In spite of the rank odor of wort and hops issuing from the aging vats, he was curious.

Ten minutes later he dug into a bowl of thick pea soup laden with ham, heavy slabs of underdone roast beef, mashed potatoes and gravy, and two sides of fresh vegetables. When the waiter returned looking amused, Talbot ordered dessert: suet pudding, which came liberally seasoned with butter and sugar.

When it was all over, he shoved his chair out from the table, gave a belch, and loosened his belt. He kicked his legs out before him and crossed his ankles.

"Will there be anything else, sir?" came the uppity voice of the waiter.

"Another stein," Talbot said. "And what time is it?"

"A quarter of ten, sir," the waiter said, glancing haughtily at the big Regulator clock over the bar.

Talbot said, "Another now and keep them coming until eleven. I have a ferry to catch at eleven-thirty and a train to catch at one."

"Of course, sir."

"Let me know when it's time to go, will you?"

The man flashed a look of exaggerated reverence. "Why, of course, sir!"

Talbot was working his way to the bottom of a third stein and feeling quite dreamy, gazing about him with warm, gauzy, half-tight objectivity. A Chinese busboy, about fourteen, strode past with a tray heaped with dirty dishes balanced on his left shoulder.

The boy had a look of concentration on his gaunt, tired face. Probably on the thirteenth hour of a fifteen-hour shift, Talbot thought.

He was watching the boy and ruminating on the harshness of life when a leg swung out from one of the tables and a shoe connected with the boy's backside. The blow pushed him awkwardly forward, head snapping back.

The tub of dirty dishes fell backward off his shoulder with a raucous crash. Glass flew. The boy gave an indignant scream that seemed meant not only for the fat, red-faced gent who'd assaulted him, but for all the gods in heaven.

"Hey!" yelled one of the bartenders above the din, fixing an angry gaze on the boy struggling to his knees. The boy's face was bunched with grief. He wagged his head and blinked back tears.

Talbot fought the impulse to intervene. Forget it; it's not your war, he told himself. You're going home.

But the voice in his head was drowned out by the image of the poor lad before him, fumbling and sobbing amid the broken glass, and of the man who'd assaulted him—who sat smoking with his compatriots, red-faced with laughter, reveling thoroughly in the boy's humiliation.

Talbot pushed his glass around on the table and brooded, hearing the grating laughter of the fat businessmen and feeling his ears warm with anger. "Ah, shit," he sighed, reluctantly pushing himself to his feet. He walked over to the man who'd assaulted the busboy. The man was short, with a paunch and a round face framed by graying muttonchops.

The three other men at his table looked like the first and were similarly dressed. Well-to-do businessmen. They were all laughing at the busboy, fat cigars clutched in their fingers.

Talbot stopped at their table and gazed down coolly at the round-faced man. "Okay, you've had your fun. Now kindly help the boy gather his dishes."

The fat man frowned and lifted his red face to the tall, broad-shouldered sailor standing before him. His laughter had died, replaced by a quizzical grin. “I beg your pardon?”

“Help the boy gather his dishes,” Talbot repeated, hating the whole mess.

“Well!” the man grunted, instantly indignant. “I guess I won’t!” He slid his eyes to his companions, who all looked equally outraged. They were not used to being challenged by those beneath them, and they were incensed by such an affront.

The Chinese boy mumbled something as he scrambled to retrieve the unbroken plates and beer steins. Talbot thrust out an open hand to him. “Wait.”

The boy looked up at him, confused.

“Stop,” Talbot said. “This man is going to help you.”

The boy squinted and parted his lips, betraying his discomfort with English. But he seemed to realize the gist of Talbot’s intervention. Instinctively he recoiled at the thought, shaking his head gloomily.

“No,” he said. “I . . . I pick up.”

“No, he pick up,” Talbot said, pointing at the red-faced man, who slid his glowering gaze between the Chinese boy and Talbot, as though he’d just found his calfskin shoes covered with dog shit.

“Who the hell do you think you are!” the man yelled at Talbot, standing slowly and puffing out his chest.

The tables around them were growing silent. The bartenders were watching, half amused, grateful for the diversion. Frozen with terror, the Chinese boy sat on his butt, watching Talbot and the fat man. His lips moved but he said nothing.

An angry red curtain welled up from the corners of Talbot’s eyes. From deep in his brain rose Pilar’s high-pitched screams for him, who was too far away to save her.

"I'm the one who just told you to help that boy pick up his dishes," he said tightly.

"I will not!" the man yelled hoarsely, looking to the other tables for help.

Talbot's voice was reasonable. "You made him drop them, you'll help him pick them up."

"And I told you I won't do it!"

Talbot's arms moved so quickly that no one in the room knew what had happened until the sailor's hands hung again at his sides. Then it was obvious from the fat man's stagger backward into his table and from the mottled glow on his cheek that he'd just been slapped. Backhanded.

The other men at the table rose slowly and backed away, watching Talbot as though he were some escaped circus animal.

Two large, muscular men in frock coats appeared from nowhere, hurrying between the tables. They'd been hired to keep order, but a "Hold it," grunted by one of the barmen, stopped them in their tracks. They looked at the barman witlessly. The barman jerked his head back, and both bouncers retreated.

Talbot did not say another word.

"Be careful, Albert," one of them whispered to the fat man. "These sailors hide knives in their clothes and know how to use them. Just itch for a reason to, in fact."

The fat man, leaning back against the table, pushed the table away. He rubbed his raw cheek and looked up at Talbot with enraged eyes.

The man's friends were silently watching behind a veil of cigar smoke, shamed by their fear and inability to help, but also amused.

The room was nearly silent. Someone coughed. Talbot could hear the quiet hiss of the gas jets. His heart was pounding but his face was taut and expressionless. The fat man looked at him. The fear in his drunken, glassy eyes was growing, the pupils expanding.

"Now help that boy gather his dishes," Talbot said.

The man took one more look around the room. No one appeared willing to lend a hand. In fact, they seemed to be enjoying the spectacle.

Figuring he could not be any more humiliated than he'd already been, and figuring the only way to end the spectacle without getting stabbed was to comply with the young brute's wishes, the man pushed himself forward, sinking to his hands and knees and gathering the dishes that had rolled under chairs and tables. Too startled to move, the Chinese boy only watched him as he worked, wheezing and cursing under his breath.

The others watched as well, though several, unable to endure the fat man's humiliation any longer, returned to their tables and their drinks. They shook their heads and smiled wryly, throwing back their drinks.

"Next time you feel like having fun at someone else's expense," Talbot told the fat man when he'd finished filling the tub and was regaining his feet, wheezing and brushing sawdust from his trousers, "remember what goes around usually comes around."

Lifting his dark eyes to Talbot's, the man said again, "You'll pay for this, you son of a bitch."

He retrieved his crisp bowler from the table and made a beeline to the nearest double doors. His ears and the back of his neck were crimson. Adjusting the hat with the first two fingers of each hand, hiding his face, he pushed angrily through the doors.

After Talbot had regained his seat, the waiter appeared with a fresh beer. "This one's on the house. It'll probably be your last." He gave a haughty smile. "Enjoy!"

CHAPTER 2

ON AN UNSEASONABLY cold Sunday afternoon in November, Homer Rinski and his hired man, Jack Thom, entered Rinski's small cabin in Rattlesnake Gulch, western Dakota Territory, brushing snow from their coats. They stomped their boots and slapped their hats against their knees.

Their faces were red from the cold, hair mussed from their hats. The chill air invaded the cabin like the gray light, which swept shadows into corners before the door closed.

The tall, rail-thin Rinski was pushing a hard-earned sixty, and he sounded like every year of it, breathing hard from his work forking hay from the wagon into the paddock behind the barn.

He hacked phlegm from his lungs, opened the door a crack, and spat outside.

Turning back into the tiny two-room cabin, he found his nineteen-year-old daughter's eyes on him. She'd been setting the table for dinner and held a plate in her hands. She had her late mother's dour countenance.

"Do you have to do that?" she snapped at her father.

"Do what?"

"Do *what?*" the girl mocked. "Spit! And look at all the snow on the floor!"

"Oh, Mattie," Homer Rinski lamented, hanging his coat

and hat on the deer antlers beside the door, "one should never raise one's voice in the house of the Lord."

"This ain't a church," the girl retorted sourly.

"The house of every good Christian is the house of the Lord, dear daughter. Besides, how you're ever gonna find a husband, with a mouth like that, I'll never know."

Ignoring the remark, the girl slammed the plate on the table and turned to the range at the back of the cabin, where several pots gurgled and sighed, sending steam into the cabin's late-afternoon murk. "Both of you wash. There's water there on the bench. Then sit up. I don't want this gettin' cold after all I slaved today."

Easing around each other in the cabin's close quarters, the men washed and sat down to table with eager but slightly bashful looks on their rugged faces—like bad boys with clear consciences.

As was his custom, Jack Thom sat silently, eyes on the table, hands in his lap, until all the kettles and pans had been set before him, and Mattie had seated herself across from her father with a sigh. The hired man punctuated Rinski's traditional five-minute table prayer with a heartfelt "*A*-men" and said nothing else until he'd scrubbed the last of the venison grease from his plate with a biscuit and downed the last of his coffee with an audible slurp.

"That sure was a fine spread you put on, Miss Mattie," he praised with a truckling smile, consciously returning his hands to his lap. He was never sure what to do with the oversized appendages, but knew from Mattie's caustic sneers they didn't belong on the table. "I thank you very kindly."

Thom was a big man with thin blond hair, a round face framed in a perpetual beard shadow, and dung-brown eyes, which Mattie thought the dumbest eyes she'd ever seen on a dog, much less a man. His clothes were old and worn from countless washings. Even fresh from Mattie's washtub, they smelled like cow- and horseshit and something distinctive but unidentifiable that Mattie attributed to the man himself.

The bunk in his shack smelled the same way.

"Yes, Jack," she replied, tiredly clearing the table.

When they'd eaten all Mattie's dried apricot pie, the men sat in their usual homemade chairs in the cabin's small sitting room. They usually played cards or checkers on the small table between the chairs, but since this was Sunday and Homer Rinski didn't think either game appropriate, they just sat there, silently staring, occasionally mentioning the weather or some chore that needed doing, regularly leaning forward to pluck a split cottonwood log from the woodbox and add it to the woodstove. They snoozed, snoring.

When Mattie had finished washing the dishes, she called from the kitchen, "Are you ready for your tea now, Papa?" Her voice had changed. It was not nearly as sharp as it had been. Homer Rinski thought the girl was happy to be through with her dishes.

Rinski smiled. His nightly tea, with a medicinal jigger of chokecherry wine. Homer Rinski did not sleep well without the toddy. He knew the Lord did not mind, for he never imbibed until he was drunk, only sleepy. Without a good night's rest he would not be able to work his six full days, and does the Lord not "judgeth according to every man's work"?

Settled back with his tea, laced with the wine to which Mattie had added several splashes of cheap corn liquor, Homer Rinski quoted from the Good Book in his droning singsong, pausing only when the flame in the wall lamp guttered and coughed black smoke.

Across from him, Jack Thom nodded his head, stifling yawns and feigning interest. He was anticipating eight o'clock, when he could return to his own shack for the night and uncork a bottle of sour mash he'd bought from Nils Spernig on Big John Creek.

Mattie darned one of her father's socks in her chair beside the stove. Occasionally she lifted her eyes to Jack Thom. His eyes met hers, then darted away. His face flushed. The girl smirked.

"Well, Jack, here is a passage I'd like you to sleep on tonight," Homer Rinski told his hired man at five minutes to eight.

Thom slid his gaze to Rinski and smiled wanly.

Holding the ten-pound tome in his gnarled hands, Homer Rinski took a deep breath and quoted dramatically, "All flesh is as grass, and all the glory of man as the flower of grass. The grass withereth, and the flower thereof falleth away. But the word of the Lord endureth for ever."

He looked at the hired man, who smiled and nodded. Rinski smiled sincerely. "Good night, Jack. Sleep well."

Thom shook his head, as though deeply touched. "I do believe you missed your callin', Mr. Rinski. You shoulda been a preacher."

"We're all God's preachers, Jack."

"Yes, sir." Thom stood and stretched, seemingly reluctant to leave such cozy, wholesome quarters. He gave Mattie a brotherly nod. "Thank you again, Miss Mattie. That was one fine meal."

The girl did not lift her eyes from her needlework, but only nodded. When Thom had buttoned his coat, snugged his hat on his head, and gone out into the cold, dark night, Mattie put down her work and stood.

"Another cup . . . since it's Sunday?" she asked her father.

Homer Rinski made a show of considering the offer. Then he nodded gravely, casting his eyes back down at the open Bible in his lap. "Guess it couldn't hurt," he muttered.

He sipped the tea for another hour. Mattie repaired several

socks and a pair of long johns, occasionally lifting her eyes furtively to appraise the old man.

Rinski's eyes were getting heavy, she could tell. He blinked often and squinted. Several times he jerked his head up from a doze.

"You're looking sleepy, Papa," Mattie said, smiling innocently.

Rinski only grunted and read on. Mattie rolled her eyes, clicking her knitting needles together and recrossing her legs under her long gray dress. Should have given him an extra shot, she thought.

When Rinski finally slammed the Good Book closed, Mattie gave a start. She'd about given up on him.

"Well, I do believe I'll turn in, girl." He rose stiffly, creakier still for the two shots of corn liquor Mattie had included with his wine. His blue eyes were rheumy and his bulbous nose fairly glowed.

"Okay, Papa," Mattie said casually. "Sweet dreams."

"You better go soon yourself."

"I will."

Mattie listened as Rinski climbed the ladder into the loft, undressed, and settled into his mattress sack. She continued darning, hands shaking with agitation and anticipation, biting her lower lip, until the old man's snores had resounded for a good quarter hour.

Then she dropped her work in a pile by the chair, stood, and tiptoed to her heavy blanket coat hanging on a peg by the door. She pulled it on, wrapped a scarf around her head and neck, then stood listening to the snores, measuring them to make sure the old man was sound asleep.

Satisfied, she turned to open the door, then slipped quickly through the narrow opening, grimacing at the whoosh of the wind under the eaves. She softly latched the door behind her and, head down, ran into the darkness.

JACK THOM'S LEAN-TO sat half a mile from the main cabin, beyond a knoll and around an aspen copse.

It had been the first cabin Homer Rinski had built after arriving in Dakota Territory from his farm in Illinois. His wife, Anastasia, had fallen ill and died on the overland journey, leaving Homer to raise Mattie alone.

Mattie moved toward the hovel along the rock-hard hummocks lining the frozen creek, twisting her ankles with every step, lifting her skirts with both hands. The tiny triangular structure stood in silhouette against the rising moon. Smoke puffed from its chimney.

Mattie mounted its one step and pushed through the door, closing it quickly behind her.

"You could have waited in the barn for me!" she said sharply, marching across the small, cluttered room to the stove. She sat on the stool before it and crouched over her crossed arms, shaking. The thought that she'd spent the first half of her life in this tiny, fetid shelter made her even colder.

Jack Thom lay on the room's single cot, under a buffalo robe, his head propped against the wall. He cradled a bottle beside him like a baby. His eyes were rheumy.

Mattie could smell the booze. It mixed with the smell of sweat and leather and mice and that other thing that could only be Jack Thom himself.

"I thought maybe your pa would go out and check the stock. He sometimes does that himself when he don't . . . you know"—his voice thickened with self-pity—"when he don't feel like he can trust me to do it."

"So?"

Thom gave a half-hearted shrug and took a swig. "He woulda seen me lurkin' there and wondered what the hell."

Mattie sneered. "You coulda told him *you* were checkin' the stock!"

"I—I never thoughta that, Mattie."

Mattie rolled her eyes and lowered her head between her knees, gave a cry, and shuffled her feet angrily. "Oh, I'm so cold!"

Thom patted the cot. "Come over here; I'll warm you up."

Mattie looked at him and smiled thinly. "You'd like that, wouldn't you?"

"Yes, ma'am." Thom nodded sincerely, as though he'd just been asked something deadly serious.

A flirtatious light rose in Mattie's eyes. It made her gaunt features appear less so. Color rose in her cheeks. "Suppose I do. What then? Will you share that bottle with me?"

"Sure." Thom held out the bottle as if for proof.

Mattie's smile grew. Slowly she took off the blanket coat and dropped it on the floor beside the stove. "You know what I like about you, Jack?" Smiling, eyes glittering, she looked at him, awaiting an answer.

"What's that, Miss Mattie?"

"You're stupid."

The big man wrinkled his brow. "I . . . I ain't—"

"I've never minded that in a man," Mattie said, thoughtfully unbuttoning her dress, her eyes on Thom. Sipping his whiskey, he watched her dull-wittedly, desire creeping into his eyes and smoothing the ridge in his brow.

"As a matter of fact, I prefer it. If they think too much, they might think about not minding what I say, and I wouldn't like that."

Mattie peeled the sleeves of her dress slowly down her arms. She shoved the garment down her waist and legs until it lay in a pile at her bare feet.

"I don't like it when my men don't mind me, Jack. You know what I'm sayin'?"

Thom swallowed, watching the thrust of Mattie's pear-shaped breasts against the wash-worn chemise. "Huh?"

Suddenly her voice rose and her face turned angry. "Are you listening to me!"

"What? Yeah."

"No, you weren't. You were staring at my titties!"

"No! . . . Well, but—"

"Oh, shut up, Jack," she said. "Here, have you a good look." She pulled the chemise over her head and tossed it on the floor. The light from the single lamp shone on her powder-white breasts, soft belly, and plump thighs.

She undid her dark hair from its bun and let it fall across her shoulders. She stared at him coolly, enjoying his eyes on her body. At length she said, "It's cold out here, Jack."

Thom lifted the buffalo robe. "Come over here, Miss Mattie. Let me warm you some."

"Thank you, Jack," she whispered, crawling in beside him. "I don't mind if I do."

She gave a girlish giggle, reached for the bottle, and tipped it back. Snapping it back down, her eyes bulged as her throat worked, audibly fighting to keep the liquor in her stomach.

Finally she coughed. "That's . . . awful."

"It has to grow on ya slow," Thom said defensively, taking back the bottle and enjoying a long swallow.

Mattie reached up and encircled her arms around the hired man's thick, beard-bristled neck, which was the color of old saddle leather from all his years—probably since he was ten—of riding range, digging wells, and brush-popping lost calves.

Mattie didn't know where he was from; she hadn't asked and he hadn't told. Theirs was not a relationship built on chatter. She could tell by looking at him what his life had been like—not all that different from hers.

The rough calluses on his hands often etched fine white lines on her flesh. The sweet pain tided her until she could sneak back to his cabin or meet him in the tall grass by the windmill.

"Pull it out, Jack," she whispered in his ear. "Pull it out and do me, Jack."

"Wait," he said, jerking the bottle back up.

She lifted her head to look into his face severely. "Pull it out and do me, Jack—not the bottle," she said tightly.

Cowed, Thom corked the bottle and set it carefully on the floor beneath the cot, then went to work under the covers, slipping out of his breeches and fumbling with the fly of his long johns. He grunted with the effort, puffing his sour liquor breath and nearly nudging Mattie off the narrow cot.

She held on and crawled on top of him. A dark, willful look knitted her brow and tightened her jaw.

"Do me, damn it. Do me, Jack," she groaned, mounting him.

They were going good when Thom heard something outside. It sounded like hooves crunching snow.

"Listen," he whispered, but Mattie—head down, lips pooched out—was riding away on top of him and groaning louder and louder with each thrust. She hadn't heard him, much less what was going on outside.

Thom listened. The sounds grew closer. A horse snorted.

"Listen!" Thom yelled, lifting his head and throwing the girl off him with a quick swing of his left arm.

As Mattie, screaming, hit the floor, the door blew open and two men ran into the cabin, shotguns aimed at the cot.

"Wait!" Thom yelled.

"You wait, ya ugly beggar!" rasped one of the men.

They were both dressed in long dusters. White flour sacks covered their faces. Holes had been cut to expose the eyes and mouth. Their breath was visible in the chill air.

To Thom they looked more like devils than anything his nightmares had ever conjured. His heart pounded. He was only vaguely aware of Mattie's screams and curses.

"You wait for this!" the man on the right shouted.

Thom covered his head with his arms. “No! . . . wait. What do you want!”

“He wants to know what we want,” one man said to the other, eyes flashing with a grin. Then, as if noticing Mattie for the first time, he said to Thom, “Fuckin’ the boss’s daughter, eh, Jack?” He hooted. “Stealin’ our beef and fuckin’ the boss’s daughter. I do believe we got us a live one here!”

“I didn’t steal no beef, you lyin’ sons o’ bitches!”

“Sure you did, Jack. I seen you.”

“You’re just sayin’ that so’s you can kill me and drive the Rinskis out.”

Both men laughed, lips parting behind their masks, shotguns held high, the stocks snugged against their cheeks.

Thom peeked out from between his elbows, rolling his eyes between the two masked figures. “Oh, Lordy,” he said fearfully. “Oh, Lordy, you’re the ones that killed poor Lincoln Fairchild last summer, and that schoolteacher from Pittsburgh!”

One of the men laughed and turned to the other. He turned back to Thom. “Naw, that was bandits, Jack. Didn’t you hear what the sheriff said?”

Thom shook his head and swallowed hard. “That weren’t no bandits. It was you two killin’ those poor people and makin’ it look just enough like bandits so that’s what the sheriff would call it. You knew the rest of the Bench would know it was the Double X drivin’ ’em out.”

“You got it all figured out, don’t you, Jack?”

“Oh, Lordy,” Thom moaned.

The man on the left turned to Mattie. She was curled up against the woodbox, covering herself with her arms and spewing epithets at the two intruders. “You can tell your pa what ya seen here tonight,” the man told her. “Tell him you and him’s next if you don’t hightail it off the Bench—ya hear?”

"Get the hell out of here, you sons o' bitches!"

"Did you hear me, girl?" the man yelled, turning to give her his full attention.

"I know who you are, you sons o' bitches!"

"Who are we, then?"

"Randall Magnusson and Shelby Green!"

Just then Jack Thom flung his right hand beneath the cot and brought it up with a .44 Remington conversion revolver. Awkwardly he thumbed back the hammer, taking too much time. The Double X men discharged their shotguns with ear-pounding blasts, instantly filling the cabin with the smell of smoke, powder, and fresh blood.

Mattie screamed, covering her face against the horrible vision of Jack Thom disintegrating before her—blood and bone splattering the wall behind him. She continued screaming, dropping her head between her knees. Spittle and vomit leapt from her lips.

Her screams settled to low moans, and she heard shotguns broken open and shells dropped to the floor. Boots scuffed.

There was a long silence. She could hear harsh breathing. Someone cleared his throat, moving toward her. The toes of his boots prodded Mattie's naked thigh.

"You know what?" he said to his partner. "I don't think this little whore's been satisfied . . . yet."

CHAPTER 3

THE WAITER'S SINISTER remark did not bother Mark Talbot. He'd spent the last six years bunking with men who carved their own tattoos and stabbed each other for snoring.

He sipped his beer slowly, then killed it when the waiter poked his shoulder and pointed to the time on the clock above the bar.

Snugging his hat on his head, Talbot picked up his sea bag and headed down the long hill toward the ferry docks whistling. He was going home, by God! He was going home!

He turned down a secondary street; rough cobbles and shipping crates and trash lined the boardwalks. Raucous music seeped through the thin walls of the saloons; lamplight and moving shadows angled from the windows. A chill breeze stirred the fog, and buoy bells rang far out in the soup.

Two men appeared out of the fog before him. They were his size, rawboned longshoremen with jug-like necks. Their tattered oilskin coats stretched taut across their sweatered chests. A foul-smelling cigarette dangled from the lips of the one on Talbot's right. He could smell the booze on them both.

"Pardon me, mates," Talbot said jovially when they closed the gap between them, not letting him pass. "You must not have seen me coming. But now that you have, kindly move your asses."

"Smart one, are you?" said the man on Talbot's left, lifting one bearded cheek with a grin. Talbot detected a faint Scottish accent.

He turned his head to see the fat businessman come up from behind the uglies. "I told you you'd pay," he said happily, puffing out his chest, a fat cigar clutched between the small, plump fingers of his right hand. "Apologize."

Talbot wrinkled his nose. "What makes you think you can treat people like freight rats, you little mackerel fart!"

The fat man screwed up his tiny, deep-set eyes. "I will not be humiliated by the likes of you, you common . . . *deckhand!*"

"Insulting deckhands now, are you? Some of my best friends are deckhands."

The fat man tipped his head to the brutes he must have recruited from a nearby tavern. They stared glassy-eyed at Talbot, swaying slightly from drink. The stench of alcohol was almost palpable. "Okay, teach him who's boss around here."

"Come on, boys," Talbot said affably. "You're too drunk to fight."

The big Scot on Talbot's left pulled back his coat to reveal a wide-bladed skinning knife in a bloodstained leather sheath. "Why don't you tell this gent you're sorry now, laddie, so we can get back to our crap game?"

Talbot sighed and shook his head. "Sorry, I won't do that."

They all stood their silently for several seconds, the fat man and his two brutes staring at Talbot, Talbot staring back. The fat man puffed his cigar and smiled.

At length, from the corner of his eye, Talbot saw the man on the right pull a knife. He was too drunk to pull it quickly, and the tip caught on the sheath. As the man fumbled with it, Talbot took one step back, turning to his right, and kicked it out of the man's hand. The man gave a yell. Talbot punched him in the gut so hard he could hear his ribs crack. The man doubled over with a groan, dropped to his knees, and aired his paunch on the cobblestones.

The other man moved in quickly on Talbot's left and slammed his fist against Talbot's ear. Talbot staggered to the right, wincing from the hot pain. He came around just as the man poked a blade at his side. Sensing it coming, Talbot deflected it with his left arm and landed a crushing right to the man's jaw, feeling the bone come unhinged beneath his knuckles.

Maintaining his feet, the man straightened. His jaw hung freely in the skin sack of his lower face. Giving an animal wail, he put his head down and charged, bulling his powerful shoulders into Talbot's ribs. Talbot smelled the fish and smoke odor of the man's hair as he ground his chin into Talbot's chest and heaved him over backwards.

Talbot flew through a stack of crates and landed with a groan. His teeth snapped together and his head bounced on the cobblestones, sending shock waves through his skull and a ringing through his ears. Still howling, the man grabbed two handfuls of Talbot's hair and smashed his head against the street.

Before the second smash, Talbot jerked both legs straight up in the air, lifted his knees to the man's head, and gripped it like a vise. Grinding the man's ears against his skull, Talbot pulled. The man went slowly back and sideways, yelling curses all the while.

Talbot staggered to his feet, trying to blink his vision clear. Feeling as though an ice pick had gone through both ears, he regarded the man on the ground, who was gaining his knees. Seeing that the man was going to keep coming, Talbot took a step forward. The man jerked to his feet, but before he gained his balance, Talbot delivered a lights-out uppercut dead center on his chin.

The man fell back on the cobbles with a grunt and a sigh, out like a light.

Talbot looked around for the other man. He was kneeling in the shadows, over a puddle of what had been his supper, gazing at Talbot with dark, fearful eyes. "Who the fuck *are* you, man?" he said breathlessly. Then he turned and disappeared in the dark fog.

Suddenly Talbot heard feet shuffling on the cobbles behind him. A sharp pain skewered him. He gave a grunt and dropped to his knees, clutching at the wound about halfway up the right center of his back.

The fat man appeared before him, running away, his right hand holding the bowler on his head. Talbot heard the clatter of the knife as the man threw it down. He could hear the man's hoarse, frightened breath and the patter of thin-heeled shoes.

"You little bastard!" Talbot yelled. Then he sank to his hands and knees, clutching his back. He didn't think the blade had done any real damage—the fat man was obviously no hand with a dagger, thank Christ—but he was bleeding like a stuck pig.

"You okay, mister?"

Talbot looked behind him. A dark, slender figure stood in the shadows before one of the two taverns sitting side by side across the street. Faded lantern light fell onto the boardwalks. Muffled music penetrated the quiet night.

Talbot waited for a carriage to pass, driven by a stiff-looking man in a silk top hat, then walked across the street bent forward at the waist and clamping his fist on the wound to slow the bleeding.

"Do me a favor?" Talbot said. "I've got a ferry to catch in a few minutes, and I need you to stop up this wound in my back."

"That was some lickin' you gave those men, mister!" said

the boy, sliding his gaze back and forth between Talbot and the injured man across the street, who was rolling around and cursing with a hand on his back.

A Negro swamper, the boy couldn't have been more than ten or eleven. He was smoking a cigarette. There was a white apron around his waist and a red knit cap on his head. His gray wool shirt was open above his breastbone. Talbot could smell the musty sweat on him.

"Would you mind?" Talbot said, stopping before the lad, wincing and breathing heavily.

The boy turned his head and looked askance at Talbot. "What you give me for it?"

"How 'bout a half eagle?"

"Half eagle!"

"Sure."

"You ain't got no half eagle."

Talbot dug inside his left coat pocket and pulled out a five-dollar gold piece. The boy reached for the coin, and Talbot jerked it back.

"That's for your apron tied around my back."

The boy smiled broadly and wagged his head. "Mister, for a half eagle I'd give ya my shirt and my pants and my long johns, to boot!"

"The apron will do," Talbot said. "And make it fast, will you, son?"

They hurried to the end of the block and stepped into the alley. With the boy's help, Talbot painfully removed his vest, sweater, and undershirt. All the garments were soaked with blood.

"Mister, you loaded!" cried the boy, eyeing the money belt wrapped around Talbot's trim waist.

"Keep your voice down, will you, son?"

Removing his apron, the boy said, "You like black girls, mister? My sister'd do you good for only five dollar!"

"No, thanks. Fold it up tight now."

When the kid had folded the apron into a long, thick bandage and had tied it around Talbot's back, Talbot struggled into the rest of his clothes.

He appraised his condition and decided the apron had slowed the blood flow. The blood that had soaked his clothes was cold against his back, but he saw it as a small discomfort, considering.

"You sure you won't visit my sistah?" the boy said. Gesturing lasciviously, he added, "Biggest melons you ever seen. Sometimes she even lets me—"

"Much obliged, kid," Talbot said with a nod. He patted the kid's bony shoulder. "Now I'll let you get back to your smoke."

The kid followed him slowly out of the alley and up the street. The boy stopped before the tavern and watched the stranger dwindle in the darkness and fog. "Mistah, where you so all-fire headed, anyways?" he called.

Talbot turned. Walking backward downhill, he said, "Dakota."

The boy frowned skeptically. "Dakota? What's in Dakota?"

Talbot grinned in spite of the pain in his back. "Peace and quiet, kid," he said. "Peace and quiet." Then he turned and hurried toward the ferry docks.

CHAPTER 4

SHERIFF JEDEDIAH GIBBON rode his gray gelding around a trail bend and past a skeletal cottonwood copse. He was nearing the scraggly little village of Canaan, Dakota Territory.

It was a clear, cold day. Frost limned the trees, the sky was cobalt blue, and the bright sun felt like sharp sand in Gibbon's eyes.

The sheriff was chilled to the bone and saddle weary. His buffalo coat and the scarf his wife had knitted, which he'd wrapped over his Stetson and tied under his chin, offered as much warmth as a man could ask for.

But nothing kept the ten-below cold from your bowels on a thirty-mile round-trip ride through snow that often rose to your horse's pecker. The small bundles of hay Gibbon had tied to his stirrups had kept his feet warm for a few miles, but he hadn't felt his toes in his boots for over two hours now.

He'd never been so happy to round the last bend in the freight road and see the two dozen tar-paper shacks and clapboard store fronts of Canaan slide out before him. Noticing the black coal smoke gushing from the brick chimney over the Sundowner Saloon, Gibbon headed that way.

Halting his horse before the raised boardwalk, he dismounted gently on his frozen feet, giving a tired groan. When he had two boots solidly beneath him, he turned to regard Miller's Feed Barn across the street. Angus Miller was out in the paddock, forking hay to a string of shaggy Percherons. His black-and-white collie lay close by, showing the horses its teeth.

Gibbon called to the man and indicated his horse. Miller nodded. Then Gibbon threw his reins over the tie rail, climbed the porch steps with painful deliberation, wincing and using the railing, and entered the saloon.

"Close the damn door," someone yelled. "You born in a barn?"

Gibbon closed the door and peered into the cave-like dark as his eyes adjusted from the bright sun. He worked his nose, sniffing. It never ceased to amaze him how horrible the place always smelled.

"Where you keepin' the bear?" he growled. "I can smell him, but I can't see him."

"How ya doin', Jed?" the proprietor, Monty Fisk, asked.

Fisk, who doubled as a barber, was shaving a local rancher in the barber chair near the big coal stove that sat, tall as a good-sized man, in the middle of the room. As was customary during cold snaps, everyone in the place had gravitated toward the stove. A fine soot hung in the air.

Behind the stove, several rough-looking, winter-weary cowboys sat around a table playing high-five. Before it, several businessmen and ranchers had gathered to gas with the boys. A coffeepot, tin cups, and several whiskey glasses sat before them.

"Been warmer," Gibbon said. "Earl, if you give me your spot there by the stove, I won't tell your wife about the fourteen-year-old soiled dove you've been diddling over in Wild Rose."

Earl jerked his gaze at Gibbon outraged. "Who told you that!"

"Oh, hell, Earl—everyone knows but Stella, and she's bound to find out sooner or later."

"And when she does . . ." remarked one of the cowboys beyond the stove, whistling.

As laughter erupted around the saloon, Earl Watson angrily grabbed his glass and headed for a vacant chair away from the stove. Gibbon eased into his place, removed his gloves, and began pulling off his boots.

When he was working on the second high-topped Wellington, Fisk said, "Trouble out to the Rinski place, eh, Jed?"

"I'll say."

"What kind of trouble?" the man in the barber's chair wanted to know. His name was Verlyn Thornberg, and he owned the Circle T ranch south of town. It was the largest spread in the county.

Gibbon's second boot came off suddenly, nearly knocking him from his chair. He dropped the boot and went to work on his socks.

"You don't really want to know, Verlyn. It'll just irritate your kidney infection."

"If it's rustlers, I have a right to know, and so do the other ranchers in the basin."

"It ain't rustlers."

"What, then?"

Gibbon dropped his socks over his boots and stuck both feet out to the warmth pulsing from the red-hot stove. The feet were white as porcelain, the hard, shell-like nails a sickly yellow-blue, but Gibbon thought he was starting to get some feeling back. "Ay-yi-yi, that feels good. . . . Give me a whiskey sling, will you, Monty?"

"Comin' right up, Jed."

"What's the problem out at Rinski's?" Thornberg persisted.

He was a thin man with a narrow, gloomy face. His hair was reddish brown, like his skin, and appeared equally faded by the wind and sun. The grim line of his mouth showed under his thin yellow mustache.

Gibbon had never liked Thornberg. Back during the Old Trouble, as everyone called it, and against Gibbon's direct orders, Thornberg had tried to organize the small ranchers against the big outfit trying to take over the Canaan Bench. The last thing Gibbon had wanted was an all-out land war. Wagging his nose at the sheriff, Thornberg went about his plans, and there hadn't been anything Gibbon could do about it. The Double X outfit was attacking the small ranchers and stealing their beef, after all. If Gibbon had charged Thornberg with anything, he would have been run out of town on a long, greased pole.

Thornberg looked at the sheriff now with dark expectancy. The left half of his face was still lathered with shave cream; Fisk had stopped to fix Gibbon's drink.

Everyone was looking at Gibbon. He waited until the toddy was in his hand. He sipped it, said over the steam rising from the surface of the deliciously warming brew, "Someone killed Rinski's hired man."

"Oh, that's all," chuffed one of the cowboys behind the stove, going back to his high-five.

"That sombitch was bound to get it from someone sooner or later," said the cowboy sitting next to him.

"No doubt," Gibbon said, sipping the toddy. He grew thoughtful and stared at the stove.

"That it?" Thornberg said. "Did Jack Thom just get caught hornswogglin' the wrong rough, or do we have a problem?"

Fisk pulled his razor back from Thornberg's throat and said, "Hold still now, Verlyn, or I'm liable to carve out your Adam's apple."

Gibbon looked at Thornberg and sighed. He knew there was no point in trying to keep it a secret. It would be all over the country in a few days. "Thom was screwin' his boss's daughter when he bought it from two masked men with scatterguns."

"Masked gunmen?" Thornberg said.

"That's right."

"Double X men."

"We don't know that," Gibbon warned.

"No, we don't," Thornberg retorted. "But who else around here has sent out masked riders in the past five years?" To the barber, he said, "Finish me up now, Monty, I gotta go," and to the men behind the stove: "Lou, Grady—get your horses."

"Where you goin'?" Gibbon said.

"Home to count my cattle," Thornberg said. "And I'm gonna send out some boys to see if I got any men left in my line shacks—alive, that is!"

Gibbon shook his head and regarded the men with gravity. "I stopped at several places on my way back, and no one had lost any men or cattle. No fences had been cut, and nothin's been burned. There's no reason to believe it was Magnusson's men who killed Jack Thom. So just simmer yourself down now, Verlyn!"

"That's what you said last summer when old Lincoln Fairchild was found dead in his cabin, and when that Pittsburgh schoolteacher and his family were found butchered on their farm over by Badger Lake!"

"Those were highwaymen," Gibbon said. "They were robbed."

"Ah, horseshit! That was King Magnusson sendin' us a message: Get out or get greased!"

"Now hold your horses, Thornberg!"

Thornberg swept the barber's smock away and bounded out of the chair and over to Gibbon's table in two fluid swings of his long legs. He planted his fists on the table. His eyes were so wide that Gibbon could see nearly as much white as iris.

"Listen, you old fossil. The message might have been too subtle for you, but it wasn't too subtle for me. When they get goin' again like they got goin' five years ago, there's going to be hell to pay. And you know who they're gonna hit hardest as well as I do. They're gonna hit me. And me and my boys are the only one's with guts enough to do anything about it. So just sit there and enjoy your booze. You just sit there all winter long and warm your big feet and drink yourself into a good warm haze—just like you did last time we had trouble. But me, I'm gonna stop trouble in its tracks . . . settle this thing the way it should've been settled five years ago."

Gibbon coolly watched the man push himself up from the table, take his ten-gallon Stetson from one of his riders, don it, and struggle into his mackinaw. The three men walked out into the bright sunlight, letting in a frigid draft, and slammed the door behind them.

Gibbon stared into his drink.

Monty Fisk quietly broke the silence. "None of us believes any of that horseshit, Jed."

Gibbon looked at him, hating the patronizing air with which the barber regarded him. The two remaining cowboys behind the stove just stared at their cards. He didn't want to look at the businessmen sitting around him. He knew they wore the same looks as Fisk.

"Oh, shut the fuck up, will ya, Monty!" Gibbon barked suddenly. "What does a man have to do to get a drink around here?"

GIBBON SAT BAREFOOT before the fire, in his bulky buffalo coat, and sipped two more toddies. The warmth of the stove conjured summer afternoons when he was a boy, fishing and napping along the creek behind the barn, the July sun beating down, branding his eyelids. Not a care in the world.

Back then, only bluegills sucking the corn on his hook brought him back from his dreaming. Now it was Monty Fisk calling from across the room.

"Jed, it's gettin' late. Go on home before Martha has to send a boy for ya."

Gibbon jerked up from his reverie, realizing a sappy grin had basted his face. He set his mug down on the table, ran his hand down his bristly cheeks, and yawned. "I reckon I better head over to the train station. The four-ten must be due."

"Go on home and quit feelin' sorry for yourself," Fisk scolded. All the other customers had left without Gibbon realizing, and Fisk was sweeping sawdust as he puffed a nickel cigar.

Pulling his hot socks on, Gibbon said, "If it wasn't for me feelin' sorry for myself, you'd go out of business. Give me a plug o' that Spearhead's for the road, and add it to my bill. I get paid next week."

When he'd stomped into his boots and pulled his gloves on, he tied his scarf over his hat, went out, and headed for the depot on the other end of town.

It was early winter twilight, and the first stars were impossibly bright. The silhouettes of supply-laden sleighs slid past, their teams crunching the packed snow beneath them. Gibbon kept to the boardwalks, glancing through windows at the lantern-lit stores, and shuffled up the shoveled cobblestone platform on which the red-brick station house sat, smoke puffing from its chimney.

He sat on a bench inside, close to the fire, exchanging platitudes with the agent-telegrapher, a half-breed who slept on a cot in the primitive office. The four-ten thundered in, twenty minutes late. Gibbon was walking out to greet it as a big-boned kid with red hair dumped the mail pouch in a battered leather buggy.

"Afternoon, Sheriff."

"Afternoon, Teddy. How's your pa?"

"He's gettin' some feelin' back in his hands, but Doc Hall doesn't think he'll ever be right in his head again."

"That's too bad. Give him my best, will ya?"

"Sure will. See ya Thursday."

Five minutes later, the conductor, shrouded in soot and steam, yelled, "All aboard!"—though no one seemed to be getting on—and the train thundered off in a cloud of hot steam, which bathed the sheriff and pleasantly sucked the cold breath from his lungs.

When the train was gone, leaving only snakes of steam curling over the cobbles, Gibbon peered up the platform. It was empty. Apparently no one had gotten off, which was just fine with Gibbon. Not having to confront miscreants—usually drunk, jobless cowboys looking for a place to winter—made the sheriff's job all the easier. He could go home now, eat a hot supper, and crawl into bed with Martha and his new *Police Gazette.*

"Sure turned cold early this year." It was the station agent, trying to drag a large crate stamped MERCANTILE across the snowy cobbles, and grunting with the effort.

"For Pete's sake, let me help you there, Henry," Gibbon said, walking over, crouching down, and trying to get a good hold on the freight carton. "On three, let's lift the son of a bitch. One, two . . ."

"One of you amigos have a light?"

The request came out of nowhere, in Spanish-accented English. It startled Gibbon and the station agent, who suddenly stopped what they were doing and looked up. Gibbon saw he'd been wrong about no one getting off the train. The man standing before him was certainly not from around here.

He was a tall, slender man in a round-brimmed black hat. He wore a coat like none Gibbon had ever seen before. It appeared to be wolf fur. Shiny and gray-black, it had a high collar that nearly covered the man's ears, and it boasted silver buttons big as 'dobe dollars.

Squatting there at the man's knees, Gibbon and the agent looked at each other, speechless. Finally, the agent straightened, brushing his hands on his trousers, and reached into his shirt pocket for a matchbox. He produced a lucifer and scraped it against the box. The man stuck a thin black cigar between his lips and leaned toward the flame, which the agent cupped, looking sheepish.

When the man got a good draw, he tipped his head back in a cloud of smoke. "Gracias, señor." The man's voice was deep and resonant, indicating a well of self-assured power.

Gibbon didn't know what to make of the man. He was no cowboy, that was for sure. What was a dandy greaser doing in Dakota in the middle of a butt-ripping winter? Gibbon wanted to ask. But the man's presence rendered the sheriff's words stillborn on his tongue.

"Now I have a question for you," the man said. "Where can a weary traveler find himself a hot bath and some girls to go with it?" His emotionless blue eyes—out of place in the Hispanic face with its high, flat cheekbones and aquiline nose—slid between Gibbon and the station agent.

After what seemed several seconds, Gibbon cleared his throat, but it was the agent who spoke. "Well . . . I reckon you can probably find both up to the Powder Horn, on the west end of town . . . wouldn't you say, Jed?"

Gibbon nodded, finding his tongue. "The Powder Horn—that's right, up the street, west end of town." He squinted at the man and took a breath, at last finding the question he wanted to ask. But before he could get it out, the man nodded graciously, spread his waxed mustache in a thin smile, and said, "Much obliged, señors." Then he hefted his baggage and sauntered down the platform, head cocked to one side, puffing smoke.

Watching him, Gibbon noticed he carried a silver-mounted saddle on his shoulder, balanced there as though it were no burden at all. There was a war bag looped over the horn. In the man's other hand he carried a scabbard containing a rifle. From its size and length, Gibbon concluded it was no squirrel gun.

"Well, what in the hell do you make of that?" the agent said, still looking after the man.

Gibbon said nothing. He watched the man disappear around the corner of the station house, recalling the man's extraordinary face. He'd seen it before . . . somewhere. He knew he had. You don't forget a face like that.

But where?

"I don't know what to make of it," Gibbon mumbled, running a gloved hand along his chin. "I'll see ya, Henry," he added absently.

Forgetting he'd been about to help the agent with the crate, he opened the depot building's doors and walked through the waiting area and out the other side. He cast his gaze up the street. It was getting too dark to see much, but he could make out the silver glint of the Mexican saddle as the man carried it up the boardwalk.

Gibbon considered catching up with the man and asking him point-blank where he'd seen him before, but decided against it. There was something in the stranger's demeanor that told Gibbon you didn't pry—unless you were Wyatt Earp or Bill Tilighman, that is, and were faster on the draw than Jedediah Gibbon.

Getting an idea, Gibbon walked over to the jail, which sat next to the livery barn and across the street from the Sundowner. It was so cold in the place that Gibbon's cup of coffee, abandoned this morning when he was called out to the Rinski place, had frozen solid.

But Gibbon didn't light a fire. He didn't plan to be here long. Martha was no doubt waiting supper for him.

He lit a hurricane lamp and set it on his desk before rummaging around in a drawer and tossing a bundle of old, yellowed wanted dodgers on his scarred desktop. He sat down and thumbed through the posters, carefully considering the rough sketch on each. Five minutes after he'd started, one caught his eye.

The likeness was so poor it was hard to be sure, but the description of the man cinched it: tall, slender Mexican with blue eyes and handlebar mustache. The man's name was José Luís del Toro, wanted for multiple murders in Texas and New Mexico. He was described as a cold-blooded gun for hire, and extremely deadly.

Gibbon stared at the picture for several minutes, feeling a chill in his loins. So Verlyn Thornberg had been right. Something was going on. One of the ranchers in the area had hired a gunman.

Gibbon scowled at the sketch of José Luís del Toro, whose very name sounded like death. It made Gibbon feel like the inadequate old coward everyone thought he was.

"Shit," he said with a grunt.

If the man who'd gotten off the train really was Del Toro, the Old Trouble was back with a vengeance. And it was Gibbon's job to do something about it.

He sat back in his chair and felt the old, lonely fear wash over him once again.

CHAPTER 5

GLOWING CINDERS FLEW back from the smokestack as the train chugged eastward into the dawn. A rolling, snow-covered prairie lifted gently under a lavender-salmon sky, relieved now and then with craggy-topped buttes and peppered occasionally with sparse buffalo herds.

A grizzled pioneer in a torn coat and scraggly beard waited at a crossing with a wagon load of hay, the yellow dog on the seat beside him cocking its head at the clattering wheels.

It was Mark Talbot's fourth and last day on the train. He'd been staring out the window nearly every waking moment. Although his back ached from the stab wound, he was able to appreciate the view, which was growing more and more spectacular. Isolated clusters of cottonwoods, frozen sloughs spiked with cattails, tidy gray cabins nestled in hollows and flanked with windmills and hitch-and-rail corrals.

Talbot reflected that most travelers, unacquainted with the Northern Plains, would no doubt find the starkness disconcerting. Born and raised here, Talbot found it restful. While growing up, he couldn't wait to see the world and fight in a war or two, search for gold in legendary Mexico. Seven years of warring and wandering behind him now, he couldn't wait to be home, on the open plains, where the scalloped sky took your breath away and the prairie went on forever.

Of course all the blood had something to do with it. You

couldn't see that much, spill that much, and not pine for home. You couldn't see friends like Max Schultz or Louis Margolies or Sergeant Maloney butchered on the burning, rocky wastes of the Arizona desert or hacked to death in their sleep in the White Mountains, the creeks in the morning flowing red with the blood of Mescaleros and soldiers alike—you couldn't see a lovely Mexican girl's slender, ruined throat—and not long for a quiet cabin on Crow Creek in western Dakota, windows ablaze with the setting sun, the quartering breeze spiced with chokecherry blossoms and sage.

The thought was interrupted by a tap on Talbot's shoulder.

He turned. A young woman and a man stood in the aisle. The woman was a dark-haired beauty in a fur coat and hat. Painted lips set off the lush brown eyes, which regarded Talbot boldly. Her hands were warmed by a rabbit muffler.

The man next to her was older but dressed with similar elegance, out of place amidst the raucous snores, stiff upholstered seats, and sooty windows of the tourist car. The man's slender frame was cloaked by a shiny bear coat and beaver hat, and his thin lips were smugly pursed. His small, silver-rimmed pipe filled the air with an aroma akin to balsam and sage.

"Yes?" Talbot asked.

The man spoke in a melodic tenor, enunciating his words very carefully. "Pardon us, sir, but the lady couldn't help noticing that you appear to be injured."

"Pardon?"

"There's blood on the back of your coat," the young woman said, pulling a hand from her muffler to point.

Talbot reached behind his back with his left hand, probing his vest with his fingers. Sure enough, the blood had leaked through. The movement sharpened the pain, and he winced. "It's nothing," he said, not wanting to make a spectacle. "Just backed up against a loading fork back on the Frisco docks. Probably looks worse than it is."

"Oh, my," the girl said. "That must have hurt."

"It's really nothing."

With small, lightless eyes, the man said, "Why don't you join us in our suite, and I'll tend it for you?"

"He's a doctor," the girl explained.

Talbot studied them, wary. Why were these two well-dressed strangers so concerned for his health? You didn't survive the Mescalero Apaches and Old Mexico during the gold boom without a healthy dose of xenophobia.

"Thanks for the offer, but I'll be fine." Talbot turned back to the window.

"As you wish, sir," the girl said. "Come along, Harry."

Talbot turned back to see the two moving off down the aisle, between sparse rows of rustic western travelers—cowboys, drummers, and gamblers who were either playing cards or curled uncomfortably on the hard seats. The girl's long chocolate curls cascaded down her slender back, bouncing lightly as she walked.

Talbot sucked his cheek, watching her. She was lovely, and she had simply offered help to a stranger. Suddenly her motivation didn't seem to matter.

"Hold up," he said, rising with his bag. "I didn't mean to be rude. I could use a fresh dressing, I reckon."

The girl's eyes brightened as she turned to regard him. She gestured to the door at the end of the car, and the man called Harrison stepped aside to let the rough-hewn stranger pass.

Two cars back was a Hotel Pullman decked out with Turkish rugs, inlaid woodwork, two red-velvet daybeds, and a potbellied stove flanked by a stack of cordwood logs split so precisely they looked surreal. Peering at himself in the gilded mirror over the sofa, Talbot gave a complimentary whistle.

"Daddy won't let me travel in anything but luxury," the

girl said, tossing aside her coat and muffler. Carefully she lifted the hat from her head, removing pins and brushing loose hair from her impossibly smooth cheeks.

Talbot furtively filled his lungs with her fresh, rosy smell, not so subtly feasting his eyes. American women.

"And on long trips, he makes me take a physician—thus Harrison here," she said. "He's a friend I met at the theater."

The man in the bear coat lifted the curled ends of his waxed mustache in a wry smile. "I'm Harrison Long. That's Suzanne." There was an ironic tone in the doctor's voice and expression, as though he envisioned himself a cultural prodigy among savages.

Talbot tore his eyes from the girl to stroll around the car, taking in the ornate hangings and plush green drapes. "So this is how the privileged live," he said. "If information about this gets out to the tourist cars, you're liable to have a riot on your hands."

Harrison chuffed. "Such rustics as I saw up there could not appreciate this kind of luxury."

"Oh, I bet they could," Talbot countered good-naturedly. "They'd have some party back here." He caught the girl smiling at him, and returned the smile.

"How long have you two been riding the rails?" he asked.

"Since August," Suzanne said. "I tend to get owly during the fall and winter on the Plains, and Daddy sends me traveling."

Talbot cocked an eyebrow. "Who's your daddy—Jay Gould?"

"King Magnusson."

"Never heard of him."

"That's not surprising," she said with a laugh.

Talbot wasn't sure whom she'd just insulted, him or her father. As he feasted his eyes on the girl's lovely lips parted to reveal a delicious set of pearly whites, on her long, slender neck and ripe bosom pushing at the low-cut shirtwaist, he didn't care. He'd been at sea a long time.

"We've told you our names," the girl said. "What's yours?"

"Mark Talbot's my handle, ma'am."

Smiling brightly, with the understated vigor of the well-bred, the girl took two strides forward and held out her long, pale hand. "Pleased to meet you, Mark Talbot."

"Likewise, ma'am," Talbot said, his gaze held by hers. Her hand was thin and fine-boned, but her shake was firm. Talbot held it, enjoying the feel of her warm, soft flesh.

Dr. Long gave a warning cough. "Let's take a look there, shall we?" he said, taking a step toward the visitor and indicating Talbot's back.

"Where?" Talbot asked.

"Right here is fine," the doctor said, holding out his hands to accept Talbot's vest.

Talbot made no move to take it off. "No offense, ma'am, but . . . with her here?"

"Oh, I won't peek!" Suzanne exclaimed playfully. "I'll ring the porter for some rags and a bowl of water. Would you care for some coffee? It's French."

Ten minutes later, Talbot was lying facedown on the sofa, crossed ankles draped over an arm, hands folded beneath his chin. Sitting on a footstool beside him, Dr. Long was sponging the wound and puffing his pipe.

Long frowned. "This was no mere hook you backed into, was it, Mr. Talbot?"

"Looks nasty," Suzanne said. She stood over the doctor, coffee cup clutched to her breast in both hands, and observed the doctor's work with an arched brow.

"Just a scratch," Talbot said.

The doctor squeezed blood and water from the sponge and dabbed at the dried blood and pus around the slit. "It looks nastier than it is, but it's no scratch. It is, I believe, a knife wound. You've outdone yourself this time, Suzanne."

"A knife wound!" she enthused. "Really, Mr. Talbot?"

Before Talbot could answer, Long said, "I think you should know, Mr. Talbot—if that's your real name—I am armed with a Smith & Wesson .35 caliber pocket pistol, and I know how to use it."

"Oh, Harrison, don't be melodramatic!" Suzanne laughed. "Besides . . . it might be fun."

"Suzanne!"

Talbot craned his head to look at the doctor. "What do you mean, she's outdone herself?"

"Suzanne has a habit—it's a game, really—of picking up interesting strangers and becoming acquainted. She spied you on a stroll through your car earlier. I agreed you did look interesting, but the blood on your vest put me off."

Suzanne shrugged. "I thought it was a good excuse to introduce ourselves, Harrison being a doctor and all." Visibly excited, Suzanne wheeled around, skirt flying, and landed in a chair. She crossed her legs and leaned forward, placing her coffee cup on her knees. Her smile was radiant.

Talbot watched her as the doctor continued to clean the wound. He couldn't help being smitten by the effervescent girl. He guessed she was no more than nineteen or twenty, and despite her means of travel and dress he sensed she was more than just a spoiled coquette. She was an educated, *well-built*, spoiled coquette.

"Come now, Mr. Talbot," she begged, "how did you come to be stabbed?"

Talbot laughed at the girl's innocent delight. "Well, I'd like to tell you I was trying to rescue a damsel from a horde of Arab slave traders, but it was really a lot less interesting than that."

Suzanne smiled delightfully. "Let me be the judge."

Talbot told her the story of the fat businessman and the

Chinese boy and the two ruffians who'd tried to clean his clock. Suzanne listened, wide-eyed. When he finished she said sincerely, "What a valiant man! Did you hear that, Harrison?"

"Yes, valiant. Hold still, Mr. Talbot; I'm just about done here."

"You're an adventurer, then, Mr. Talbot," Suzanne said admiringly.

"I reckon I had an adventure or two," Talbot allowed. "But I'm going home now, to Dakota, and I plan to stay there. I've had my fill of knockin' about. Once a shitkicker, always a shitkicker, I reckon. Pardon my French."

"Dakota! Well, that's where we're headed. Where abouts, Mr. Talbot?"

"A little town called Canaan, on the Canaan Bench. My older brother has a ranch thereabouts."

Dr. Long was taping a bandage to Talbot's back. "I appreciate this, Doctor," Talbot said. "I was getting tired of that wet apron wrapped around my chest."

"I think you'll find this considerably more agreeable," Harrison said. "You can slip into your clothes again, if you'd like."

Suzanne frowned thoughtfully. "My father's place is on the Canaan Bench, and Canaan is . . ." Suddenly her eyes widened. "My gosh, that's only a two-hour ride from where we live!"

"Is that right?" Talbot said, sitting up and reaching for his clothes.

"Yes." Her smile widened, and her eyes flashed. "We're practically neighbors!"

She got up, retrieved a china cup from the tray the porter had set on the trestle table in the middle of the car, handed it to Talbot, and filled it from a silver pot. Turning to the doctor, who stood rolling down the sleeves of his crisp white shirt, she said, "Would you like a cup, Harrison?"

"No, I think I'll go smoke and leave you two to your hometown chatter," he said dryly.

When he'd donned his broadcloth jacket and his heavy bear coat and hat and left, Suzanne turned from the door with a mischievous flair. "He's jealous, you know?"

Talbot frowned, opened his mouth to speak, but she cut him off.

"Oh, not of you, of me. He's . . . he's one of *those*—couldn't you tell?"

Talbot raised his eyebrows. "One of *those*?"

"Yes. I do love Harrison dearly—he's the best friend a girl could ever have—but he's quite irrevocably . . . one of those." In two light-footed strides she'd fallen onto the couch beside Talbot, smoothing her skirt beneath her, turning to the side and gracefully crossing her long, coltish legs. "When you had your shirt off, I thought he was going to start foaming at the mouth—elegantly, of course."

A curl slipped from behind her ear and fell gently along her cheek. Talbot stared at it, fighting the urge to smooth it back behind the delicate ear. Her smell was fresh and subtle, like the rain in Chihuahua. Her eyes softened, as if reading his mind.

"To tell you the truth," she said breathily, "I didn't blame him one bit. You cut a handsome figure, Mr. Talbot." Her lips stretched back, revealing all those perfect teeth, faintly gleaming.

"Mark," he said, coloring a little at her candor. He was surprised that a girl of her station could be so forward.

"Mark," she said, lowering her eyes, turning suddenly girlish and shy.

Talbot's heart tom-tommed in his chest, and he could feel the sweat pop out on his forehead. The girl was like a drug, a tonic washing over him. His head fairly swam, and he wondered for a moment if he weren't dreaming.

Of its own accord, Talbot's hand rose from his knee. Slowly it traversed the space between him and Suzanne and rested on her chin, cupping it gently in his first two fingers. Lifting it, he leaned toward her. Her head tilted back, offering her slightly parted lips.

Suddenly the car jerked and slowed, and they fell back against the couch. Suzanne sat up and turned to look out the windows. "Oh, my goodness—we're finally stopping!" she said with cheer.

"Great," Talbot said wryly, dazed from the attempted kiss.

The girl seemed to have forgotten all about it. She knelt on the sofa, cleared the steam from the window with her hand, and watched the first few cabins and shanties slide by as the wheels clattered on the iron seams. The car slowed, shuddering as the breaks worked against the locomotive's giant wheels.

Suzanne read the sign attached to the station house. "Wibaux."

"Wibaux?" Talbot said with surprise, turning to see for himself. "That's where I switch to the branch line."

"Oh, Mark, no—I stay on until Big Draw!" Suzanne exclaimed, swinging her eyes to him. "We were just starting to get acquainted!"

I'll say we were, Talbot thought. Reaching for his war bag and awkwardly gaining his feet, he laughed mirthlessly and wagged his head. "You sure made the time fly, Miss Magnusson."

"Oh, fudge, Mark," she lamented, pursing her lips in a pout. "Promise me you'll look me up . . . once we're both home and settled? I want to hear all about your adventures. They sound so . . . so . . . romantic." Her voice had become a resonant purr.

"It's far from that, but I'll tell you about it," he promised. As he moved out the door, Suzanne was on his heels. The train had nearly stopped, its couplings clamoring like thunder, steam fogging the windows.

"Promise? . . . Oh, no you won't! Before you even think of me again, the local girls will be pounding on your door."

Talbot laughed. He jumped down from the car and turned to her, standing between the cars with both hands on the rail, her breath visible in the cold air. He knew that if anyone was going to have suitors knocking their door down, it would be she.

"No local girl could hold a candle to you, Suzanne. I'll look you up. You can be sure of that."

He tipped his head and returned her smile, laughing heartily. "Thanks for everything. Say good-bye to Harrison for me."

"I will. Travel safe . . . until we meet again."

Talbot turned to walk down the platform. He turned back to her, still watching him like a lovelorn heroine from a British romance. "If I'm going to look you up, I'll need the handle for your father's ranch."

"Oh . . . it's the Double X," she said.

"The Double X," Talbot echoed. He hadn't heard of it, but he supposed a lot of new outfits had moved in since he'd left. "I'll find it."

He waved, hefted his war bag over his shoulder, and strode toward the station house to await the branch line that would carry him on the last leg of his journey home.

CHAPTER 6

TEX MADSEN WAS a tall, rail-thin cowpoke with dull, deep-sunk eyes and a walrus mustache. He was only twenty-nine years old, but climbing the stairs of the Powder Horn Hotel in Canaan, he wheezed like a geezer. He cursed as his weak lungs constricted, stopping on the landing to catch his breath.

He leaned against the wall as a loud coughing fit gripped him. The paroxysm raked his insides like sandpaper. When it subsided, Tex lifted his head, wiped his nose and mouth, and peered grimly at the blood-laced fluids soiling his handkerchief.

"I knew I shoulda stayed in Texas," he mumbled, continuing down the narrow hall between closed doors. "Cold like this ain't natural. It's . . . it's taken my youth."

Tex had been stricken with the virus nearly a month ago, and being sent out into the subzero weather to round up some gunslick wasn't going to help him get over it. Hell's bells, he'd probably end up like old Yancy Kellogg, the old Double X hostler who'd died of pneumonia last winter and whose body was ravaged by mice and owls as it awaited a spring burial in the barn loft.

Cursing the ranch foreman who'd sent him out in this chilblain weather, Tex stopped at room 15 and knocked, stifling another cough.

"Who is it?" came a Spanish-accented voice.

Sniffing, Tex leaned toward the door. "Tex Madsen. I'm supposed to show you out to the Double X. If you're Mr. del Toro, that is."

"Si," Del Toro grumbled. "Give me a minute."

You can have the whole goddamn morning for all I care, Tex said to himself. It wasn't exactly steamy in the hotel, but he was in no hurry to go back outside where he could hear the brittle wind howling. His cheeks and toes were still numb. His head and back were chill with fever.

Tex was waiting with his back against the wall when the door opened and a blond girl stepped out. Her face was puffy with sleep, her hair and dress disheveled. Tex didn't know her name, but he'd seen her working in the saloon downstairs. Not bad-looking for a soiled dove in these parts. She softly latched the door behind her, paying no attention to Tex, and drifted down the hall, her short red dress swishing against her legs.

Tex gave a fragile grin and turned back to the door as it opened again. Another blond poked her head out and looked around. A beret hung loose in her hair. Bigger than the first girl and rawboned, she scrutinized Tex dully, gave a little smile, stepped out, and shut the door behind her. Smoothing her dress, she whined at a tear and headed for the stairs.

"Well, I'll be . . ." Tex muttered wonderingly.

He waited another five minutes, noting the feeling returning to his toes. He couldn't believe it when the door opened again and another girl slipped out, carrying two empty whiskey bottles and three water glasses. She was not wearing a dress, but had wrapped a sheet around herself. A brunette with a pretty, round face, she looked haunted and struggled awkwardly with her load while holding the sheet closed at her bosom. When she saw Tex she gave a start, her grip on the sheet loosening, giving Tex a momentary shot of her chafed, red-mottled breasts.

Tongue-tied, Tex tried a smile and fingered the rim of his big Stetson.

Stiffly the girl marched up to Tex. Fire sparked in her eyes. "That man is an *animal*," she hissed, then scurried down the hall, tripping on the sheet. Tex heard the crash of a bottle; it clattered as it rolled down the stairs.

The door opened once again. Tex turned to it, expecting to see another rumpled girl, but this time a tall, straight-backed, lean-faced Mexican man stood before him. The man's gray coat appeared to be wolf hide, and the nickel-plated pistols he wore strapped to a wide cartridge belt were Colts with mother-of-pearl grips—butts forward, holsters bent back and tied to the man's thighs.

The pistols were probably the finest Tex had ever seen, but it was the man's lake-blue eyes in the long, narrow face, its hollows filled with shadows, that held the Texan's attention. The eyes looked both humorous and menacing, flashing like blue glass in a muddy stream. Tex felt the skin behind his ears prick as the man sized him up, chewing on a thin black cheroot.

"Don't let her fool you—she loved every minute of it," the man said, grinning with his eyes.

The comment caught Tex off guard. "Pardon me?"

"The girl calls me an animal, but she never once asked me to stop." The man's lips parted around the unlit cigar, showing little square teeth, slightly discolored.

Tex turned to look down the hall, as though the girl were still there. "Oh . . . oh, sure," he said.

"Have you ever spent a night with three women, amigo?"

Tex laughed. "Who? Me? Nah."

"You should try it. It is the closest thing to heaven a man will experience on earth. Light?"

Tex dug inside his coat for a lucifer, scratched it on the door frame, and lit the man's cigar, careful not to betray his anger. He didn't like playing servant to some uppity greaser, no matter how many men the gunman had slain, no matter how many women he'd diddled in one night.

When the cigar was lit, the gunman turned into the room, picked up his war bag and rifle, and tossed them to Tex. Then he picked up his saddle and started down the hall, leaving the door hanging wide behind him.

Tex stood there, grappling with his sudden burden and silently cursing the man. He peered into the room, where the bed stood in complete disarray, the mattress hanging off, the sheets and quilts twisted and strewn. The dresser had been pulled out from the wall, and its mirror was shattered. A tattered dress lay on the floor.

Tex shook his head slowly, not knowing what to make of the Mexican gunman.

Three women in one night? Tex thought, starting down the stairs. *A man like that could do some damage around here.*

THE GUNMAN RODE beside Tex on the snow-covered wagon road, on the black stallion Tex had led to town for him, and never uttered a word. Tex decided the man was either too uppity or ornery for idle banter, and that was just fine with Tex, who was too cold and feverish for conversation.

"The boss and the others are waitin' for ya inside," he told the man when they'd passed through the front gate of the sprawling Double X headquarters. "I'll take your horse into the barn."

The man did not reply, but sat staring at the three-story terra-cotta mansion with its cylindrical towers, arched windows, balconies, and ornate woodwork. From the look on his face, Tex figured the man hadn't been expecting to see such an elaborate hacienda this far off the beaten path.

His eyes played along the wide verandah to the carved oak door, in which the Double X brand had been burned, and up past the massive gable, with its deep-set window to the great stone chimney. Smoke lifted and was torn away on the wind.

One sleigh and a saddle horse stood before the verandah, the shaggy horses turning their drooping heads and twitching their ears at Tex and the gunman, clouds of breath jetting from their nostrils. Finally the man dismounted and handed Tex his reins. Wordlessly he walked up the wide steps, and the big door opened as though of its own accord.

Leading the stallion toward the barn and looking over his shoulder, Tex watched the gunman enter the house, the door closing behind him.

"There she blows, boys," Tex mumbled darkly, turning away. "There she, sure as shit, blows."

KING MAGNUSSON WAS sitting in the stuffed leather chair behind his desk, hands laced behind his head. His foreman, Rag Donnelly, and his business partner, Bernard Troutman, president of the First Stockman's Bank in Big Draw, had joined him in his den, and were sitting on the couch against the wall, to Magnusson's right.

The banker's beaver hat sat between him and Donnelly on the overstuffed cushions. They were drinking coffee and cognac and chatting easily, waiting for their meeting to start.

Magnusson was a tall, lean man in his late fifties, with hard, weathered features and thick, wavy blond hair combed back from a slight widow's peak. His eyes were blue; his friends said they had an amiable cast. His enemies called them the eyes of a liar, calculated to take your mind off the knife he was about to stick in your back.

Minnie McDougal, the housekeeper, was bending before the visitors, offering coffee and cognac from a silver tray. A hot fire sparked in the enormous stone hearth to Magnusson's left, filling the room with the smell of pine.

Magnusson lifted a coffee cup and saucer from the tray Minnie offered him now, declining more cognac—he wanted to stay clear this afternoon—and turned his eyes to his visitors. Minnie left the tray and returned to her chores.

"So when's this man supposed to get here, King?" Troutman asked. His red hair was matted and his pale, freckled cheeks were still mottled from the cold.

"At one o'clock, but who knows how badly drifted the road from Canaan is. It blew all night, and it's still blowin'."

"Why in hell did he take the train to Canaan? That's way the hell north—a two-hour ride in good weather."

Magnusson shrugged. "It's enemy territory," he said. "Said he wanted to check it out while he was still anonymous. Sounds like a good idea, if you ask me. Tells me the man knows what he's about."

The nervous Troutman didn't seem to be listening to Magnusson's explanation, but forming his next question. "How much did we agree he was worth?"

Magnusson suppressed a scowl. "We've been all over this, Bernie. Six thousand now—today—and another six when the job's done."

"How do we know when the job's done?"

"We'll know."

"And how do we know if he's caught he won't sing?"

The foreman, Donnelly, turned his cool wrangler's eyes to the banker. "Calm down now, Mr. Troutman—before you start giving *me* the jitters." He turned the smile to Magnusson, who dropped his eyes and plucked a long nine from the cigar box on his desk.

Biting the end off his cigar, Magnusson said, "He comes highly recommended. I can't say by whom, but . . ." He let his voice trail off and sat quietly smoking and listening to the clock.

A thought occurred to him and he turned to Donnelly. "How many beeves did you say Jack Thom was trying to get away with the other day?"

Donnelly shook his head. "I didn't see it. Randall and Shelby Green said they saw him hazing five off toward the Rinski place."

Magnusson's eyes grew dark, and he shook his head. "That arrogant son of a bitch."

"Shelby also said he saw several of our brands in Grover Nixon's pens—right there at his headquarters!"

Magnusson puffed and stared off into space.

Troutman piped up thoughtfully. "Well, the army came in and sided with them, so now they think they can do whatever they goddamn well please."

"Not for long," Magnusson said, darkly wistful. "Not for too goddamn much—"

He was stopped short by a tap on the study door.

"Come," Magnusson called.

The door opened. Minnie McDougal reappeared, nervously feigning a pleasant smile. Something had disturbed her. "There's a gentleman here to see you, sir."

"Send him in, Minnie."

She threw the door wide to let del Toro step past her. The smile vanishing, she left, closing the door behind her.

"Mr. del Toro!" Magnusson said buoyantly, standing and moving around his desk. "I'm so happy to see you made it. How was your train ride?"

Del Toro shrugged. "Pleasant enough, señor."

Magnusson shook his hand. "I'm King Magnusson. This is Mr. Troutman, my business partner, and Mr. Donnelly, the Double X foreman."

Both men stood and shook the gunman's hand. Donnelly

was smiling, coolly sizing up the Mexican. Troutman appeared flushed and tongue-tied as he eyed the man's wolf coat and fancy, prominently displayed pistols.

Magnusson had to admit that the man's presence was . . . unique, to say the least. He imagined the man even gave off the odor of death, however subtle. The blue eyes were downright startling. Magnusson mused he couldn't have handpicked a man this obviously appropriate for the job.

"Please sit down."

When the gunman had seated himself in the stuffed chair angled before the fire, crossing his long legs, Magnusson gestured toward the tray Minnie had left on his desk. "Coffee and cognac?"

"Just the cognac," the man said, looking around the room, at the western oils and watercolors hung in gilt frames, at the game trophies, and at the bear rug before his chair. "It was a chilly ride."

He seemed to be quite taken with the room's furnishings. Magnusson thought the man was probably more comfortable in bawdy houses and gambling dens.

When the rancher had given the man his cognac and had retaken his seat behind his desk, he said, "Well, let's get down to business, shall we, Mr. del Toro?"

"That's why I'm here," Del Toro drawled.

Magnusson retrieved his cigar from an ashtray before him and inspected its ash. "It's really very simple, and I'm not going to beat around the bush. There are about fifteen ranches north of us, on the other side of the Little Missouri, giving us trouble. Stealing our beef, taking our summer graze. We want them out."

A thin smile broadened below the gunman's mustache. "I thought you tried driving them out five years ago."

Troutman growled, "Heard about that, did you?"

"I heard they called the army in from Fort Lincoln to settle things down," the gunman continued.

"That's right," Magnusson said with a nod. "At that time the army, not knowing the full story, sided with the small cattlemen."

"What makes you think things are gonna be any different now, señor?"

"An old friend of King's was just elected governor," Troutman said with a grin.

Magnusson looked at Del Toro, his eyes hard. "I've been wanting those goddamn human coyotes off the Bench for a long time. None of us can increase year after year if we're sharing the Bench. There's simply not enough grass to go around, and the acreage I need to keep turning a profit and satisfying my eastern investors has forced me to get nasty. It's a simple matter of economics . . . and survival of the fittest."

He paused, stared thoughtfully through the variegated smoke cloud hanging in the study. Gray winter light penetrated the window behind him, outlining him against it and angling down on the leather top of his desk like quicksilver.

"I tried once before to clean off the Bench," Magnusson continued. "I failed because I didn't have the right men behind me. Now with Charlie Sparks in the governor's office . . . well, let's just leave it at that, shall we, Mr. del Toro?" He smiled, self-satisfied.

From the shadows on the far side of the fireplace, Del Toro looked at each man in turn. He removed his hat, primly smoothing his shiny black hair, and planted the hat on his knee. Returning his hand to his lap, he looked at Magnusson and said, "So how many do you want to disappear?"

"Disappear?" the banker said, frowning.

Donnelly snickered.

Magnusson said, "That gunman's talk for *die*, Bernard. Go to the henhouse. Buy the farm. *Comprende?*"

Troutman looked at him, scowling. "It ain't every day you hire a gunman, King."

"No. And let's hope we won't need to ever again."

Turning to Del Toro, Magnusson continued, "You see, we want this to be taken care of much more quietly than what happened five years ago. Five years ago, we let our tempers get away from us, and we lost control of our men." He shot an accusatory look at Donnelly, who dropped his eyes. "Things got very messy, to say the least. Out of control. This time, we want to be sure of every step we take. We want the right people excised with the precision of a well-schooled surgeon."

"And we don't want anything to point back to us," Troutman added.

Magnusson slid his chair out from his desk, opened a drawer, and produced a legal-size sheet of paper. "To that end, my two colleagues and I have drawn up a list."

Del Toro smiled, loving it. "A list of those to disappear, uh?" He got up to retrieve the paper. "A death list."

"Exactly."

Donnelly said, "Once you're done with it, burn it."

"I know my trade, señor," Del Toro said absently, standing before Magnusson and regarding the list. He took it to his chair and sat down. "Ten names."

"Yes," Magnusson said.

"How much?"

Magnusson decided to start low. "Eight thousand. Four thousand now. Four when you're through. We'll wire it to you after you're gone from here in a hurry."

Del Toro shook his head. "Uh-uh. Fourteen thousand. Nine now, five when I'm done."

Troutman chuffed. Donnelly smiled at Magnusson.

Magnusson sighed and puffed his cigar, studying the calendar clock on the fireplace mantle. He regarded his partners, then the gunman. "We'll go no higher than twelve. Two increments of six thousand."

"Let's see it," Del Toro said.

Magnusson opened another drawer. He counted out a pile of bills, slipped them into an envelope, and slid the envelope across his desk.

The gunman turned his head to the banker. "Would you mind bringing it to me, señor?"

Troutman gave Magnusson a flabbergasted look, mouth and eyes drawn wide.

"Oh, for Christ's sake," Donnelly said, standing and grabbing the envelope from the desk.

He took it to the gunman. Del Toro casually accepted it in one hand while offering his empty glass to Donnelly. The tall, rangy foreman refilled the glass, then returned it to the gunman. By this time, Del Toro had counted the money. He'd stuffed the envelope and the list in his coat.

"Gracias, señor," he said, accepting the glass from Donnelly. He sipped, then asked Magnusson, "Is there only one lawman in the county?"

"Yes, and he's harmless. Believe me."

Troutman and Donnelly both gave a laugh.

"Sí, I saw him at the train station," Del Toro said. "A soft old bear who hibernates all year long, eh?"

"You got that right," Troutman said. "Sleeps and drinks. When we tried clearing off the Bench five years ago, he hid out at the Sundowner in Canaan. When he finally decided he needed to take action, he called the army in."

"But that won't happen this time," Magnusson said importantly.

"Very well," Del Toro said, nodding. He polished off his cognac. He stood and donned his hat, adjusting it carefully.

Magnusson walked around his desk and shook the gunman's hand. The other men did likewise. There was a knock at the door as the gunman turned toward it.

"Yes?" Magnusson called.

The door opened and a pretty dark-haired girl, flushed from the cold, poked her head inside, gazing around Del Toro at Magnusson. "Hello, Father. I just wanted to let you know I'm home."

"Suzanne!" Magnusson said, his face fairly glowing, the hard features dissolving under the shine of parental adoration. "Get Minnie to heat you some chocolate. I'll be right out."

The girl smiled and gingerly withdrew from the door, latching it quietly.

Del Toro turned to Magnusson. "Your daughter?"

"Yes."

"Muy bonita, señor."

"Yes," Magnusson said, his smile turning cold. "And completely off-limits."

"Of course, señor," the gunman said with a lascivious smile. He tipped his hat at the men and left the room.

Magnusson stared at the closed door, feeling an icy finger probe his spine and wondering if he hadn't just made a pact with the devil.

WHEN HE'D SEEN Bernard Troutman off on his sleigh, King Magnusson heard boots crunching snow across the yard. He lifted his eyes to see his son, Randall, walking toward him from the barn.

Randall Magnusson was two inches shorter than his father, with a bearded, moony face and weak brown eyes. Long hair hung down the back of his buckskin coat. He wore a floppy flat-brimmed hat with a snakeskin band, secured with a cord beneath his chin.

"Hello, son."

"Pa."

"How's that heifer?"

Halting beside his father and turning to look at the sleigh dwindling in the distance, Randall said, "Eating a few oats now, anyway. Who's the greaser?"

"Name's Del Toro. He's gonna help us clean off the Bench, once and for all. Let's keep it under wraps, shall we?"

"Gunslick?"

Magnusson nodded.

Randall turned to his father. "You never told me you was hirin' no gunslick."

"Didn't want the word to get around."

"I can keep my mouth shut!"

King turned to him. His eyes were overtly patronizing. "We both know that isn't true, son. Especially after you've had a few drinks with the boys."

"Sure I can!"

"Randall," King admonished, arching an eyebrow. Having punctuated the conversation, he turned toward the house.

Puffing up his chest, Randall said, "You didn't need to go hirin' no gunman, Pa. Hell, me and Shelby Green can do what he can do, and we're a hell of a lot cheaper!"

King regarded his son skeptically. "Now, son, I appreciate that fine bit of detective work you and Shelby did out on the range. Finding Jack Thom with those beeves was a real help to me. It confirms what I've suspected all along about the smaller ranchers trying to ruin me. But I think it best if we leave the dirty work to those who've been schooled in that arena. Don't you?"

He smiled and put a broad, thick hand on Randall's shoulder, squeezing. "You may be a lot of things, son, but you're no gunman. That's a credit to your character, not an allusion to your poor marksmanship. You just keep working those mustangs, and one day you'll be as good a broncobuster as Rag."

King smiled, parting his thin, chapped lips.

Randall smoldered. Rag this, Rag that.

"Come on inside," King said, giving his son's shoulder another squeeze. "Your sister's back from Frisco."

King turned away.

Randall said to his back: "Yeah, well, tell that guman not to worry about the Rinskis."

"What?"

Giving an evil grin, the younger Magnusson stared into his father's eyes for a full three seconds. He wanted to tell him about what he and Shelby had done to old man Fairchild and that fancy-pants schoolteacher from Pittsburgh, but he resisted the impulse. When it came down to it, not even the old man had the stomach for what needed to be done to clear the Bench for the Double X.

"Me and Shelby caught Jack Thom butchering one of our steers Saturday. He held us off with a rifle, so we let him go. The next night we rode over to his cabin and let him have it."

He gave a self-congratulatory smile and sucked his cheek. "You can be sure the Rinskis won't be collarin' any more Double X beef."

Magnusson looked dully at his son. He lifted his chin and breathed sharply through his nose. "Let me get this straight. You and Green killed Jack Thom?"

"That's right."

"Did anyone see you?"

Beside himself with pride, Randall said, "We wore masks."

"Anyone else around?"

The young man's smile dulled. "Um, well . . . yeah. I mean . . . no."

"Well, which is it? Yes or no?"

"No. I mean . . . well, Rinski's daughter was there."

King looked surprised. "Daughter?"

"Yeah, well . . . she and Thom seemed to be . . . you know—carryin' on . . . with their clothes off and such." Randall laughed uneasily.

Magnusson drilled his gaze deeper into his son's face. "You shot Jack Thom while he was diddling Rinski's daughter?"

Randall wasn't sure if his father found the information humorous or horrifying. He looked for evidence of either as he said, "Yes, sir."

"So the girl saw you?"

"But . . . we were wearin' masks."

"Well, at least you had sense enough to do that." King looked around, digesting the information. "You didn't harm the girl, did you?"

Randall swallowed. "N-no, sir." He swallowed again and smiled.

King nodded. "Well, I reckon if you caught Thom red-handed, he deserved what you gave him." He sighed. "But from now on, you leave that work to the gunman. This Del Toro knows how to get things done quickly, cleanly, and quietly. Best of all, no one knows him, and no one knows who he's working for."

"Pshaw, I could—"

"You listen to me now, Randall," King said, waving a crooked finger in his son's face. His tone was again patronizing. "Just because you were lucky enough to catch Jack Thom in a . . . uh . . . compromising situation, and got the drop on him, that doesn't mean you're going to have that kind of luck again. You don't think I'd risk my only son getting killed over a few rustled beeves now, do you? So you leave well enough alone. You just hang tough with those broncs, and leave the gun work up to Del Toro."

He gave Randall a wink. "Maybe one of these days I'll be

able to tell my poker buddies that my son can ride as well as Rag Donnelly."

He turned and went into the house.

Randall glowered at the door. "Rag Donnelly this, Rag Donnelly that," he muttered, curling his upper lip. "You'll see who's who and what's what around here, you old duffer."

CHAPTER 7

EARLIER THAT SAME day, Mark Talbot's train steamed into Canaan screeching and hissing. Talbot disembarked with his war bag, wincing at the cold, which stung his face like a resolute slap.

He stood looking around to get his bearings while the only other passengers disembarking, two drummers in store-bought suits and muttonchop whiskers, hurried around the freight depot, no doubt in search of a warm spot to light.

But for the shiny new train tracks curving along the river buttes south of town, everything appeared pretty much as it had before Talbot had left. Sod and log shanties and clapboard shacks sat willy-nilly around the central business district of false-fronted stores and the livery barn with its fragrant sprawl of paddocks and corrals. The red train station and water tank abutted the settlement on one end, the lumberyard on the other.

Everything had the same feeble look of impermanence, and Talbot wondered how long it would take Canaan to decide to thrive or return to the sod.

His shoulders screwed up against the cold, he started toward the false fronts of the main street. The frigid air funneling up his thin cotton breeches told him he wasn't dressed for this kind of weather. Before shopping for new duds, he decided to shore himself with a stiff drink.

A gruff voice said, "I'm guessin' you're gonna freeze up solid within the hour, and I'm gonna have to find a place to hide your body from the rats until the ground thaws."

Talbot turned. A dozen feet to his left, before the frosty station-house doors, stood a round bear of a man with gray sideburns and a tin star.

"It is a mite chilly," Talbot agreed with a grin.

"You might want to think twice about lettin' that train go."

There was an ominous note in the big man's voice. Talbot knew that, with his shaggy beard and hair and mismatched seaman's clothes, he'd been pegged as riffraff, and that he'd just been invited to leave.

Talbot smiled pleasantly. "Don't worry, I'm not here to rob a bank or hold up the stage. I'm from here, born and bred, and I'm comin' home."

The sheriff tipped his head and squinted as he considered the newcomer. After a moment he said thoughtfully, "I thought you looked familiar. You're . . . you're . . ."

"Mark Talbot."

"Sure, Owen Talbot's youngest boy. Didn't recognize you under all that hair." The sheriff moved forward and held out his hand. Talbot could smell the liquor on his breath.

"Jed Gibbon," he said as Talbot shook his hand. "I ranched out in the sandhills before my water and credit dried up. I knew your pa, a good man. Used to play poker with him winters. Damn shame how the smallpox took him and your ma. You couldn't have been more than twelve."

"Fourteen. My brother was sixteen, but he grew up fast after the folks died—having to fill in for them and all." Squinting, Talbot studied the sheriff. "Oh, sure," he said. "I remember you. You treated me and Dave to hard candy and soda pop when you and Dad were chin-deep in cards. I don't know why I didn't recognize you."

"Yes you do," Gibbon said with a self-deprecating laugh. "What brings you home?"

Talbot shrugged and smiled wanly. "Just homesick, I guess. Decided to come back and see if my brother, Dave, had room for me on the ranch."

Gibbon's eyes dulled and his face fell. "You . . . you didn't hear, then?"

"Hear what?"

"No one sent you a telegram?"

Frowning, feeling his gut roll, hearing a high-pitched inner scream, Talbot said, "I doubt it would have got to me if they had." He studied the sheriff keenly. "What's this about, Sheriff?"

"Aw, shit," Gibbon grumbled, looking off. He rubbed his chin with a gloved hand, looking away. At length he nodded his head toward the street. "Come on. Let's go back to the jailhouse. It's warm there and we can talk."

Talbot followed the big man up the street, feeling his heart drumming in his chest, trying not to anticipate the bad news he knew he was about to hear.

Inside the jail, Gibbon shed his big coat, hung it on a nail by the door, and added a stout log to the potbellied stove. A fire was already burning and the room was warm. A blue enamel coffeepot gurgled on the stovetop shelf.

"Coffee?" Gibbon offered, gesturing to it.

Frowning, Talbot absently shook his head. Gibbon found a tin cup and emptied its dregs into a wastebasket. He filled the cup three-quarters full of hot coffee and topped it off from a flat bottle he produced from a desk drawer. Indicating the chair before his desk, he said, "Have a seat," then collapsed with a sigh into his own swivel rocker, which squeaked with his weight.

"Come on, Sheriff, spit it out," Talbot said impatiently.

Gibbon took a deep breath, sat grimly back in the chair,

and stared at his coffee. His face was pale. "Your brother's dead."

Talbot gazed into the sheriff's eyes, absorbing the information, feeling his stomach flip-flop and his heart wrench. After several seconds he squeezed his eyes closed and leaned forward in his chair. Slowly he rested his elbows on his knees and laced his hands together.

"How?" he asked quietly.

"He was shot."

Talbot lifted his head sharply. He'd expected to hear that Dave had had an accident or fallen ill with such common killers as influenza or pneumonia or smallpox. He'd never expected to hear that his brother, an eminently peaceful man, had been shot.

Not here . . . not at home!

"Did I hear you right?"

Gibbon had folded his hands over his hard, prominent belly. He was staring at the scarred desktop littered with pencil stubs, scrawled notes, and cigarette makings. He nodded slowly.

"Who?" Talbot asked, feeling anger grow heavy in his loins.

"Don't know for sure."

"When?"

" 'Bout five years ago."

Feeling sick, Talbot rested his head in his hands, trying to work his mind around the idea of his brother being dead for five years.

Five years . . .

Talbot stood and walked to the window, gazed out at the street. Horsemen passed. Lumber drays and buckboards rattled over the icy ruts. There was a sleigh parked before the mercantile; a small dog sat on the seat, gazing at the store for its owner.

"Tell me about it," Talbot said.

Gibbon sighed again and leaned forward. He rested his elbows on the desk and started building a cigarette.

"We had some trouble here about five years ago," he began slowly. "Your brother was one of the first ones killed."

Talbot turned sharply away from the window. Sweat beaded on his forehead. "First ones?"

Gibbon nodded as he shook tobacco from his pouch. "We ended up with about seven dead altogether. It all started when a new outfit moved in. It had more cattle than its government allotments provided grass and water for. Instead of culling its herds, it tried culling the smaller ranchers around it."

A grim cast to his eyes, Gibbon twisted the ends of his cigarette and scraped a match along a drawer bottom. "Your brother included."

Talbot gritted his teeth. "Who runs this outfit?"

Gibbon touched the flame to the end of his cigarette. Blowing smoke, he said, "King Magnusson. He's from Missouri."

"Magnusson," Talbot repeated, frowning. "Where have I heard that name?" Then it dawned on him, and he pictured the lovely dark-eyed Suzanne. How could the father of such a delicate, beautiful creature have killed his brother?

He tried working his mind around the question as Gibbon continued his story. "Several of the smaller ranchers got together to stand against this Magnusson," the sheriff said. "But it's harder than hell to fight against guerrilla tactics. And that's what these guys were using. They'd strike at night or first light, kill a man or two, burn a cabin, steal a few cows, and disappear before anyone knew what happened."

"Figured they could squeeze the others out without actually having to kill everybody, that it?" Talbot said.

"That's it," Gibbon said, sitting back in his chair and

crossing a leg over a knee. The cigarette smoldered in his right hand.

"I'm assuming you did something to stop it."

Gibbon flushed and inspected his quirley. "Well," he said tentatively, "the army had somethin' to do with that."

"You called the army in?"

Gibbon nodded. "The smaller ranchers put together a small army of their own, and were about to raid the compound of this outfit." His tone grew defensive. As he spoke, he stared at the floor.

"They . . . they wouldn't listen to me. Not that I had that much to say. I was new then, you understand, and someone had shot my deputy. Blew his head clean off his shoulders." Gibbon wagged his head and snapped his jaw at the memory. "Christ." He looked at Talbot as if for understanding.

Talbot frowned. "You arrest anybody?"

Gibbon lowered his gaze once more. "No. The army came in, Magnusson hemmed and hawed and denied everything he'd done, said it was the small outfits stealin' from him that started the whole mess in the first place. Which it probably was—who knows? It helped, of course, that one of Magnusson's main investors was in the territorial legislature. He's governor now."

"Christ," Talbot sighed, shaking his head. "So they got off scot-free."

"What the hell was the army gonna do? They're soldiers, not judges and juries. Besides, they had the Injuns to worry about. They weren't about to waste their time out here in the middle of nowhere. When everyone went home and things looked settled, they went back after Sitting Bull."

"You arrested no one for killing my brother, then," Talbot said. His tone was accusatory.

Gibbon raised his shoulders and spread his hands defensively. "Who was I going to arrest, for Christ's sake? Your brother was found out by one of his stock wells with two bullets in the back of his head—at least a week after he'd been killed."

He looked at Talbot and blinked nervously, licked his lips. He seemed to wait for a reaction. Receiving none, he said, "There'd been a good rain, so by the time I got out there, there were no tracks to speak of. No shell casings. Nothing. Period. I had nothing to go on. And that's the way it was with all the other killin's. It was one godawful mess around here!"

"So you called the army and they called it a draw and everyone went home," Talbot said tightly. "Except my brother and the six other dead."

Gibbon swallowed. His eyes retreated to his desktop. "That's right."

"Then the men who killed my brother are still out there." Talbot felt as though a saber had laid open his chest, exposing his beating heart.

"I reckon that's right," Gibbon allowed, nodding. He took a long drink of his toddy. After several seconds he mustered the courage to raise his gaze to Talbot, whose face was ashen with befuddlement and rage.

"I hope you're not thinking of getting even with the Double X," he said, his voice gaining an authoritative tone. "King Magnusson will screw your horns backward and twist your tail but good. Besides, your brother was killed five years ago. It's been quiet around here now . . . mostly. I don't need any trouble."

Talbot looked at him. "What do you mean, mostly?"

"It's still the frontier," Gibbon said defensively. "Things are bound to happen now and then." He inspected the coal of his cigarette and lifted it to his lips, taking a long, contemplative drag. Around the smoke issuing from his lips, he said directly, "The best thing for you to do is go get yourself a hot bath and hop the next train out of here."

Talbot walked over to the stove and stared at the glowing iron. His mind was numb, his body sick. A blade-like chill caressed his spine. He crossed his arms against it, vaguely aware of the cold sweat on his forehead and above his lip.

Dave has been dead for five years.

Talbot knew enough about land disputes to know how messy they were. The men who pulled the triggers were often not the only ones responsible for the killings. They were just your average soldiers riding for whoever was paying the wages and giving the orders.

But the man who'd hired Dave's killer was still around, smug in his certainty he'd gotten away with murder. And that man was lovely Suzanne Magnusson's father.

No matter where you were, it seemed, life was one war after another.

Watching him struggling with the news, Gibbon said, "It's a terrible tragedy, but your brother's dead, and nothin's gonna bring him back. If you try to get even with Magnusson, you'll not only be instigatin' another war, but committin' suicide. You'll be compoundin' the tragedy, understand?"

"I understand," Talbot said absently, knowing the man was right but feeling the urge for vengeance just the same.

"Good," Gibbon said, brightening. He scrutinized his blotter. "Now there's another train due in at four-ten tomorrow."

Talbot opened the door and said, "Maybe I'll be on it, maybe I won't."

He closed the door behind him and squinted against the cold wind, not sure of anything anymore.

CHAPTER 8

HEAD REELING FROM the news of his brother's death, Mark Talbot walked across the street in a daze. It wasn't until ten minutes later that he finally stopped walking and realized he'd been drifting aimlessly up one side of the street and down the other. His toes and face were nearly frozen.

Seeing the sign for the Sundowner Saloon, he headed that way.

"Help you, mister?" the barkeep asked. A stout man in a crisp white shirt and armbands was standing behind the bar reading the newspaper spread open upon the polished mahogany.

Talbot walked as far as the roaring cast-iron stove in the middle of the room. "Give me a boilermaker, will ya?" His voice was low and taut, and he did not look at the apron as he spoke. His mind was on his brother and on the man or men who had killed him.

He set his war bag on one chair and himself in another, only a few feet from the stove. He looked briefly around and saw that the two cowboys on the other side of the stove, nursing whiskeys and playing a friendly game of cards, were the only other patrons.

The cowboys' good-natured banter was an irritating contrast to Talbot's dark mood. Still, the tavern was as good a place as any to get warm and to digest the news of Dave's death, to try and get a handle on what he was going to do now.

The barkeep came with the beer and whiskey, and Talbot paid him. Obviously curious about the bearded, shaggy-headed stranger, the man lingered, attempting small talk. Discouraging it, Talbot offered only curt replies to the man's questions, and soon the apron drifted back behind the bar.

Talbot warmed his cold feet by the stove, nursed his beer, and sipped his whiskey, which soothed his chill body but did nothing to quell the torment of his soul.

Lost in his own brooding, he did not see one of the cowboys stand and walk slowly past him, regarding him warily until he'd made the door and stepped outside. Neither did Talbot notice the other cowboy get up and move to the bar. The man turned to Talbot and tucked his coat behind his gun.

It wasn't until Talbot had finished his whiskey and turned to the bar to ask for another that he realized the barman had disappeared. Only the cowboy stood there, a lean man with a hawkish face, regarding him darkly. Talbot's gaze dropped to the man's gun, prominently displayed.

The front door opened. Boots thundered across the floor, on a wave of chill air. Talbot twisted around to see three red-faced men approach. Their spurs beat a raucous rhythm on the rough pine boards. All wore blanket coats and hats snugged under knit scarves. The tips of their greased holsters showed beneath their coats.

Talbot saw the other man who'd been playing cards earlier. He walked past Talbot to rejoin the cowboy standing with his back to the bar. Both stared at Talbot as though he were something a dog had left on the floor.

One of the other two men stopped directly behind Talbot and about five feet away. His anger growing at the obvious confrontation, Talbot was craning his head to regard the man when the other moved around the table, pulled out a chair, threw his gloves down, and started unbuttoning his coat.

Talbot nearly laughed at the man's arrogance. "Sit down and make yourself at home."

As though he hadn't heard, the man—a slender individual in his fifties, with reddish-brown hair flecked with gray and a close-cropped mustache—regarded the bar. "Bring over a couple of whiskeys, boys."

"Thanks, but I'll drink alone," Talbot said.

Again the man did not respond. He regarded Talbot blankly and sat down, throwing his coat out from his gun. It was an obvious threat. He sat staring at Talbot until the whiskeys came. He threw the drink back and slammed the empty glass on the table.

Talbot felt rage burn up from the base of his spine. His heart beat erratically. A muscle twitched in his cheek. He was in no mood for indulging the insolence of strangers.

The sandy-haired man calmly wiped his mouth with the back of his hand. Suddenly his right arm jerked, and he lifted a revolver above the table, aimed at Talbot's heart. "All right, who are you and who you workin' for?" he said, red-faced and nearly shouting.

Talbot let two seconds pass. He set both hands on the table's edge and leaned forward, staring into the stranger's eyes. He said through gritted teeth, "None of your goddamn business!"

Then, springing to a crouch, he gave the table a violent shove forward, thrusting it into the man's chest, knocking his pistol up and sending him over backward with a startled yell. The pistol cracked, sending the slug into the rafters.

A half-second later Talbot was on his feet and wheeling toward the man behind him. The man had been pulling his .44, and as Talbot lunged for him, he brought the butt of the gun down hard against Talbot's head. Talbot dropped to a knee, shaken.

The cowboy stepped forward and was about to bring the gun down on his head again when Talbot heaved himself forward and bulled the man over backward. They both hit the floor. The man punched Talbot in the jaw and rolled aside. When Talbot looked up, all the cowboys stood around him, guns drawn and aimed at his face.

Behind the cowboys, the older man had risen to a knee and was regarding Talbot with wide-eyed anger. He was breathing heavily, and his hair was awry. His crushed Stetson lay several feet away.

"You had enough, Slick, or should I have my boys ventilate you now?"

Talbot breathed heavily. Blood dripped from his swelling lower lip. He felt a goose egg growing on his temple. "This the kind of homecoming you're offering these days?"

"Homecoming?" the man said with a skeptical grunt.

"That's right."

"Who are you?"

"Who'd you think I was?"

The man blinked. "I don't know, but you got *trouble* written all over you, and we've had our fill of trouble around here."

"Looks can be deceptive," Talbot growled.

"When you're dealin' with killers, you can't be too careful."

"I'm no gunman. If you'd taken the time to look, you'd have seen I'm not even armed."

The man nodded and shot a sharp look at the man who'd summoned him. "I see that now," he said to the sheepish-looking cowboy.

The cowboy said, "Y-you said to let ya know if we seen any strangers, boss, and this man here . . . well, he sure looks like a tough, he acts like a tough, and he sure ain't from around here."

"Shut up, Virgil," the man snapped. To Talbot he said, "The cowboy's right. A cowboy was murdered by two toughs a few days ago. If you're not a tough, what are ya, then?"

"I'm Mark Talbot. Owen Talbot's son."

The man cocked an eyebrow. "Owen's boy?"

Talbot nodded. "Been away for a while." Talbot climbed to his feet and wiped the blood from his lip. "Now I have a question for you. Who poked that burr up your ass?"

One of the cowboys laughed, then covered it with a cough. The older man's face turned a deeper shade of red. He cowed his men with a look and said gruffly, "All right . . . holster those irons and get yourselves a drink. We'll be heading back to the ranch soon."

When the men had returned to the bar, where the bartender furnished drinks, the rancher said to Talbot, "You'd be suspicious, too, if you been through what I been through around here."

"Are you talking about the same trouble that killed my brother?"

"One and the same."

"The sheriff told me the army came in and settled that mess five years ago."

The man nodded, his jaw tightening. "That's what I thought. But a week ago a man was shotgunned out east of here. Two days ago a Mex gunman shows up, slinks around town, and disappears into the countryside. We thought maybe you were another gunman Magnusson was bringing in."

"So you think it's starting all over again," Talbot said.

"Hell, it never really stopped. There were always killin's . . . hangin's and such. But when Rinski's hired man was killed by two masked men with shotguns—before a witness!—well, that told me all bets were off. Suzy, bar the door."

Talbot searched the man's face gravely. "Who killed my brother?" he said tightly.

Shrugging and shaking his head, the man picked up a chair and sat down on it. "Who knows?"

There was a pause as the man looked around the room, his eyes thoughtful and afraid. Finally his gaze returned to Talbot and his features softened. He said, "I apologize for the trouble. Can I buy you a drink?"

Talbot nodded and sat down across from the man.

"Monty, bring a bottle," the man called.

"And a beer," Talbot added.

When the barman had brought the bottle and a beer, and two fresh shotglasses, he filled the glasses, set the bottle on the table, and returned to the bar. At a table on the other side of the room, the other cowboys had started a new game of five-card stud.

The older man shoved his open hand toward Talbot. "Name's Thornberg," he said. "Verlyn Thornberg. I ranch south of here, along the Little Missouri."

Talbot shook the man's hand. "Mark Talbot."

"I met your brother in the mercantile once or twice. Don't believe I've ever seen you before."

"I lit a shuck out of here about seven years ago. Must have been before your time. I left the ranching up to my brother. Figured I was too good for it. Wanted to see the world."

"Did you see it?"

"Enough to know if there's such a thing as the good life, it's here."

"Maybe it *was* here, back before I came, right before the trouble," the man said, thoughtfully sipping his whiskey. Swallowing, he shook his head. "But it ain't here no more. When did you find out about your brother?"

" 'Bout an hour ago."

"Jesus, I'm sorry. That's tough, comin' home after seven years to find your brother dead."

Talbot shook his head, scowling and staring into his whiskey. "It wasn't exactly what I was expecting, no. You know what happened to our ranch? I was Dave's only kin, and I was out of reach. I hope Magnusson didn't get it."

The man thought for a moment. "I believe the Kincaid girl is grazing her beef on it. It abuts her land, as you know, and it's got good winter cover."

Talbot lifted his head. "The Kincaid girl? Jacy Kincaid?"

The man nodded.

Visibly surprised, Talbot said, "Why, she can't be but fourteen years old!"

"I've seen Jacy Kincaid," Verlyn Thornberg said with a humorous air, "and I can tell you she's no fourteen-year-old. She fills out a cotton shirt and a pair of Levi's 'bout as well as any girl in the territory, and she's a better hand on roundup than half the men. Broke most of the hearts on the Bench, too, I might add."

Talbot did some quick math on his fingers. Sure enough, the girl he'd known on the neighboring ranch would be in her early twenties by now. But the knowledge that she'd taken over the Talbot ranch was too much to grasp.

Talbot said, "You must mean her father assumed the Circle T."

Thornberg wagged his head. "Nope, Miller Kincaid died of a heart attack two springs ago."

Talbot remembered the towheaded little tomboy who used to ride her horse over to the Talbot ranch hot summer afternoons when he and Dave were kids. She'd played cowboy and Indians with Talbot and Dave, always accepting her role as the savage warrior good-naturedly. She snared gophers with the Talbot lads, too—as rough and tough as any boy.

She'd had a splash of freckles on the bridge of her nose

and down her cheeks, and for that reason Talbot and Dave had called her Freckles. She'd taken issue with the nickmame, however, and given them each such hard kicks to their shins that they finally had to cease and desist or risk permanent hobbling.

"Well, I'm glad Jacy's got it," Talbot said now. "If she turned out anything like her old man, she'll be good to it—won't muddy up the springs or overgraze the creeks."

"She'd turn it back to you," Thornberg speculated. "Since you were neighbors and all."

Talbot shook his head. "Nah, it's hers. She earned it . . . while I was off on my high horse." He took a big sip of beer and threw back the last of his whiskey.

Thornberg folded both his hands on the table and leaned toward Talbot, regarding him gravely. "Come to work for me, then."

Talbot laughed. "Doing what? I haven't ridden a horse or swung a lasso in a coon's age. I figured my brother would put up with me 'til I got the hang of it again, but I wouldn't expect anyone else to."

Thornberg shook his head. "I don't mean as a rider. I've seen you fight."

Talbot blinked. "As a fighter?"

Thornberg nodded and smiled conspiratorily. "If it came down to a tussle between you and that Mex gunman the big outfits brought in, I'd place my money on you."

Talbot just stared at the man, hollowed by the thought that his home had turned into a graveyard and a battlefield, just like the rest of the world.

"How good are you with a gun?" Thornberg continued eagerly.

Talbot blinked and considered the proposition for a moment. He had to admit it was tempting. But the possibility of finding Dave's killer was slim at best, and the probability of his getting enmeshed in the very life he'd finally turned away from was great. That life had cost him too much to return to it here at home.

Talbot finished his glass of beer, stood, and reached for his war bag. "Thanks for the offer, but I don't think so."

Thornberg frowned. "Where you goin'?"

"To find a place to sleep," Talbot replied quietly. "Thanks for the drinks." He swung the war bag over his shoulder and headed for the door.

"What about your brother?" Thornberg cried, incredulous.

Talbot turned back to the man. "I expect I could spend the rest of my life seeking vengeance and end with nothing to show for it but hate. If you had known my brother, you'd know he wouldn't have wanted that."

He looked at Thornberg, then at the barman and the other cowboys, who had ceased their game to see what all the commotion was about. Talbot turned away and opened the door.

"Besides, I'm no longer in that line of work," he mumbled, and went outside, looking for a peaceful place to light.

He wondered if he'd ever find it.

CHAPTER 9

TALBOT WENT UP the street to Zimmermann's Hotel, which had added another story and a coat of paint since he had last seen it, and asked for a room furnished with heat and extra quilts.

In the small room consisting of a bed, a chair, a dilapidated wardrobe, and a coal-oil heater, he sat and smoked a cigarette and wished he hadn't come home.

The wind howled beneath the eaves and blew snow against the windows. Someone in the room above him was scuffing around in his boots and hacking phlegm from his throat. Somewhere a baby was crying. Out in the silent street a cat mewed.

From somewhere out of the blue, Talbot remembered the old spotted horse he and Dave used to ride to their swimming hole, hot July afternoons. Then a twelve-year-old, Dave was jumping from the barn loft, tucking his knees to his chest and wrapping his arms around his legs and careening through shafts of afternoon light into a mountain of sweet-smelling hay.

"I bet you can't do this, Mark!"

Talbot walked to the window and peered out without seeing anything. With Dave dead and only memories left, Talbot had no idea what to do, but he felt the need to see his old home place again and to visit Dave's grave. He'd hang around the country for a month or so. Maybe at the end of that time he'd know whether he still belonged here or somewhere else.

He plucked the quirley from between his lips and studied the ash grimly. He lifted his war bag onto the bed and opened it. Dipping a hand inside, he rummaged around on the bottom, then pulled out his six-shot revolver, an old model Colt he'd worn in a covered holster during the Apache campaigns. He hadn't worn a gun since Mexico, and he'd lost his government-issue holster in a poker game aboard the *Bat McCaffrey*. He regretted the loss; in self-defense, he supposed he'd have to wear the hog leg on his hip.

Welcome home, he thought, dropping the iron back in the bag and stowing the bag under the bed. He stubbed the cigarette out in an ashtray and headed for the door.

"Where'd be the best place to find new duds around here?" he asked the old woman who ran the place. She was watering a half-dead plant hanging in the window downstairs. Talbot didn't remember her and assumed she was a recent arrival, as were most of the people he'd seen so far.

"Check McDonald's up the street," she said.

"McDonald's? You mean McCracken's."

"McCracken's burned two years ago. McDonald rebuilt."

"Much obliged," Talbot said, feeling as though time had left him in its wake.

Talbot found the mercantile sandwiched between a clapboard establishment advertising hardware and tinware and a wholesale tobacco shop. The proprietor stood behind the counter in a derby hat and wool vest, one fist on his hip, the other on the countertop. He watched Talbot with silent suspicion, and Talbot found himself thinking he was liable to get shot in the back in his own hometown.

"At ease, friend. I'm one of the good guys," he said, resenting his outsider status among these newbies. People sure seemed quick to label and reject around here. That wasn't how Talbot remembered this town.

The man said nothing. His expression did not change.

With the proprietor watching but offering no assistance, Talbot picked out a sheepskin coat, a union suit, heavy denim jeans, a flannel jersey shirt with leather ties, a black Stetson hat, wool-lined leather gloves, wool socks, and fur-lined knee-length moccasins.

After he'd picked out a soft leather holster, a cartridge belt, and a .44-caliber lever-action Winchester, which he'd heard were all the craze among cowboys these days, and three boxes of shells, he got the grim proprietor to throw in a scarf and a sack of tobacco, and paid the man.

"Nice doing business with you," he said dryly, hefting the parcels onto his shoulder. "I'll be sure and hurry back."

He hauled the merchandise two doors down, to Gustaffsen's Tonsorial Parlor for a shave, a haircut, and a long, hot bath.

When he'd finally hauled himself out of the steaming iron tub an hour and a half later, he felt like a stranger. The face that peered back at him from the proprietor's handheld mirror bore little resemblance to his more youthful conception of himself.

Cut to half its former length, his wavy auburn hair was combed straight back behind his ears, and his face, minus the beard, was big and hard-lined and ruddy. An Apache arrow had left a healed-over dent to the left of his right eye.

With the beard gone, he saw age in the spokes around his eyes and in the leathery skin pulled taut over his high, chiseled cheeks. Several gray hairs appeared in the two-inch sideburns. His eyes lacked their youthful luster and his lips were sullen.

In seven years he had grown from reckless youth to wry middle age, though he was only twenty-seven.

"You like?" Gustaffsen asked in a Swedish accent heavy

enough to sink a clipper ship. His sharp eyes glanced from the mirror to Talbot and back again.

"No."

"Huh?"

"I mean . . . it's fine," Talbot said, handing the man his glass. "What's the charge?"

When he'd dressed in his new duds, he buckled the six-shooter and the new holster around his waist. The gun felt so foreign and looked so malign, hanging there on his hip, that he took it off in frustration and shoved it back in the war bag.

If they wanted to shoot him, let them shoot an unarmed man. He wasn't ready to start killing again. Not even in self-defense.

When he'd wrapped his old clothes in a bundle for Gustaffsen to dispose of, he went over to the town's only café for a supper of pork chops, sauerkraut, and fried potatoes.

He and the two drummers he'd gotten off the train with were the only customers, the cold weather apparently keeping everyone else home. The drummers' idle banter across the room depressed him; instead of lingering over his coffee and dessert, he went back to his room and crawled into bed.

He lay awake for a long time, listening to dogs barking in the distance, staring at the ceiling, and pondering the notion that his brother was gone and that he'd been homeless for five years without knowing it.

Five years . . .

AFTER BREAKFAST EARLY the next morning, Talbot found a feed barn and a livery stable and picked out a saddle horse and tack. An hour later he was cantering a deep-chested speckled gray gelding along the mail road east of town.

Mid-morning, he left the road and followed a long, shallow

valley between low rimrocks. He remembered the way easily, noting landmarks and pausing occasionally to study eagles' nests and wolf prints in the snow, feeling good to be back in the saddle and back in the country.

It was a cold, windy day, with low, fast-scudding clouds. Talbot snugged the strap under his chin to keep his hat in place.

When he came to the canyon in which lay the valley where the Talbot Circle T ranch was located, Talbot took the first ravine to the west. He rode for another hour, following the ravine's devious course until it rose into a bowl surrounded on three sides by hogbacks spiked with tawny grass poking through the snow. In the distance sprawled a long, wedge-shaped mesa where Talbot and his brother used to trap rattlesnakes every summer.

Below the hogbacks, in a natural wedge that broke the wind, sat the Circle T—a two-story log cabin with a lean-to sloping off its east wall, a big gray barn with a connecting paddock, and several small corrals straggling down the ravine to a stock pond and windmill.

The place had a forlorn, abandoned look, and Talbot's heart ached to see it like this—the cabin dark, with no smoke lifting from its chimney; the corrals barren of saddle stock; the weathered gray blacksmith shed looking as hollow as an old tree stump.

Three pigeons started from the barn loft. They flew around the yard, then settled again in the loft and watched between the planks of the closed doors. Behind the cabin, the outhouse door squeaked in the wind funneling through the draws. It sounded like a moan. The air was heavy with the smell of skunk.

Entering the compound, Talbot saw that one of the pole barns had lost a pole and its roof had partially fallen in. The snow around the compound was pocked by hooves and littered with frozen discs of cow dung. A drift had formed on the cabin porch like a frozen wave. The old Talbot lease was apparently being used as winter range, and the cabin probably served as an occasional outpost for grubliners and bandits.

Talbot spurred his horse forward and dismounted before the cabin, looping the reins over the tie rail. He turned the knob and pushed the door open. He stood in the doorway and looked around the cabin, letting his eyes adjust to the shadows within.

When the living room swam into focus, he saw that the newspapers he and Dave had tacked to the walls had turned yellow. Torn strips curled toward the floor. Most of the furniture had been hauled off by other settlers, no doubt.

A few stools and a homemade chair remained near the fireplace. The floor planks were floury with dust, coated in grime and mouse shit. The few remaining lamps were chipped and smoke-blackened, and cobwebs hung from the ceiling joists.

Opening the door and walking down the short hall to the kitchen, Talbot saw that this part of the house was in the same state of disrepair. The two remaining chairs were broken, and the plank table sat askew, littered with dirty dishes, tins, cigarette stubs, and playing cards.

There were yellowed newspapers and magazines scattered about the cupboard tops. A mouse-chewed flapjack lay on the floor by the range. Two torn gray socks hung from a rafter. This room was an add-on, and Talbot recognized his own notches in the logs. It was a bittersweet recognition, shaping his nostalgia to a sharp point.

Talbot sucked his teeth, listening to the mice scuttling in the walls and thinking, It's no more than a line shack.

Outside he looked around the yard for his brother's grave but saw no sign of it. Surely someone had buried Dave on the premises—the sheriff or one of the neighbors. The wind had blown most of the snow against the buildings and corral posts, nearly covering an old horse mower and a dump rake but clearing the open ground. A marker would have been evident.

Puzzled, Talbot started back to his horse. A rifle cracked nearby. Talbot and the horse jumped simultaneously. While the horse kicked and pawed the ground, Talbot crouched and looked around.

"Hold it right there, asshole!"

It was a female voice.

"Throw your gun down."

Talbot shuttled his gaze from the barn to a figure standing on the other side of the corral, hunkered behind a post from which a rifle poked.

"I'm not wearing a gun," he said, raising his hands to his shoulders.

"Gordon, check the son of a bitch for a gun!" the woman yelled.

Talbot heard boots crunching snow and turned to see a lanky, stoop-shouldered man walk out from behind the pole barn, a Navy Colt held before him. Appearing to be in his fifties or early sixties, he was swarthy with a bushy gray mustache with upswept ends, patched denim breeches, and a big sugarloaf sombrero pulled low over his eyebrows. His torn mackinaw was stretched taut across his broad chest, its frayed collar raised against the cold.

He scuttled toward Talbot sideways, his eyes wide and cautious. Chew stained the corner of his mouth.

"Easy, now," the man growled as he approached Talbot sideways and gave him the twice-over with his watery-blue eyes. He patted the sides of Talbot's coat with his free hand.

Finally he looked at him sharply and said, "Where in hell's your gun?"

"In my saddle boot."

"No hog leg?"

"In my war bag. Wasn't inclined to wear it today."

"Well . . . I'll be." Turning to the woman, he said, "He ain't wearin' no iron, Jacy."

The woman said nothing for several seconds. Then the rifle went down, and she said, "Keep your eyes on him, Gordon. I'm comin' over."

She walked around the corral, and Talbot watched her, smiling, wondering if she'd recognize him. She hadn't been more than fifteen when he'd left home—just a scrawny, freckle-faced girl. She'd turned into an attractive young woman.

She appeared about twenty or twenty-one, and tall for a woman, maybe five-eight or -nine. A bulky green-plaid coat concealed her figure, but from her legs and hips Talbot could tell she was slender.

Under the wide-brimmed, flat-crowned black hat, her face was fine-boned and smooth, with full lips and green eyes that slanted a little, betraying her Slavic heritage. Her skin was vanilla, like the remnant of a summer tan, reminding Talbot a little painfully of Pilar. Rabbit fur moccasins rose to the patched knees of her faded jeans, and the rifle she held was a Henry with a seasoned stock and an oiled barrel.

As she moved closer to Talbot, she cocked her head to the side and squinted one eye. Recognition growing slowly on her face, she stopped before him but said nothing. Her eyes regarded him with frank amusement.

He smiled.

"Well, I'll be goddamned," she said.

"Hi, Jacy."

"Damn near got yourself shot."

"Nice to see you, too."

Turning to the older gent who stood regarding them quizzically, still holding the Colt, she said, "Remember Mark Talbot, Gordon? Dave's brother? He's finally come home."

The man squinted at Talbot, nodding slowly. "Well, I'll be goddamned."

"I didn't recognize you at first either, Gordon. How are things?" Talbot offered his hand to the old cowboy.

Gordon Jenkins shook it and shrugged. He'd been working for outfits around the Bench for as long as Talbot could remember. He was one of those men you always saw on horses among others just like him but didn't think much about. They were professional cowboys living their lives on the open range, brush-popping steers from sunup to sunset, and spending the winters holed up in brothels and bunkhouses from Bismarck to Abilene.

"Pretty much the same, Mark. How 'bout you?"

"I've been better."

"What happened to your lip?" Jacy asked.

Talbot probed the swelling with his tongue. "Had a little homecoming party in town last night."

"This isn't the same country you left, Mark," Jacy said darkly. "Dave was killed five years ago. I'm so sorry."

Talbot looked off and squinted. "I heard. Thought I'd ride out here and look for his grave."

"Did you find it?"

Talbot shook his head.

"Get your horse and follow me." Jacy turned and started walking around the pole barn for her horse.

Talbot was mounting up when he heard horses blowing and turned to see Gordon driving a spring wagon loaded with supplies.

"Came from town," he explained, driving past.

Jacy rode her line-back dun through the coulee south of the ranch, following a cattle trail in the snow. They rode single file, Talbot following Jacy, Gordon bringing the wagon up behind Talbot.

The wind was still blowing, shepherding shadows across

the snow, which shone in gray, wind-drifted patches here and there along the coulee. Small flocks of redpolls wheeled above the weed-tips. A coyote spooked from a frozen seep and disappeared up a crease in the ridge. The only sounds were the wind and the horses crunching snow.

It was a grim ride; no one said anything.

After ten minutes, the coulee fanned out on both sides, revealing a line of big cottonwoods standing along Crow Creek. The creek bottom was about a quarter mile wide, and dense with willows, chokecherry, hawthorn, and occasional box elders.

It was a haven for whitetails, Talbot remembered. But you had to beat the brush for them, and you had to get them before they dashed up the opposite ridge and were gone across the prairie.

"I remembered how you and Dave liked it down here," Jacy said, as if reading his thoughts. "I couldn't think of a more fitting place to bury him."

Talbot kept his eyes focused on the corduroy ridge on the other side of the creek, not wanting to lower them, wanting to stay with his memories of old deer hunts and Dave whooping and hollering in the willows while Talbot sat in a declivity on the ridge, waiting for the hazed deer that would bound over the natural levee only a few yards away.

Finally Talbot dropped his eyes to the homemade cross beneath the cottonwoods. Its thin gray shadow angled over the rock-mounded grave beneath it.

Dave.

Talbot dismounted, handed his reins to Jacy, and studied the grave. Fallen leaves clung to the nooks and crannies between the rocks. Tracks of coyote and racoon made light impressions in the snowy grass. A weasel had been poking about.

Talbot studied the grave for a long time, remembering his big, blond, grinning brother who could toss a hundred-pound feed sack into the haymow like it was straw. Finally he looked up at Jacy, blinking away the film of tears from his eyes.

"You . . . you buried him here?"

"Dad and Gordon dug the grave. I thought it was fitting," she said matter-of-factly.

He lowered his eyes again to the grave. "Thank you."

"I'm sorry. What a thing to come home to."

Talbot gave a dry laugh. "I figured maybe Dave had got married, had him a youngun or two, maybe built one of those nice big clapboard houses. I sure never expected this."

"It was a horrible thing, what happened here," Jacy said thinly. "Frank Thompson, Paul Goodnough—hanged on their own ranges. There were five cabins burned, and Hutt Mills was taken naked from his lean-to and forced to walk back through knee-deep snow. He lost both his feet and nearly all his fingers to frostbite."

"Any idea who shot Dave?"

Jacy looked at Gordon, who sat the wagon seat, elbows on knees, sucking a tooth to distraction, his eyes wide and distant. A scuttling breeze toyed with the brim of his sombrero.

Jacy said, "Gordon said he saw Randall Magnusson and another man crossing our range one morning a few days before he and Dad found Dave's body. They were heading toward your place."

Gordon moved his head slowly from side to side. "I sure wish I woulda looked into it at the time, but I was just so thrilled to see 'em riding away from me, I didn't give much thought to where they were goin'."

The cowboy's slow voice betrayed a high, Ozark twang. "That Magnusson kid—he was only about sixteen, seventeen at the time—is the ornriest little bastard I seen outside of Blackfeet country. A coward and a cold-blooded killer with more than a few screws loose to boot."

"Did you tell the sheriff?"

"Sure I did."

"And?"

"And Jed Gibbon just crawled all the deeper into his bottle. Wasn't about to fool with the likes of the kid or the kid's father, King Magnusson."

Talbot sighed and bit his lip. "Christ."

"Yep," Jacy said, drawing out the word darkly.

Talbot mounted his horse, a thoughtful look wrinkling his brow. "King Magnusson," he muttered. "I can't imagine a killer like that raising a girl like his daughter."

Jacy frowned. "You know Suzanne?"

"Met her on the train."

Jacy and Gordon shared a sneer. "Was she comin' from back east or out west?" Jacy asked snidely.

"West."

"You never know with little Miss Queen of England. When she gets tired of the smell of cowshit, her daddy sends her to New York for a new wardrobe."

"I take it you and her aren't close," Talbot said ironically.

"It's not so much her I hate as her family—a bunch of highfalutin scalawags, getting rich off the land they steal from others." She watched Talbot; his eyes were cast in thought. "You taken with her?"

His eyes rose to hers, his mind racing to reconcile the vivacious, cultivated young woman from the train with the family Jacy had just described.

Changing the subject, he said, "I heard your pa died."

Jacy nodded matter-of-factly. "Had a heart attack in bed, but it was King Magnusson that killed him. All the worry about the ranch and what would happen to me if night riders came . . ." Her voice trailed off.

"Your ma?"

"She married Harold Offerdahl last spring. Harold took her off to Mandan to open a harness shop, and I was glad he did. This battlefield is no place for a nervous lady like Ma." She smiled. "She writes me twice a month and sends me cookies and pies."

"Maybe you should have gone with her."

Jacy tilted her head. Her eyes were sharp. "Why's that?"

Talbot shrugged. "Well, because you're . . ."

"A girl?"

He shrugged again.

"Girl or no girl, I wasn't about to let King Magnusson take everything my pa had worked so hard for," Jacy snapped.

Talbot smiled, admiring the girl's spine but thinking her foolhardy just the same.

"Well . . ." he said, and reined his horse around and started along the creek. Jacy caught up with him and rode parallel, several yards to his left. Gordon brought up the rear in the clattering wagon.

Several white-faced cattle appeared at the mouth of a draw, chewing cud in the gold sun, breath puffing around their heads. Snow and dirty ice clung to their coats.

"I've been wintering some older stock on your range," Jacy explained. "I'll get them out in the spring, and me and Gordon will help you get your cabin back in shape."

"I'm not sure I'm gonna stay," Talbot said, "but I appreciate the offer."

"Where would you go?"

"I don't know."

"This is your home."

Talbot forced a chuckle. "That's funny. It sure doesn't feel like it."

He was craning his neck around to watch Gordon, who had broken off the trail and now directed the shaggy draft horses toward the cattle. The old cowboy leaned out from his wagon perch, inspecting the brand on a Hereford within a loose pack of seven beeves.

"Hey, Jacy," he called. "There's a Double X brand over here."

Jacy turned to look toward the cowboy and the milling cattle. "Good," she said angrily. "Coyotes got the rest of that steer you butchered last week."

"Whatever you say," Gordon said, drawing his pistol.

To Jacy, Talbot said, "You're gonna shoot that Double X stray?"

The young woman shrugged and pursed her lips. "You know what they say—nothin' tastes better than the neighbor's beef."

Her sentence was punctuated by the flat report of Gordon's Colt. The first was followed closely by a second. The herd bounded into an awkward run up the draw. The one Gordon had shot remained behind—lying on its side, its legs kicking spasmodically.

Talbot regarded Jacy with heat. "Isn't that the sort of thing the Old Trouble was about?"

"Magnusson started it."

"That's no defense, Jacy."

She jerked a sharp look at him. "Several of Magnusson's cowboys rode through Jamison Gulch last week on their way to town, and drove four of my best steers over a butte. Gordon was out riding the line and saw it. Wasn't much he could do and not get himself killed. That wasn't the first time Magnusson killed my stock. I found three heifers shot last fall. He kills mine, I kill his. It's the only defense I have."

"Are the other small operators having the same trouble?"

"In spades."

Talbot shook his head. "You're gonna get yourself killed, pulling stunts like that."

Jacy grunted. "I only wish they'd try pulling something on me like they did over at the Homer Rinski place last week. Then it'd be more than their cows dyin'!"

Talbot remembered what Gibbon had told him. "It was Rinski's hired hand they shot?"

Nodding, Jacy added, "And whose daughter they savaged like animals. Mattie's in a bad way, and her father doesn't know what to do with her."

"Does she know who they were?"

Jacy gave her head a shake and sighed. "Don't know—she won't talk about it. She tries to act like nothing happened, only she can't settle down. She works like a butcher all day and can't sleep at night. She's not in a good way."

Talbot paused, watching Gordon begin to dress out the dead steer. "My God, what's become of this country?" he said weakly.

Jacy turned her sea-green eyes from Gordon to Talbot and brushed a stray lock of tawny hair from her cheek with a gloved hand.

"My place ain't the cheeriest these days, but it's good for a hot meal or two." Her lips cracked a smile. "Her teats might be bigger than mine, and she may walk a little straighter, but I bet Miss Magnusson has nothing on me in that department. If you're squeamish about stolen beef, I can boil you up a porcupine."

Talbot's face warmed at the girl's salt. He had to laugh. "You know, I bet you're right, Jacy Kincaid."

"Is it a date?"

If I had any sense, Talbot thought, I'd take the sheriff's advice and head east, keep riding until I was a safe distance from here. Maybe Minnesota or Iowa, possibly Wisconsin. This country, like so many other places from which he'd fled—the desert Southwest, Mexico during the gold boom—was a powder keg sitting only a few feet from a lit fuse.

But this was home.

"It's a date," he said with a slow nod, returning Jacy's smile, then cutting his eyes down the coulee toward his brother's grave.

CHAPTER 10

JOSÉ LUÍS DEL Toro quietly levered a shell into the breech of his rifle and waited for a rift in the wind. If there was such a thing up here. With snow on the ground, there was practically what the gringos called a whiteout every time the wind blew—which was nearly all the fucking time.

It was blowing now, and even though the sky was clear as crystal, each gust caused a whiteout. There was no snow falling, only blowing, and during a gust you could hardly see your fucking hand before your face. A ground blizzard. That's another word the gunman hadn't heard before coming north.

No wonder gringos were such a chilly race of people.

Del Toro's rifle was a Sharps .50-caliber, factory engraved with a horseback rider shooting buffalo, and inlaid with gold. It had a silver finish and butt plate, and its smooth black walnut stock felt firm and familiar against the gunman's cheek.

The Big Fifty fired a two-and-a-half-inch-long case loaded with ninety grains of black powder that could blow a dollar-sized hole in a man at six hundred yards. That kind of distance didn't come into play here, however. If all went as planned, the first man on Magnusson's list would pass within seventy-five feet below him, on the meandering cow path at the bottom of the draw.

If it hadn't been for all the snowy brush covering the hillside on which Del Toro sat, rifle on his knees, it would have been a chip shot. But with the winter dead foliage limned with hoarfrost between him and the trail below, he'd need a steady hand not to clip a clump of frozen berries or a hawthorn twig, and nudge the slug wild.

The swirling snow wasn't helping any, either. Visibility was only about thirty yards. About twenty yards beyond that now, the man was coming on a brown horse—just as he came every night from town, lit up with cheap liquor and singing like a stud lobo at the end of March.

Del Toro could hear the man's voice, make out the words of the song he was singing—attempting to sing.

"Oh, Su-zanny, don't you cry for me, I've gone from Al-a-ba-my . . . with a banjo on my kneeeee."

The voice was so high and ludicrous and off-pitch and gringo cocky that it made Del Toro grate his teeth together. But his face remained expressionless, his jaw set in a hard line. He closed his left eye, stared through the sliding leaf sight, through the tunnel of motionless foliage.

It was about four-thirty, a still, cold night this far north in December. The sun had fallen into the prairie, but the sky remained blue. Amid the blowing snow, which swirled down the draw like some living thing, the brush was dark, a solid black shape against the opposite, boulder-strewn ridge.

Horse and rider were approaching now. When the wind died and the snow settled, Del Toro could see the horse and the dark shape of the man.

He lifted his head from the rifle stock, gave a high, short whistle, then returned his eye to the sight. The rider stopped suddenly, drawing back on the reins.

"Whoooa. What was that?" he said. His voice was thin and barely audible above the wind.

The horse had stopped, jerking its head against the bit pulled taut against its jaw.

The man opened his mouth, lifted his upper lip like a curious horse. He looked around, listening. "Who's there?" he said after several seconds.

Del Toro was counting his heartbeats and staring through the sight at the vague shape in the snow. He waited for the present gust to break so he'd have a clear shot. The last thing he wanted was to wing the bastard and see him flee on his horse. That would be messy. Del Toro did not like messes.

The snow swirled like silk flags waving this way and that, catching and tearing on boulders and tree limbs. Gauzy forms assembled and scattered. The man waited, looking around. He did not have the animal's keen nose, but he sensed the hunter's presence just the same.

He was frozen there in his tracks, sensing death there on the hillside just a few yards away. "Who's there?" he said again, quieter this time, voice thin with fear and suspicion.

A gust died for half a second; the snow thinned.

Del Toro cursed in Spanish. He should have taken the shot. It might have been the only one he'd have.

But just as the thought vanished, the wind settled again, and the man sat there clearly, both hands holding his reins, looking up the hill.

Del Toro squeezed off the shot just as the man turned up the trail and started to flick the reins. Fire spit from the end of the barrel and the report echoed like an immense drumbeat, circling before it died.

Del Toro lowered the smoking gun and stared down the hill, frowning. The wind and snow had closed in, thick as ever. He could see nothing but the irregular, free-forming shapes of the ground blizzard, but he heard the horse whinny loudly, heard the hooves stomping and the bridle chains jangling.

The man yelled out, cursed.

The horse pounded off. A pistol cracked once, twice, three

times. Del Toro ducked low behind a tree and listened to the slugs thudding into the ground around him—the closest about ten feet away.

The reports echoed. When they died, Del Toro tipped his head to listen. Below rose the soft crunching of boots in the snow, nearly indiscernible above the wind.

The man was off his horse and was running away!

Cursing himself, the gunman stood, reloaded the single-shot rifle, and started down the hill. Gravity pushed him down the snowy slope at a breakneck pace. Sliding and stumbling, he broke the speed of his descent by grabbing branches and careening off boulders, holding the rifle out for balance.

Hurdling a deadfall, he came to the foot of the hill and stood in the horse's tracks, looking around and catching his breath. His lungs were not used to air this cold. It was like breathing sand.

Sweeping his gaze along the ground, he saw the man's horse had thrown him—there was a splash of blood in a broad, scuffed area where he'd fallen—then bolted up the trail. Boot prints showed the man running back the other way, in the direction from which he'd come.

Del Toro sighed, clutched his rifle in both hands, and followed the man's tracks, walking. There was no reason to hurry. From the amount of spilled blood, the gunman knew the man wouldn't get far without a horse. Also, the man could be lying in wait for him, pistol drawn. There was no reason to add injury to insult by getting bushwacked.

As he walked, he considered letting the man go. He'd either die from the wound or freeze to death. But there was always the possibility of his finding help from a fellow traveler or of retrieving his horse.

No, Del Toro needed to finish the job. There was nothing he hated more than a mess.

He wrinkled his nose to loosen the frozen nasal hairs and

began moving forward, following the erratic tracks of his wounded quarry. There were occasional splotches of blood next to the boot prints, and they looked brown in the fading light. Del Toro stopped every few steps and listened before moving on.

He knew the man would stop sooner or later, since he was losing blood fast and he had a gun; he would hunker down in the brush along the trail and wait. Like a cornered lynx.

A fine goddamn mess, Del Toro thought. Shoot a man with the biggest rifle on the market and miss! Like something a damn gringo would do.

It was this hellish weather—all this snow and cold fucking wind. The conditions for killing were horrible.

Del Toro stopped. About fifteen feet away, the tracks began bearing off to the left, toward the shrubs and brush. A small wedge of red-orange flame poked through the blowing snow. A crack followed and a bullet whistled, thunking into a tree somewhere behind the gunman.

Del Toro dropped facedown in the snow and cursed. He rolled to the right and heard the pistol fire twice more. The lead thumped the snow. He unholstered one of his two pistols and fired at the place in the snow he had seen the pistol flash. The lead twanged off stone.

The man was behind a rock. Shit.

Del Toro angrily fired off four more rounds, then rolled again to his right. The pistol barked and flashed again. Two more quick bursts, then one more about five seconds later.

That was six shots. The man's gun was out of bullets.

Quickly, Del Toro climbed to his feet and ran slipping through the snow, peering through the whiteout, trying to brush it away with his hands. Suddenly the wind settled to reveal the big stone—a flat-topped slab of granite grown up with dead weeds and moss. A stunted cedar grew out from under it at an impossible angle.

The gunman grabbed a cleft in the stone for leverage and peered around the rock, lifting his rifle to his chest with one hand.

"No!" the man screamed. "Leave me be!"

He lay on his back, chin to chest. His pistol was in his right hand, shielding his head. The pistol's cylinder hung out, and empty cartridges lay scattered on the ground.

"Please don't shoot me," the man pleaded, kicking his feet and cowering like a whipped dog. Blood oozed from a hole in his dirty blanket coat. The air around had the rotten-egg odor of gunsmoke.

Del Toro said matter-of-factly, enjoying the man's misery, "I have to shoot you, señor."

"Why?"

"Because you're filthy gringo scum. Because you butcher cattle that do not belong to you. Because you occupy land you do not deserve, and because you multiply like brush wolves and fill the land with more mangy scum like yourself."

"King!" the wounded man cried. "King Magnusson! He's the one who hired ya."

"That is right. Allow me to introduce myself, señor." The gunman took his rifle in his left hand and held out his right. "José Luís del Toro."

The man stared at the hand, lips quivering, eyes bright with fear. Tears rolled down his heavy, leathery cheeks. "Please . . ."

When he saw that the man was not going to shake his hand, Del Toro shrugged and lifted his rifle to his shoulder, aimed at the man's forehead. "No, I am sorry, señor. I have a job to do."

"What about my wife? What about my kids?"

Del Toro did not reply, and there was no indication on his taut face that he'd even heard what the man had said.

The man saw this, and his breathing slowed. The fear in

his eyes gave way to resignation, though a good dose of the fear remained. He dropped the empty pistol in his lap.

His head tilted to the side and his chin came up. The eyes rose to the gunman's, sighting down the octagonal barrel.

"No," he begged one last time.

Fire and smoke geysered from the barrel, and the big gun bucked. The man's head snapped back from the impact of the slug destroying his forehead. The head bounced off the ground with such force that the man's back rose nearly perpendicular to the ground. Blood and brain matter sprayed. Then the man fell back again. The man's head turned to the side, and he lay still.

The air left his lungs with a sigh and a groan.

Del Toro stood the rifle against the rock and rummaged inside his coat, producing a pencil stub and a small leather-bound notebook. He licked the stub and scrawled something on one page of the notebook. He tore the page from the book, folded it, and stuffed it in the pocket of the man's coat. Then he licked the stub again and scratched out the first name on his list. With a slow, satisfied nod, he replaced the pencil in the book and returned the book to his coat.

He snugged his collar against his neck, retrieved his rifle, and headed back toward the hill and the tree to which he'd tied his horse.

"This goddamn gringo weather," he grumbled.

CHAPTER 11

TALBOT'S HORSE ASCENDED a crumbling clay bank, putting its head down and digging its front hooves into the hard ground. Beside Talbot rode Jacy, then Gordon Jenkins, the field-dressed beef lying behind the dry goods in the wagon box.

At the top of the knoll, they halted to give their horses a breather, and Gordon rolled a cigarette. Talbot swept his gaze around, reacquainting himself with the lay of the land—a rolling, sage-pocked prairie creased by ravines and coulees, capped by a low, gray sky. Bromegrass and wheatgrass shone where the wind had swept the snow away. Here and there cattle grazed.

Jacy pointed to a grove of trees marking the line of a distant creek. "That's the Rinski place. I thought we'd take a little detour and check on Homer and Mattie."

"I remember Homer," Talbot said. "A God-fearin' man, as I recall. Don't recollect his daughter."

"You probably never saw her," Jacy said. "From just about the time she started walking, that girl had to take care of her father. I doubt she ever went to a dance or had a boyfriend."

"None her father knew about, anyway," Gordon said, letting cigarette smoke drift out with his words. "Pardon my talk, Miss Jacy, but word has it Jack Thom wasn't the first of her daddy's hired hands she was a mite friendly with, if you get my drift."

Jacy grunted a laugh and grinned at the old cowboy. "If I had a life like Mattie's, I'd probably be chasing you around the bunkhouse, Gordon."

"Shee-it," Gordon said, blushing and wagging his head.

Jacy clucked to her gelding, and Talbot and Gordon followed her down the knoll and across the prairie. As they rounded another knoll about twenty minutes later, the Rinski ranch appeared, fronting a creek tracing a brushy path below buttes.

Jacy halted her horse about fifty yards from the low, ramshackle cabin. "Mr. Rinski, it's Jacy," she called.

A tall gray-haired man appeared in the doorway holding an old-model rifle. He wore a fur coat and a round-brimmed black felt hat. He pulled the door closed behind him. Gazing at the three visitors sitting their horses at his ranchyard's perimeter, he said nothing. He just stood there, blinking, holding his rifle low across his thighs. Hogs grunted under a thatch-roofed pole barn, giving off their distinctive smell.

Finally Jacy spurred her horse forward. Talbot and Gordon followed suit.

"Who you got with ya?" Rinski asked.

"This is Mark Talbot; remember him?"

Talbot smiled, noting how the man had aged since he'd last seen him, and recognizing the haunted cast in his eyes, due no doubt to what had happened to his daughter and hired man. "How are ya, Mr. Rinski?"

"You're the one went off to fight the 'Paches," the old rancher said, remembering. "Your brother bragged ya up some, he did."

"I don't doubt it," Talbot said with a weak smile, feeling guilty all over again for having left his brother to ranch alone.

"The Lord been kind to you, young Talbot?"

"I reckon he was kind enough to keep me alive. Quite a feat when dealing with Victorio's Mescaleros. I wish he'd been that kind to my brother."

Rinski's eyes seemed to focus on something beyond Talbot. He worked his lips a moment before he spoke. "The Lord works in mysterious ways."

"I'm sorry about the trouble you've had here."

Jacy inquired about Mattie.

"Nothin' wrong with my daughter time and the Good Lord can't heal," Rinski said automatically. Then his conviction seemed to flounder, and his eyes flickered doubtfully. "Does seem awful . . . *nervous*, though."

The old man's heavy eyebrows knitted together as he dropped his chin, pondering the ground as though looking for something. It had no doubt been a nightmare for the man to reconcile his faith to what had happened in his hired hand's shack last week.

Jacy said after an awkward silence, "How you getting along, Mr. Rinski? Do you need anything?"

"I'm fine," he said, though his ghostly countenance indicated otherwise.

Turning to her hired man, she said, "Gordon, why don't we leave the beef liver with Mr. Rinski? I know how he likes fresh beef liver."

Rinski said nothing. The wind poked at his hat and at the gray hair hanging beneath it.

As Gordon dismounted and went around the wagon to retrieve the liver, Jacy said, "Do you mind if I go in and see Mattie, Homer?"

"She'd like that."

When Jacy had gone inside, Rinski turned to Talbot again. "You come to fight a war closer to home, did ya, young man?"

Talbot shook his head. "I thought by coming home I was getting away from war."

"Well, you weren't." Rinski's voice was louder now, his gaze more certain. His eyes grew large and dark. "There's a devil at work here now, and we're gonna need help in fightin' him. Verlyn Thornberg is trying to get some of us smaller outfits organized, but he don't seem to have the leadin' spirit. No one wants to follow him against this big outfit that's been moved by Satan to savage our women and swallow up our land."

Rinski spoke as though he were standing behind a pulpit. His forehead was creased and his lips were pursed, dimpling his chin. "It happened once before. With the Lord's help we got the demon back in hell, but he's slipped out again, sure enough. We need you on our side, young Talbot, to fight against the Beast."

"What you need is the law," Talbot said.

"The law is without fortitude in this matter," Rinski said without batting an eye.

Talbot was about to respond when Rinski said, "Follow me," and started walking east around his barn and corral, where a half-dozen winter-shaggy horses milled, manes ruffling in the wind.

Talbot tried to study him out, puzzled, then spurred his horse in Rinski's direction. When he caught up with the old man, the rancher was standing in the doorway of an old lean-to cabin, looking in. His back was stiff and his shoulders were slumped forward.

When Talbot had dismounted and dropped his horse's reins, Rinski turned to him. "Have you a look at the devil's work, young Talbot," he said, stepping aside.

Talbot ducked as he stepped through the low door. The room was small and dark. A small stove hunkered in the back right corner. The air smelled coppery.

His eyes swept the room, stopping on the back wall above a cot. The logs of the wall bore a large stain, at least three by five feet wide. Talbot moved forward and saw that the cot was covered, too. The blood had frozen on the green wool blankets, which were twisted and mussed and had turned a crusty, flaky brown. Talbot guessed that the white specks of bone in the substance were what remained of Jack Thom's skull.

Talbot felt his stomach clench. He winced as he imagined the screams and yells and the two loud booms from the shotguns. The old rancher watched him darkly.

"Thought you should see for yourself the blood that's been spilled here in the name of the devil," Rinski explained.

"Do you know who did this, Mr. Rinski?"

"Magnusson's son and Shelby Green."

"Has your daughter named them?"

Rinski's face was stony, his eyes hard. "She won't talk about it, but when I asked her if it was those two mavericks—they been terrorizin' folks for years—her eyes grew big as silver dollars."

Talbot looked at the frozen blood drops on the wall. "What are you going to do?"

Rinski shrugged and stared at the rough wood floor. "Whatever the Good Lord tells me to do, young Talbot."

Talbot stepped past the man and walked outside. Rinski watched as he mounted his horse and rode back to the cabin.

"Where did you go?" Jacy said. She and Gordon were standing on the porch.

"To the hired hand's shack."

"What did you think?"

Talbot shrugged. "Nasty business. You might stop stealing beef."

"They steal ours—"

"So you steal theirs, I know," Talbot said, nodding his head. "How's the girl?"

Jacy shrugged darkly. "She won't sit still—just keeps scrubbing and straightening, like she can't get anything clean enough. Doesn't talk much, either."

As they were leaving the ranchyard, Rinski appeared, walking around the corral.

"The liver's in your skillet," Jacy called.

"Obliged," Rinski called back, not looking at them.

THEY RODE THE horse trail along Haughton's Bench to Wolf Creek, and cantered out upon the long, rolling reaches above the Little Missouri. As night came down, the rambling buildings of Jacy's Bar MK appeared, dark and shapeless below the tip of a grassy, tongue-shaped mesa.

They unloaded the wagon, stabled their horses in the timbered barn, hung the dressed Double X beef high above the floor, and threw hay to the saddle stock. Jacy and Talbot headed for the cabin, and Gordon walked to the bunkhouse.

The cabin was a long, low, solidly built structure of saddle-notched logs and wood shingles. A peeled-log gallery ran the length of the porch, and Talbot remembered his father and Miller Kincaid sitting out here, jawing away a summer evening.

"I'll have supper ready in half an hour, Gordon," she called.

"No thanks, Jacy. Think I'll mosey up to Spernig's . . . you know, see about a friendly game of poker."

"A friendly Mrs. Sanderson, more like," Jacy said.

Gordon wagged his head and went into the bunkhouse.

"He's got a woman who works at Spernig's Roadhouse," Jacy explained to Talbot as they mounted the porch steps.

The kitchen in which they gathered was built of big,

square-hewn logs with plastered walls and a four-globed light hanging low over a long cottonwood table. Oval pictures hung on the walls, and several magazines were spread across the table. Coffee cans on the cupboard tops held utensils, and braided rugs fought the cold air seeping up from the floor. It was a big, homey kitchen, the kind of kitchen that took your mind off your problems. Talbot was grateful for such a kitchen just now.

"Sorry about the mess," Jacy said as she struck a match and lit the lamp on the windowsill. "I'm afraid I'm not much of a housekeeper. Don't really see the point, I guess . . . living alone."

Talbot had picked up several pieces of kindling from the porch. He tossed the wood in the box by the range and sat in a chair by the door. "I'd have thought you'd be married by now."

"Was," she said, throwing paper and kindling into the big stove. "For about a week. Met him at a shindig over at Spernig's—one of those come-one-come-all barn dances. He rode for Verlyn Thornberg. I thought he was the best thing since Winchesters and mustangs. The day after I married him, he turned shiftless and mean." She laughed without mirth, blowing on the fledgling fire. "Guess I should have realized he was marrying me for my ranch, but I was young and lonesome."

"What happened?" Talbot asked.

"I called him on it. The next morning he was gone. Took two of my best horses. Haven't seen him since. Heard he went to Montana, the son of a bitch."

Talbot said nothing, watching her.

She had her back to him while she worked on the fire. "What about you?"

"Well, I never married, if that's what you mean. The last seven years have been . . . crazy, I guess is the word." He didn't want to talk about Pilar. He hadn't spoken the girl's name aloud since she'd died.

"So why didn't you come home sooner?"

He shrugged. "I liked crazy for a while. You don't get bored when you're always on the move."

She had turned to him now with her coat and hat still on. The cabin was cold. "So why did you come home now?"

He thought for a moment, shrugged. "There's no place like home. Or so I thought."

She smiled. "I'm glad you're home." She flushed slightly. "I . . . I looked up to you guys—you and Dave."

He frowned, skeptical. "Really?"

"I didn't have any brothers, you know."

"We tormented you."

"I loved it."

He laughed. "The scars on my shins tell a different story."

"I was only really angry when you didn't take me serious," she confessed, then flushed even more and turned away to the fire. It was burning well now, and the iron range was ticking as it heated.

She pumped water and heated it on the stove, insisting he wash first since he was company. He did so after he'd hung his coat and hat on pegs by the door. She was slicing potatoes into a skillet in which grease popped.

"Your turn," he said, drying his arms and face on the towel she had draped over a chair back.

He sat at the table, feeling good to be sitting down to table again in Dakota. He reached into his shirt pocket for his tobacco pouch and started rolling a smoke. He worked on it thoughtfully and deliberately, lifting his eyes to Jacy as she washed.

She was a girl no longer, he saw as she removed her heavy wool coat and hat and swept her hair back from her neck with both hands. She was every inch a woman, with all the right curves in all the right places, though genes and hard work had streamlined them some, taken some of the female plump and turned it to muscle.

Without a trace of modesty, she unbuttoned her blue workshirt and tossed it onto a chair, then rolled up the sleeves of her faded red long johns and bent over the steaming washtub. From his side view, Talbot couldn't help noticing that she was not wearing any of the underclothing most females used to nip and tuck here and pull and press there.

Her small, conical breasts pushed invitingly against the thin, wash-worn fabric of the long johns, the pronounced nipples sliding this way and that as she scrubbed her face and behind her ears and neck.

"That feels good," she said breathily. Strands of wet, tawny hair stuck to her face. "It's a long ride to town and back."

Talbot stuck the quirley between his lips and struck a phosphor on the underside of the table, lighting up. "Do it often?"

" 'Bout once a month. It's nice to get away, see something else for a change, and get the pantry stocked, of course." She glanced at him, did a double take.

"What are you lookin' at?"

It was too late to avert his eyes. He'd been caught. He smiled, flushing and blowing smoke at the ceiling. "You."

She was drying her arms. "What about me?"

"You've . . . grown up, Miss Jacy."

"Yes I have, and now I can really give your shins a bruising." She tossed away the towel and produced a long knife from the counter. Brandishing it, she said, "Why don't you go out and cut us a couple of nice steaks from that Double X beef—or cut me one and bring yourself a porcupine. You'll probably find one or two at the trash heap."

With a flick of her wrist, she flung the knife through the air. It landed point-first in the table, about six inches from

Talbot's right hand, the handle vibrating for about two seconds after impact.

Impressed, Talbot pushed himself to his feet as though he'd just discovered a diamondback under the table. "Whatever you say," he said melodramatically. Sticking his cigarette in the corner of his mouth, he reached for his coat, pulled the knife out of the table, and headed out the door.

Jacy turned to the sizzling potatoes, smiling.

Talbot returned several minutes later, hands full of raw, marbled beef, kicking the door closed behind him. "Here's your grass-fed Double X," he said dryly.

"Drop it in the pan. I've got the potatoes warming in the oven. Where's your porcupine?"

"Plum got away. I guess I'll be dining on the Double X this evening. Along with you and the Rinskis. I just hope King Magnusson doesn't decide to check out your barn. That brand is hanging there, plain as day."

Jacy poked the meat around in the skillet and grew serious. "You're making too big a deal out of this, Mark. King Magnusson started putting his brand on our cattle the day after he moved into that big house of his."

"Then you should have brought in stock inspectors and federal marshals, and hauled him in front of the federal magistrate."

Jacy shrugged. "Hindsight is twenty-twenty. Besides, you know how these old guys around here feel about the law. Hell, half of 'em are wanted for some penny-ante thing back east, and the other half believe the law belongs to only those who can pay for it. And the only one who can pay for it around here is King Magnusson."

Talbot sighed and sat down. Jacy had convinced him of the situation's complexity. Still, two wrongs didn't make a right. Stealing from King Magnusson only made the water muddier.

Just the same, the smell of cooked, seasoned beef wafting

up from the range made his mouth water, and he decided to enjoy the meal in spite of his philosophical differences with the cook.

"How do you like your steak?" she asked him.

"Bought and paid for, but I'll settle for well done."

JACY FILLED THEIR plates, and they wolfed down the meat and fried potatoes like true Dakotans. Afterwards, doing his part, Talbot cleared the table and washed the dishes while Jacy sat at the table, watching him while she rolled and smoked a cigarette.

"Sorry, I know it's not very lady-like," she said, indicating the quirley. "Drinkin' whiskey probably isn't, either, but would you like a glass to wash down that Double X beef?"

Talbot shrugged. "I reckon it wouldn't be polite to make a woman drink alone."

When he had dried and put away the dishes, he and Jacy took their glasses of whiskey and retired to the sitting room, where she had started a fire in the big fieldstone hearth.

Talbot sat in the rocker near the flames, noting the deer and bear heads eyeing him from the walls and remembering that Jacy's father had been quite the hunter and trapper in his day. Jacy sat on the sofa and removed her moccasins, nudged them near the fire with a stockinged foot.

"Tell me about Dave," Talbot said after several minutes of contemplative silence.

"What about him?"

Talbot shrugged. "Did he have a girl? Before I left he was taking a shine to Maggie Cross over to Big Draw."

Jacy took a drag off her cigarette. "Maggie died, you know."

"She did?"

"You didn't know that?"

"No."

"Suppose you wouldn't. It was the milk fever."

"Jesus. Had they been close?"

"Rumor was they were going to marry. I asked him about it, but he wouldn't say. You know how shy he was about women."

Talbot leaned forward in his chair, taking his whiskey in both hands and resting his elbows on his knees. He sighed heavily.

Jacy continued, "After that he kept himself busy on the ranch. Dug several wells, added another herd he brought up from Kansas City, mixed in some white-faced stock. He had three cowboys workin' for him when . . . when he died."

"Where did they go?"

"I hired one. Thornberg took the others."

She disappeared into another room and returned with a document, dropping it in his lap on her way back to the sofa. "That's his will. I found it among his papers. It leaves the ranch to you."

Talbot sighed and stared at Dave's boyish signature at the bottom of the sheet, beside the official seal. "What if I don't want it?"

"It's your home. And it's some of the best graze on the Bench. No wonder Magnusson went after it first. What I wouldn't give for one or two of your creeks."

"They're yours."

"Don't say that."

"Why not?"

"We can be partners. I'll help you get started again."

"Why?"

She shrugged. "Old time's sake."

Jacy finished her whiskey and set the empty glass on the lamp table beside the sofa. She went into the kitchen and returned with the bottle, then refilled Talbot's glass. She straightened, holding the bottle by its neck. "I had a crush on you once. Did you know that?"

He looked up at her.

"But you never paid attention to me after you started taking Rona Paski to dances."

He shook his head, surprised. "I didn't know that."

She smiled. "Then you went away."

Jacy took the bottle and sat down. She refilled her glass and set the bottle on the table. "I was just a kid to you, I reckon."

"Well, you were a kid," he said defensively.

There was a long silence. They each sat drinking and thinking, listening to the fire crack and the wind howl under the eaves. Talbot had the feeling again of having been left behind. The plan had been simple: Go home and help Dave on the ranch. Get hitched, build his own place, raise a few kids . . .

He worked his mind back around to the moment, toying with the idea of taking over the ranch. He had the money; he could feel it in the homemade pockets around his waist.

"How many head are you running?" he asked Jacy.

She was lounging with her head about a foot below the top of the sofa's back. She looked tired and her hair fell carelessly to her shoulders. She'd crossed her ankles on the stool before her.

"Close to a thousand," she said. "I had a good increase last year. I'm hopin' for an even better one this year. I only keep Gordon on during the winter, but I have about four men on my rolls during the spring and summer. Want another drink?"

They each had another. He tossed his back and looked up. She was still sitting there in the same way, but now tears were rolling down her cheeks.

"Jacy, you're crying," he said.

She smiled through her tears. "I'm just drunk."

"What are you crying about?"

"I don't know. I just get to feeling loco in the winter with nothing to do but feed cows and stare at the clouds." She sniffed. Her voice sounded far away. "And I don't know if I can keep this place . . . if I can stand against old Magnusson."

"You will," he assured her.

"Oh, I know—I'm just drunk."

"Why don't you go to bed?"

"I think I will."

Deliberately, she uncrossed her ankles and set her feet on the floor. She tried to push herself up but fell back down. "Or . . . maybe I won't."

"I'll help," Talbot said.

Smiling, she threw up a hand. He clutched it and pulled her to her feet. Feeling how unsteady she was, he bent down, picked her up in his arms, and carried her down a short, dark hall. She was light, and she felt good in his arms, her loose hair brushing his forearm and wrist. She smelled musky but feminine.

"Which is your room?" he asked her.

"That one."

He pushed the door open with his boot and laid her on the iron bed. She pulled the quilt back and crawled clumsily beneath it. Talbot walked to the door.

"Good night, Jacy."

"You can sleep here. . . . This is the only bed in the house."

"What about your father's?"

"It's buried under tack; you'll never find it." She patted the quilt beside her. "Come on. I won't bite."

He stood in the doorway, watching her. His breath came short, and he couldn't help feeling aroused. It had been a long time since he'd slept with a woman, with or without sex. His last lover had been Pilar, three years ago. He knew he should grab a quilt and lie on the couch, but he couldn't make himself do it. He wanted to lie next to Jacy.

So he removed his shirt, money belt, and jeans and lay on the bed.

She turned to face him, snuggled up against his chest.

"It's been a long time since I've had a man to keep me warm," she said drowsily, getting comfortable against him.

He kissed her ear, ran his hand down her thigh.

She looked up suddenly. "What's that?"

"Sorry . . . I, uh . . . seem—"

"I'm not a loose woman, Mr. Talbot," she said haughtily. "Here, I'll take care of it."

She thrust her hand through the front opening in his long johns, grabbed his member, and squeezed, slowly pressing it down.

"There—how's that?" she asked.

He gave his head a quick shake and smiled against the pain. "Yeah . . . yeah, that should . . . do it," he said with a sigh.

"Good."

Then she wedged her head against his chest and went to sleep.

CHAPTER 12

SPERNIG'S ROADHOUSE SAT in a horseshoe of the Little Missouri River, along a well-traveled freight road snaking across the broken prairie between Mandan and Glendive, Montana.

The roadhouse sat in a hollow between low buttes. Doubling as a dance hall, it was a long, barnlike building constructed of milled lumber and boasting a redbrick chimney poking through its shingled roof. A corral flanked the building on the left, and a long hitch rack paralleled its front porch.

In spite of the cold weather, or because of it, Spernig's was hopping tonight. The corral was nearly filled with saddled horses, and two spring wagons and a buckboard were tied to the hitch rack. Dull yellow light spilled from the windows, and the sound of laughter, shuffling feet, and broken piano music penetrated the still, cold night.

Inside, Gordon Jenkins sat a table nearest the piano. His big hand was wrapped around the handle of a soapy beer mug and his attention was glued to the woman playing the piano—or trying to play, as the others saw it. No one but Gordon could understand why the woman had been hired, for she could play no better than a gifted cowhand, and her half-assed renditions of "Little Brown Jug" and "The Flying Trapeze" were raucous at best.

But night after night, Gordon listened and watched as

though he were being personally serenaded by harp-wielding cherubs. And tonight was no different.

Now as the woman finished a ponderous "I'll Take You Home Again, Kathleen," letting the final notes fade with a dramatic flair, lifting her pudgy nose to the rafters, Gordon rose to his feet. He brought his sun-darkened paws together slowly at first, issuing reports like those from a heavy Sharps rifle, then more quickly as he gained momentum. The woman turned her round face to him and smiled.

Gordon returned the smile with a wet-eyed one of his own, then turned his head to glance about the room. The other men and Spernig's two soiled doves were not clapping. They weren't even looking the piano player's way.

Gordon's expression turned so dark that the others seemed to sense its heat before they saw it. Gradually, one pair of hands at a time, the room filled with applause. One of the soiled doves even removed the cigar from her mouth and gave an obligatory whistle before going back to her card game.

It was enough to satisfy Gordon, who smiled broadly and held up his beer as the lady at the piano beamed and flushed, dropping her eyes demurely.

As the applause died and everyone returned to their jokes and their card games, Gordon pulled a chair out from his table, and the woman made her way to it. She was dressed in a shiny green gown with puffed sleeves and feathered felt hat. Gordon loved the way her full bosom bubbled up out of her corset like giant scoops of vanilla ice cream.

"That was some fine playin', Doreen, some mighty fine playin'. Yessirree, doggie—can you *play* that thing!"

"Well, thank you, Gordon."

"No—thank *you*, Doreen. You know, after listenin' to you of a night, I'll hear one of those tunes all the next day while I'm goin' about my chores—just like you was playin' a little piano inside my head."

Doreen Sanderson laughed gaily, red lips parting and blue eyes flashing. Gordon didn't know how old she was—he guessed she was somewhere around forty-five or fifty—but he thought her the best-looking thing for the years as you'd find in Dakota in the wintertime, and her a widow with full-grown children to boot!

"Really?" she said, beaming.

"Would I lie to you?"

"Well, no, I guess you probably wouldn't, Gordon."

"Here, have a seat. I'll order you a drink."

She frowned and pursed her lips, hesitating. "Oh, Gordon—you know, I'm awfully tired, and Mr. Norton wants me to start inventory early in the morning, before the doors open." She only moonlighted as a piano player, working full-time as a clerk and bookkeeper in Big Draw. "I'm awfully sorry, but I think I'm going to head back to town."

Gordon's face fell. "So early?"

She smiled painfully and touched his hand. "I'm afraid so."

"Well, I'll drive the buggy around."

"Oh, you don't need to see me home. It's early yet. You stay and have fun."

Gordon shook his head, reaching for his coat, which he'd thrown over a chair. "Wouldn't think of it. It's a dark, cold night out there. It'd take a pretty small man to send a lady off alone."

"Oh, Gordon . . ."

He gave her a look of mock severity. "Now, Doreen, don't argue with me. You get bundled up while I go out and get the buggy."

Five minutes later, Gordon pulled the Deere & Weber Company two-seater around the front of the roadhouse, and tied his roan gelding on behind. Doreen stepped through the door in a wash of yellow light and a wave of laughter.

She wore a long wool coat, fur hat, and fur gloves. She

clutched a round box, in which she'd placed her feathered hat for the journey home.

"Easy now, these steps are slippery," Gordon said as he mounted the porch and began guiding her down.

"Oh, Gordon, how you do dote on me!"

"Well, some women just call for dotin'."

"If only my dear dead Charlie could hear that!" she said with a throaty laugh.

When they were situated in the buggy and Gordon had thrown a buffalo robe over Doreen's legs, he flicked the reins against the harnessed sorrel's back, and they moved off down the trail leading south along the frozen river. Buttes lofted on their right, white with snow in the frosty darkness. The riverbed pushed up on the left side of the trail, thick with brush and dotted here and there with isolated willows and box elders.

Owls cooed and small night critters moved in the brush—raccoons, no doubt. Occasional wolves howled. When one such howl rose so loudly from a nearby knoll that Doreen's eardrums rattled, she slid close to Gordon and gave a shiver.

"Oh, I just hate it when they do that!"

"They do tend to get brave out here," Gordon allowed. "But don't you worry none. I've lived in the Territory for fifty years, and I've never once heard of a wolf attacking people. Besides, I've got this here"—he lifted the carbine he'd stood between his left knee and the buggy's fender—"and a Winchester Sixty-six is about as good a luck charm as you'll find." He grinned.

She squeezed his arm. "Mr. Jenkins, you certainly know how to make a woman feel secure."

"Well, thank you, Mrs. Sanderson."

They were riding around a bend when another howl rended the quiet night. Gordon jumped this time, as well as Doreen, who cried, "Oh!" The harnessed sorrel started, ruffling its mane, and Gordon could feel the resistance when his own horse, tied behind, paused briefly to snort and look around.

"It's okay, Earl," he told the horse. "Keep on, now."

"Such a noise," Doreen said, huddled close to Gordon. "I've never heard one that close. He must be stalking us!"

"They don't stalk people," Gordon said.

"Well, apparently this one hasn't been told that."

The wolf howled again. The bewitching noise lifted from somewhere ahead, just beyond their range of vision. Gordon let the sorrel come to a halt, then draped the reins across his knee and picked up his Winchester. He stared ahead, squinting, trying to pick the critter out of the darkness. Behind him, his horse whinnied and shook its head, jarring the buggy.

"Come on, you," he growled. "Show yourself."

Doreen squeezed his arm. "Let's turn around, Gordon. I got a funny feelin' about this."

"It's just a wolf," Gordon said, but his voice was tense.

"Just a wolf!" Doreen cried.

"He's just tryin' to scare us," Gordon said. "He's out havin' fun."

"Maybe he's after the horses."

"Well, he ain't gonna get 'em." He tossed the reins. "Giddyup, horse."

They continued on for another mile and were beginning to feel less fearful, starting to chat again, when the wolf howled again—this time from behind them. It sounded as though the animal were only a few feet away. Gordon's horse plunged forward and around the buggy, jerking its right wheels several inches off the ground.

Doreen screamed as she bounced from side to side, flailing for Gordon's arm. Gordon yelled, "Hey, hey, horse! Whoah! Whoah! . . . Eeeeasy."

Then it was over and the sorrel was pulling the buggy

again, shaking its head from side to side, agitated, and Gordon's horse was following along behind—tensely snorting and jerking its head around to see behind it.

"Gordon, please, let's go back!" Doreen yelled.

"Hell, the goddamn thing is behind us now!"

"Oh, Gordon . . . I'm scared!"

"Don't be scared. I'll get you home." He pulled back on the reins, slowing the sorrel to a halt. "But first I better loosen the lead so old Earl can't topple us."

Doreen grabbed his arm as he prepared to leave the buggy. "Gordon, don't leave me!"

"Just for a second, Doreen. I've got to loosen that lead."

"Oh, Gordon, hurry. I have such a bad feeling . . ." She turned to stare ahead, her eyes wide and brimming with animal fear. "There's something awful out there."

Gordon wanted to assure her that it wasn't something so awful, but he wasn't sure himself anymore. He, too, had a bad feeling. About as bad a feeling as he'd ever had—and he'd ridden herd through Blackfeet country!

He handed the reins to Doreen. "Hold on to these real tight now. Don't let go."

"Just hurry, please, Gordon."

He crawled down from the buggy and patted his horse to settle him, then went to work untying the lead. He tried to hurry, but the horse's commotion had twisted the leather into one hell of a tight knot. He cursed as he tried to work it apart with his bare, cold hands, nearly prying his fingernails off. The cold air burned and ached in his fingertips.

"Holy shit in a sandstorm," he muttered.

"Gordon," Doreen said quietly. Too quietly.

He looked at her. "What?"

"Someone's coming."

"Huh?"

She did not reply. Gordon followed her gaze around behind him. Sure enough, a rider was approaching. Gordon could make out only a silhouette, but that was enough to make his heart lighten. It was probably one of the men from the roadhouse heading home. He'd ride with Gordon and Doreen, and they'd be all right. There was safety in numbers.

"Hello, there," Gordon called, holding his horse by the bridle.

The rider came on but said nothing.

"Gordon," Doreen said thinly.

Gordon ignored her. "We sure are glad to see you," he said, grinning, staring off down the trail. The horse and rider took shape as they approached.

"The lady got a little scared," Gordon said. "We've been hearing wolves."

Doreen gave a breathy, frightened sound that seemed to crawl up slowly from deep in her chest. "G-Gordon."

Gordon turned to her, frowning. "What is it?"

"He . . . he's got a gun."

Gordon turned back to the rider again. Sure enough, the man was holding a rifle out from his belly. The barrel was pointed at Gordon's head. It was a big gun, bigger than most of the guns used around here for ranchwork. It looked like a hide hunter's Big Fifty.

Gordon regarded the man's gray-black coat and dark, featureless face, from which a cigar glowed beneath the round brim of a black hat with a brown leather band. He did not recognize the man. His fear returned, stronger. His tongue swelled and his heart began to pound. Cold as he was, sweat popped out on his back. He caught the smell of the man's cigar.

He stood there frozen, smile fading, holding his horse's bridle.

"Gordon," Doreen cried softly.

"Who . . . who are you?" Gordon said.

The man halted his horse about ten feet in front of him. The horse tossed its head. The man steadied it with an iron grip on the reins. Smoke puffed from around the cigar protruding from his dark face.

Gordon wanted to reach for the pistol on his right hip, but his right hand held fast to the bridle.

"Oh, Gordon," Doreen cried again, in a high voice broken by sobs. "I knew it . . . I knew it . . . was something . . . awful."

Gordon watched as the man lifted his left hand to his face and removed the cigar. Then the man slowly tipped back his head and howled. There was nothing at all human in the howl. It was not a man's howl.

It was a wolf's howl.

It lifted to the sky and set the night alive with its evil . . .

And it was the last sound Gordon Jenkins ever heard.

CHAPTER 13

"I JUST WANT you to know I wouldn't have touched your dick if I hadn't been drunk."

Talbot opened his eyes. Jacy was leaning over the bed, gazing into his face. She was dressed and washed and ready to go. Her hair was pulled back in a ponytail.

"Huh?"

"I was drunk, or I wouldn't have touched your dick last night," she repeated.

"You flatter me. What time is it?"

"Nearly seven o'clock. What's with the men around here? Gordon's not up yet, either." She moved to the door, picked up his clothes from the chair, and tossed them on the bed. "Rise and shine. I don't serve chuck all morning."

She walked out the door, and a moment later Talbot heard her knocking pans around in the kitchen and whistling while she worked. His mouth watered at the smell of frying bacon and freshly brewed coffee. Wondering how he could have slept until seven o'clock in the morning, he threw the covers back, hauled his saddle-sore ass out of bed, and dressed.

"You didn't have to wait breakfast for me," he said, entering the kitchen and buckling his belt.

Jacy was standing at the range, stirring eggs in a cast-iron skillet. "It's nothing," she said, "just the usual—bacon and eggs. Help yourself to coffee. There's a mug on the table. How did you sleep?"

"Like a dead dog," he said. "You?"

"Good."

Talbot filled a mug, returned the pot to the warming rack on the range, and sat down at the table. He sipped his coffee and noticed that she had recovered from last night's melancholy and was her old self again—a real Toledo blade, Dakota style. Tough and tomboyishly pretty.

As she lifted the pan from the range and shoveled eggs onto a plate, he realized he'd been staring at her, and turned and looked out the window. Gray light angled in and shone like quicksilver on the worn floor.

"Looks like we got some snow, huh?" he said conversationally.

"Looks like."

She grabbed a couple of pot holders and opened the oven door. Smoke wafted. "Shit!" she cried. "Goddamn it, anyway—I burned the biscuits!"

She dropped the pan on the range top and slammed the door, throwing the pot holders on the cupboard.

"They don't look burned to me," Talbot said, politely ignoring the smoke.

"They're burned on the bottoms."

"Throw one on my plate; I'll give it a shot."

"I'll scrape the bottom first," she said, waving at the smoke clouds webbing toward the rafters.

After scraping the burnt crust off one of the biscuits, she set it on the plate, then set the plate before Talbot. "Here you go," she said fatefully. "Nothing fancy, but this isn't the Hotel Deluxe and I'm no French chef."

"Looks good," he said, studying his plate with a wooden smile.

The charred biscuit was nearly raw in the center, and the

underdone eggs looked like marmalade preserves that hadn't jelled. But Talbot maintained the smile and gave his head an appreciative wag. "Now there's a breakfast! How did you know I like my eggs runny?"

Jacy shrugged, smiling. "Just had you pegged for a runny-eggs guy, I guess."

She poured herself a cup of coffee, then sat across from him and watched him eat. After several minutes a cloud passed over her face. "I wonder what's keeping Gordon this morning."

"Must have had a hell of a time last night."

She shook her head. "It's not like him to sleep this late, no matter how much fun he had the night before."

"I'll check on him as soon as I'm through here."

"Would you? If I go pounding on his door, and he's drunk, I'll just embarrass him."

"No problem."

When he'd finished the massive pile of scrambled eggs, and sopped up the bacon grease with a biscuit, Talbot tipped back the last of his coffee, dressed in his new winter garb, and headed outside. He could tell from the fresh snow limning the corrals and water troughs that they'd gotten a good three or four inches last night.

The sky was as gray as an old coin; it hunkered so low that the top of the box elder behind the bunkhouse was nearly indiscernible. A couple of fat crows lit out from a hay rack, cawing, and winged out over the corrals toward the mesa.

Talbot walked across the yard and around the corrals, noting the lack of smoke puffing from the bunkhouse chimney, and knocked on the door.

"Gordon?"

No answer.

Talbot opened the door and stepped inside. The long, low room, provisioned with an eating table and several cots, was dark and empty. The air was stale and tinged with the smell of old sweat and tobacco. Talbot touched the big iron stove in the room's center: cold as ice. It hadn't been fired for at least eight hours.

Thoughtfully, Talbot walked out behind the bunkhouse and looked around, wondering if Gordon was in the habit of staying out all night. Something told him he wasn't.

As he stared out across the gray prairie, he heard sleigh bells and voices. The sounds seemed to be coming from the cabin's direction. He wheeled and headed back across the yard, then stopped dead in his tracks.

Sitting before the cabin was a sleigh drawn by a stout silver-gray gelding wearing a halter and bells. Inside the sleigh were two fur-clad people—a woman and a man—looking like Russian royalty out for a winter romp with the Cossacks. The man puffed a pipe. The horse bobbed its head and stomped a front hoof, eager to get moving again.

Then Talbot heard the unmistakable voice of Suzanne Magnusson, smelled the distinctive aroma of the doctor's pipe. They had stopped before the cabin and were talking with Jacy, who spied Talbot now, walking toward the sleigh.

"There he is," she said. "Mr. Talbot, you have a couple visitors from the Double X ranch," she called, her voice taut and sarcastic, brimming with unconcealed hatred. "You know Miss Suzanne and . . ."

"Dr. Long," the doctor said thickly, giving a gentlemanly bow. Rheumy-eyed, he appeared half drunk.

Suzanne had turned to Talbot. Shock and surprise brightened her exquisite face, her cheeks flushed from the cold. "Mark, it's you! Hello!"

Talbot smiled tightly, aware of Jacy's caustic glare. "Suzanne. Harrison. What are you two doing here?"

Suddenly petulant, Suzanne said, "You were supposed to call on me, Mr. Talbot."

Talbot slid a look at Jacy, who stood glaring at him across the sleigh. "Well, I've only been here two days, Suzanne."

"When you didn't come to me, Harrison and I decided to come to you. We stopped here to ask directions, and learned from Miss Kincaid that you were here!" Suzanne was smiling beautifully, eyes flashing, but there was a question there as well.

Talbot said, "Jacy and I are old friends. My cabin needs a little work, so she offered me a bed."

"How nice of her," Suzanne said, her smile losing its luster as she shuttled it to Jacy.

Changing the subject, Talbot said, "How are you, Harrison?"

The easterner had produced a leather-sheathed traveling flask from his coat and was unscrewing the top. He raised it to Talbot and said with dramatic flair, "Out here on these magnificent Great Plains to which Miss Magnusson was kind enough to drag me? Where there are as many trees as balmy days, and the air is absolutely frigid? Never better!" He tipped back the flask for several good-sized swallows.

Suzanne gave the man a playful poke. "I keep telling him to think of it as an adventure."

"No, Crete was an adventure," Harrison retorted, offering the flask to Talbot, who waved it off. "How is your back, Mr. Talbot?"

"Good as new," Talbot replied, noticing Jacy's questioning glance. "I had a little accident before I left San Francisco," he explained.

"Some accident!" Suzanne said admiringly. To Jacy she gave a short, dramatic account of Talbot's adventure. "It's like something you read in novels," she said when she'd finished the story.

"Did all that really happen?" Jacy asked Talbot.

Talbot shrugged modestly. He hadn't felt this uncomfortable with his clothes on.

"Thanks again for the patch job," he told Harrison, who grunted and shook his head. "I'd ask you both to light and sit a spell, but it's not my cabin, and . . ." He stopped, deferring to Jacy.

She only sneered. "I haven't straightened up," she said dryly. Then she wheeled around and went into the cabin, slamming the door behind her.

"I sense a distinct hostility in that girl," said Harrison facetiously.

"Well, with the tension between the small ranchers in the area, and Suzanne's father, I guess there's bound to be some hard feelings," Talbot said, thinking of Dave.

Suzanne turned a cold eye to the cabin door. "I guess they're supposed to be able to steal as much of my father's beef as they want, and not get called on it," she said.

Talbot grew testy. "They claim your father's been handing out death warrants, that he killed people five years ago and that he's starting again now." He debated telling her about Dave's murder, and decided to wait for a better time. The information might make her even more defensive.

Suzanne looked hurt. "Mark, if you knew my father, you'd know how ridiculous that is. Papa is the gentlest man alive. I know he's been trying to buy the nesters out. They've been stealing our cattle and overgrazing the range, not to mention destroying all the water holes and befouling the bloodlines. But he would never kill anyone . . . for any reason."

She shook her head sincerely, firmly believing what she'd professed.

She almost had Talbot believing—at least questioning what he'd been hearing from Jacy and the others. He shrugged and forced a smile. "Maybe you're right, Suzanne. I haven't been here long enough to find out the whole story."

"Well, let me help you get the whole story, Mr. Talbot," she said, brightening. "What we came out here for was to invite you to a birthday and pre-Christmas celebration at the Double X tomorrow night. Won't you come?"

"Whose birthday?"

"Mine, of course."

Talbot frowned and looked off, thoughtful.

"Oh, please, Mark," Suzanne begged. "I want you to meet my father and see what a fine man he is. Of course, there will be plenty of food and drink and"—she grew subtly flirtatious—"I'll be there." She arched a delicate eyebrow and smiled brightly.

Talbot felt himself softening. He had no solid proof that King Magnusson had killed his brother, and Suzanne certainly wasn't involved. A visit to the Double X might even prove helpful in sorting through this mess. He found himself ignoring the small voice in the back of his head reminding him it was not his mess to sort through.

"All right," he said. "What time?"

"Six o'clock."

"What should I wear?"

"Come as you are. You'll feel right at home."

Doubting that, Talbot said with a nod, "Six it is."

"Okay, then," Suzanne said, pinning him with a smoldering gaze. "See you there."

Harrison flicked the reins along the silver gray's back, and said, "Cheers!" as the sleigh started off with a celebratory jingle of the bells.

Talbot stood watching them as they made a large circle in the yard, and headed back the way they had come. Suzanne looked back and waved, and Talbot returned it. Then he walked to the cabin door and turned the knob. It was locked.

He knocked once. "Jacy?"

The silence that answered was answer enough, and he knew

it was all the answer he was going to get. Jacy had heard everything, and she wasn't about to let him explain.

"Gordon's not in his cabin," he said to the door. "Let me know if you want help tracking him down."

He turned around and headed for the barn and his horse, feeling a stone grow in the pit of his stomach. Something told him that the next couple of days were going to put an end, once and for all, to any and all hopes he still entertained of finding peace.

CHAPTER 14

THAT AFTERNOON, JED Gibbon was nursing a beer in the Sundowner and reading *The Saturday Evening Post* when something caught his eye out the big window to the right of the front door. A cowboy had ridden up on a deep-chested claybank, and was looping his reins over the tie rail.

His expression was grim, and his horse was blowing like he'd been ridden hard. The man had bad news written all over him.

Darkly, Gibbon watched the man mount the porch and push through the door. When he'd closed the door behind him, stomping snow from his boots, he stood looking around. Gibbon knew the man was waiting for his eyes to adjust.

"Howdy, Luke," Fisk said from behind the bar, recognizing the cowboy.

"Monty."

"What can I do ya for?"

"The sheriff here?"

Gibbon cleared his throat. Reluctantly he said, "Over here, Luke."

The man shuttled his eyes to his right, where Gibbon sat under a big elk head, in shadows cast by the stove and center post.

"How's things over to the Nixon place?" Gibbon said as the man's eyes found him, trying a smile.

Luke Waverly was tall and lean to the point of emaciation, with a thin, droopy mustache and deep-sunk eyes. His face looked like rawhide that had been soaked and dried too quickly over a hot fire. His eyes hung low in their sockets, like a chastised dog's.

"Mr. Nixon's been shot."

Gibbon took a deep breath and ran a hand down his face. "Don't tell me that, Luke. I don't want to hear that."

"He didn't come home last night," the cowboy continued. "I went out lookin' for him this mornin' and found him behind a rock with half his head gone. Found this in his coat."

The cowboy stepped forward and laid a scrap of paper on the table before the sheriff. Gibbon lowered his eyes. On the paper was a big number one drawn boldly in pencil.

Gibbon felt his bowels loosen, and he was afraid for a moment he would soil himself. It was starting again. If he'd entertained any doubts before, he didn't now.

He cursed and lifted a hand to his forehead, took the bridge of his nose between thumb and index finger, and squeezed, trying to steady himself, trying to imagine what he should do, what he had the balls to do.

"Bushwhacked?" he said at length, through a grimace.

"Executed, more like. Just like Jack Thom. More of the Double X's handiwork." The cowboy's voice quaked with emotion.

"Where is he?"

"At the cabin."

Gibbon fought off the very real urge to run. He stood, tipped back his beer, draining it, and wiped the foam from his mouth with the back of his hand. Turning to pluck his coat off the rack to his right, he said ominously, "Let's go."

AN HOUR LATER Gibbon and the cowboy made the Nixon ranch, a motley collection of log and milled-lumber buildings and corrals scattered in a deep, wooded draw. High, rocky buttes poked up behind the trees. A yellow-brown mongrel ran out from the barn and scolded Gibbon's horse.

"Shut up and lay down, Buster!" the cowboy yelled.

The dog put its head and tail down and slunk off to the middle of the yard, where it sat growling, ears flat against its head. Dismounting at the barn, Gibbon heard a woman's muffled cries. He turned an ear to the cabin.

"No," she screamed in German over and over, the screams spaced about two seconds apart. "Nein! . . . Nein! . . . Nein!"

It was a haunting refrain, pricking Gibbon's spine. It even spooked his horse, which craned its neck to get a fix on it.

The cowboy took Gibbon's reins. "I took the kids over to the neighbors and gave the wife some whiskey to calm her down, but it don't seem to be workin'."

"Mrs. Nixon?"

Waverly nodded. "I haven't heard her speak anything but English for years." The man lead the horses toward the corral. "I laid the boss out in the barn. You can go on in."

Gibbon didn't really want to go into the barn alone—the dead always made him feel nightmarish and lonely—but he slid a heavy door open anyway and stepped inside.

The air was heavy with the smell of hay and ammonia. A milk cow gave an inquisitive moo. Heavy stock—probably draft horses—knocked against their stalls. There were several windows along each wall, but the gray winter light was too weak to penetrate the afternoon shadows.

Finding a hurricane lamp on a post, Gibbon lifted its globe and lit the wick. The light lifted shadows from an open-ended work wagon in which an inert body in tattered range clothes lay on its back, arms at its sides.

Gibbon held the lamp high and moved toward the wagon's spring seat. The light revealed the man's head—or what was left of it. Most of the forehead had been blown away. One eye bulged hideously. The other was missing. Gibbon swallowed to keep his lunch and beer down.

"Jesus Christ," he murmured, needing a shot of something strong.

"Big-caliber bul—"

Gibbon jumped at the voice and turned to see the cowboy standing beside him. He hadn't seen or heard the man enter the barn.

"Sorry," Waverly said. "I was gonna say it looks like a big-caliber bullet blew the top of his head clean off."

"I got eyes," Gibbon said, testy, remembering the big gun Del Toro had carried away from the train. "Fifty caliber. I've seen their work before, and not just on buffalo. I see he took another one to the side."

The cowboy shook his head, eyes wide with foreboding. "What am I gonna do now? What's the woman gonna do? She has five younguns."

Trying to stay focused, Gibbon said, "Could you tell by the tracks in the snow how many men were after him?"

"One as far as I could tell."

"Was Nixon armed?"

"Yep."

"He return fire?"

"Yep."

"You got anything else to say except yep, Luke?"

"Yep." The cowboy's eyes slid to Gibbon's. "Double X got him, Sheriff. Sure as shit up a cow's ass. And him's only the first," the cowboy said.

"The first killed by Del Toro anyways," Gibbon said, remembering Jack Thom.

"Who's Del Toro?"

"Let me put it this way, Luke. A blue-eyed bean eater

decked out in wolf fur comes callin', you shoot the son of a bitch out of his saddle. Blow him from here to old Mexico. No questions asked."

The cowboy rubbed his jaw and eyed Gibbon warily. "Where you goin'?" he said with an insinuating drawl. "Back to the saloon?"

Gibbon stopped at the door and turned around. His face and ears flushed, as though he'd been slapped hard. A moment ago, he hadn't really known where he was going; his mind was a mess of half-conceived ideas and very real fears that probably would have led, in the end, to a drink. But the cowboy's barb pricked him, set a fire in his brain. He was tired of the jokes made at his expense. What's more, he was tired of deserving them.

He took a deep breath fighting panic and was nearly overcome by the unfamiliar sound of his own courage. "To talk with King Magnusson over to the Double X. Please relay my condolences to Mrs. Nixon, and assure her that I'll bring her husband's killer to justice."

Waverly tipped his hat back. "The Double X! By your lonesome?"

"Posses take too long to gather. Besides, a bunch of trigger-happy cowboys would just touch off a powder keg. No, I'm gonna give old King Magnusson a nice, civilized ultimatum."

When Gibbon had mounted his horse and was riding away, the cowboy stood between the open barn doors watching him and scratching his head.

"That son of a bitch is gonna get his ass shot off."

AS HE MADE his way south along a thin wagon trace, Gibbon was thinking the same thing. While he'd been standing in the barn with Waverly, inspecting Nixon's body, he'd felt something very close to courage seep into his veins. It was like a heady shot of liquor after you'd gone without for several days. It was a courage born of anger and shame. Magnusson was acting like he owned the whole damn country, and he paid as little heed to Gibbon as he would to a stable boy.

Alhough he was still feeling plucky after ten miles of hard riding, his heart was starting to race by the time he made the ridge over St. Mary's Creek, the Double X's primary water source. He pointed the horse east along the game trail that twisted through the ponderosas above the draw, and felt his mouth dry up and his knees grow heavy with apprehension.

"I'm liable to get shot out of my saddle and left to the wildcats," he told himself. "This is a big country, and even if anyone came lookin', they'd never find me."

But he was only about two miles from the Double X compound, and he could not turn back now. Not if he wanted to hold on to what little pride he had left.

He stopped his horse behind a snowdrift at the lip of the ridge, rummaged in his saddlebags, and produced a whiskey bottle. Uncorking it, he lifted it high and felt a little of his nerve return almost instantly.

He recorked the bottle and was about to return it to the saddlebags when he reconsidered. "Hell, I'm gonna need all the metal I can muster," he mumbled, biting the cork from the bottle, spitting it out, and spurring the horse forward.

He was good and soused by the time he made the two-track wagon trail climbing the tawny-snowy bench toward the Double X headquarters. It was the kind of drunk he used to feel back before the Old Trouble—a cocky, courageous drunk. A powerful, light-headed drunk that made him feel potent and vigorous and heroic.

When the Magnusson mansion rose up on a knoll a half mile ahead, two riders appeared on either side of him. They each had a carbine resting on their hips, and they rode up fast—scruffy, duster-clad cowboys in Stetsons.

Gibbon tossed his nearly empty bottle into a clump of sage.

"State your name and business," the cowboy on his right demanded.

Gibbon told him who he was.

"Mr. Magnusson expectin' you, Sheriff?"

"Should be if he ain't," Gibbon said, trying to steady himself. His tongue felt half a size larger than it was.

"What's that supposed to mean?"

"Just what I said. Now kindly get your hammerheads out of my way and let me through."

The men looked at each other knowingly, then reined their horses off the trail. They followed Gibbon through the open Texas gate, under the horizontal rail in which the Double X brand had been burned, and into the compound. They kept their distance, but they watched Gibbon with curious, wary eyes.

When Gibbon was nearing the mansion, taking in the breadth of the place while trying to keep his nerve up, one of the men spurred ahead and dismounted near a cluster of cowboys that had gathered outside a corral. The corral sat to the right of the mansion, up a slight rise and near several wagon sheds and a blacksmith shop.

Gibbon halted his horse before the mansion and waited, watching the group. A pretty girl and a horse seemed to be the center of attention. In a buffalo coat and round-brimmed, green-felt hat, King Magnusson stood near the girl, smiling down at her.

"Oh, Papa, he's beautiful! Where did you ever find such a horse?"

"Had him shipped all the way up from Tennessee," Magnusson said. Turning to the men crowding around, he added,

"The conductor told me he nearly took his own private car apart board by board!"

A whoop broke out from several men, and Gibbon figured it was instigated more by the girl than by Magnusson's blabber or even by the horse. In a big wool poncho and riding hat, raven hair cascading down her back, she stroked the horse's fine, arched neck. Gibbon could tell by the looks on the cowboys' faces they were imagining her stroking something else.

"He's just a beauty, Papa, just a beauty," the girl went on.

Magnusson was about to say something else when Gibbon's cowboy interrupted him. The man spoke to his boss, who frowned and lifted his head to look over the crowd at the sheriff. Gibbon tipped his hat and grinned.

Magnusson's big, ruddy face flushed. He turned sharply to the cowboy and moved his lips. The cowboy nodded and pushed through the crowd.

Approaching Gibbon, he said, "Sorry, Sheriff. The boss is busy today. It's Miss Suzanne's birthday."

Gibbon lifted his eyes from the cowboy to Magnusson, laughing with his daughter and running his hand over the thoroughbred's muscled shoulder. Gibbon touched his spurs to his mount's flanks, moving toward the crowd.

"Hey, where do you think you're goin'?" the cowboy yelled.

Gibbon ignored him and rode to the edge of the crowd. "Mr. Magnusson, I'll thank you for a minute of your time."

The rancher turned sharply, frowning. "I'm busy here, Gibbon. You're gonna have to come back some other time."

"Can't do that."

"What's that?"

Gibbon's anger burned at the man's snide demeanor. He held on to the saddlehorn and yelled, "I said get your ass over here so we can talk in private! . . . Unless you want your lovely daughter to hear about the cold-blooded killin's her father's been committin' on open range."

The girl turned to her father and wrinkled her nose, curious. She said something Gibbon couldn't hear. Her father stared at the sheriff, his face turning red, then white, then red again.

The girl said something else. Magnusson ignored her. He was staring at Gibbon with a demon's eyes. The cowboys had turned to him, too, cutting looks between him and their boss, who did not appreciate getting read out before his hands, much less his daughter.

"What do you say, King?" Gibbon asked, swaying a little in his saddle. It felt so good to air his spleen that he was finding it hard to shut up. He saw the holsters hanging beneath the cowboys' coats, but he was unconcerned. He felt large—too large to kill—and teeming with saintly virtue.

King turned to his daughter and moved his lips. She frowned and dropped her head, then handed the thoroughbred's reins to one of the wranglers. The crowd parted as she moved toward the mansion.

When she was safely inside, the men stepped back to form a corridor, and King Magnusson sauntered over to Gibbon. A man the sheriff recognized as Rag Donnelly followed him. Another man fell into step behind Donnelly.

A stout man with a head like a broad chunk of oak and a red mustache that curved around to meet his sideburns, he looked like either a politician or an eastern financier. He puffed a stogie in the side of his mouth and stuffed his fists in the pockets of his calf-length beaver coat.

Magnusson approached Gibbon. His face was set firm and frozen, like a gambler waiting to see his opponent's busted flush. "All right, Gibbon, what's on your mind?"

"Two men have been killed on the Canaan Bench—that's what's on my mind, you son of a bitch."

Magnusson said nothing. He just stared at Gibbon. Humor crept into his eyes. Gibbon met the gaze head-on. He'd made it this far, and with each passing second he felt more and more fearless. More and more invincible.

Magnusson cut his eyes to Rag Donnelly standing grimly beside him, then back to Gibbon. "What makes you think that has anything to do with me?"

"Precedence," Gibbon growled.

"Precedence without evidence won't get you very far in a court of law, Sheriff."

Gibbon leaned out from his saddle. "Call him off, King."

"Call who off?" Magnusson said, as though indulging the village idiot.

It took a couple seconds for Gibbon to get his tongue around the words. "José del Toro. Your Mex gun for hire."

"José del who? I'm afraid I didn't catch the name."

"You know the name."

Magnusson turned to Donnelly. "Rag, do we have a greaser gunman named José—" He turned to Gibbon with an expression of mock perplexity. "What was this fella's name again?"

The well-dressed gent puffing the stogie gave a loud guffaw and clapped his kid-gloved hands.

"Very goddamn funny, Magnusson, but if you don't call him off the small ranchers on the Bench, the only one's gonna be laughin' is the hangman—as he's escortin' you to the gallows."

"My, what pluck we're exhibiting here today, Mr. Gibbon! I don't believe I've ever seen you in such rarefied form. It's due to the alcohol, I suspect. Good Lord, man, you smell like a still!"

Rag Donnelly said through tight lips, "Fairly reeks of it, he does."

Gibbon flushed. "I may have had a shot or two on the way

out from town. It's a long ride." His features bunched with anger. "And anyway, my drinkin' ain't the point! The point is you're breakin' the law just like you did five years ago, only this time I ain't gonna stand back and watch it happen. I ain't gonna sit back and watch you kill to your heart's content, until you've freed up every square foot of the Bench for your own beef. It's murder, goddamnit, Magnusson. Cold-blooded murder!"

Magnusson laughed. "Sheriff, I'm afraid your sympathies lie in the wrong camp. I'm certainly not condoning cold-blooded murder, but if certain men were caught stealing my beef, and my boys . . . well, that's frontier justice. It may not be legal in the purest sense of the word, but I highly doubt any judge would rule in the favor of stock thieves." Magnusson laughed again.

Gibbon fairly shook with outrage. "Then it goes both ways. I've seen their brands in your holding pens."

"If their beef was in my pens it's because they were eating my grass."

"What is your grass—the whole goddamn Bench?"

"My grass is whatever I can rescue from those goddamn ignorant farm-stock sons of bitches—men like yourself, Gibbon. Drunkards, cowards, and common thieves." Magnusson was angry now himself. His face had turned bright red, setting off the frosty blue of his eyes.

"Why, you highfalutin son of a bitch!" Gibbon was trying to get his gun out from under his coat. As he fumbled angrily, growling like a wounded bear, Magnusson reached up and grabbed his left arm and pulled. Gibbon came out of the saddle and hit the ground like a sack of grain. His foot stayed in the stirrup and his leg twisted at the ankle.

Gibbon cried out and Magnusson kicked the foot free, still holding the sheriff's left arm. Then he kicked Gibbon hard in the gut with the toe of his boot. He followed it up with two more brutal kicks, yelling, "How dare you bring a firearm onto these premises! How dare you pack an iron onto my land and try to shoot me in my own yard—you scumsucking, ignorant old drunk!"

Gibbon yanked his arm free and fell into a hard patch of dirty snow. The cowboys gathered around, cheering their boss. Gibbon caught a glimpse of their grinning, tobacco-chewing faces as he got his hands beneath himself and tried to gain his feet.

He'd gotten only as far as his knees when the tall, iron-bodied rancher—grinning now, showing off for his men—delivered another stovepipe boot to the sheriff's round paunch.

Gibbon groaned as the air exploded from his lungs.

The kick propelled him backward, and his head hit the hard ground, sending lightning bolts beneath his closed eyelids. The blow made him sick to his stomach. It dawned on him that, coming here alone, he'd made a mistake. Probably the biggest mistake of his life . . .

The thought was still resonating when he felt himself being drawn up by two hands pulling at his coat. The ascent took several seconds, for Gibbon was a big man, and his legs would not cooperate. He wasn't quite sure what was happening—his head hitting the ground had fogged his brain.

When he was half standing, balancing there with the rancher's help and still trying to coax air into his lungs, Magnusson drew his arm back like a bowstring and let it go. His fist slammed into Gibbon's face once, twice, three times.

The powerful right jabs propelled Gibbon into a straight-backed stance for half a second before he collapsed again on his back. His eyes watered from the pain daggering through his nose and deep into his skull. Blood gushed from his lips and nose, flooding his face. He felt his eyes swell.

"If I'd known you were having this much fun out here,

King, I would come a long time ago!" he heard the well-dressed gent say around a deep-throated laugh.

Standing over him, his chest rising and falling, Magnusson said tightly, "Some lawman, Gibbon. I've never seen a sorrier excuse for a man, much less a sheriff!"

Gibbon heard men laughing just below the high-pitched whistling in his ears.

Magnusson said to Donnelly standing beside him, "What do you think, Rag? Should we kill the sorry bastard or send him home to his mother?"

"Well . . ." Donnelly said, scratching his head and playing along, "I'd say his mother's dead. Dead of a broken heart, no doubt. Might as well kill him and put him out of his misery."

Magnusson faked a grimace and shook his head. "I don't know, Rag. Those sorry ten-cow ranchers are gonna need someone on their side. At least he's a figurehead for 'em. Seems like it wouldn't be fair to take their general so early in the battle—sorry as their general is."

"I know," Rag said. "Why don't we tie him to his saddle and send him back to his troops? Sort of like a message from us to them."

"A little frontier justice!" the well-dressed gent bellowed, as though he were attending a staged spectacle. "I love it!"

"Grand idea, Rag! Grand idea," Magnusson agreed.

Turning to the other men, who'd formed a half circle around him, Donnelly, and Gibbon, the rancher said, "Now that's the kind of creative thinking I like to see in my men. Boys, let Mr. Donnelly here be an example to all of you."

Picking his son out of the crowd, he said, "Randall, you and Shelby toss our conquering hero over his horse and send him home. I'm sure the good citizens of Canaan will want to give him a hero's welcome."

Donnelly chuckled and shook his head.

Randall said, "What if the horse can't find his way home, Pa?"

"I'm sure that horse has had plenty of practice finding his way home without the good sheriff's assistance," Magnusson said, cutting his eyes to the passed-out Gibbon with a sneer.

Ten minutes later, Magnusson had retired to his den with the well-dressed gentleman and Rag Donnelly. Most of the cowboys had gone back to their work around the compound.

Randall Magnusson and Shelby Green draped the big unconscious lawman over his saddle and used the reins to tie him to the horn.

"I say he shoulda shot the son of a bitch," Randall said as he gave the horse a resolute slap to its backside.

The horse bounded off, whipping its head around at the oddly mounted burden on its back. Gibbon cried out in his stupor, his old bones creaking against the saddle. The horse galloped through the gate and out of the yard, descending the gradual grade toward St. Mary's Creek and the purpling flats beyond.

"But I have to admit, it's a pretty damn good joke!" Randall laughed as he and Shelby Green turned around and started toward the barn.

"Yeah, your pa has quite a sense of humor," Shelby agreed.

Above their retreating backs, Randall's sister, Suzanne, stood in one of the mansion's upstair's windows, staring out at the horse and its bound rider dwindling in the wintery distance.

CHAPTER 15

JACY SPENT THE rest of the day pulling firewood out of a draw with the two Percheron crosses her father had added to their remuda the year before he died. She had decided that Mark Talbot was a lecherous dope for having accepted Suzanne's invitation. Although she had never known Gordon to act so irresponsibly, it was apparent that the old cowboy had either eloped or gotten involved in a marathon poker game.

Jacy saw now that she had grossly overestimated each man's character. Like the rest of their lot, they were fools and would always forsake their responsibilities for big-breasted women and the quest for fun and money.

Early the next morning she continued her work, trying hard not to think about either man. Around noon she was leading the horses back to the yard, towing a heavy box elder trunk, when she stopped suddenly by the corral.

Something at the cabin had caught her eye, and she stared at it, trying to make it out. It was a piece of paper attached to the cabin door. It fluttered and rattled in the breeze.

She tied the horses' lead to the corral, then walked to the cabin, mounted the steps, and plucked the sheet from the rusty nail. Having to steady it with both heavy-mittened hands, she squinted her eyes at the penciled words: CLEER OUT.

That's all it said.

Jacy stuffed the note in her coat and looked around the yard, drawing the heavy Colt pistol she had taken to wearing around her waist. Her jaw was set tight and her eyes were cool; only her ashen features betrayed the storm within.

Concluding that the yard was clear, she turned back to the cabin and pushed open the door, letting it swing back against the wall. She knew that the men who'd left the note were probably gone—for now—but she entered stiffly and looked around, extending the pistol before her.

Thumbing back the hammer, she started moving through the kitchen, checking every nook and cranny, looking behind every chair and cupboard. Then she proceeded through the rest of the house in the same way—slowly, tensing herself for sudden violence, ready to shoot at anything that moved.

When she was sure the cabin was safe, she returned to the kitchen, holstered her pistol, and picked up the Winchester standing by the door. Retrieving a shell box from a cupboard, she set the rifle on the table and began feeding ammo into the breech. It was clumsy maneuver; her hands were shaking.

"Goddamnit anyway—go in there!" she screamed, nudging the box and spewing shells on the floor. Knowing that Magnusson's men had been here made her feel violated, and she couldn't have felt much more incensed if they'd ransacked the place.

When she'd slid the last bullet into the receiver, she jacked a shell in the chamber and lifted the rifle to her cheek, aiming at a pan on the wall, trying to steady herself, to even out her breath, and to hold the tears of fear and outrage at bay.

It didn't work. She jerked back the trigger. The rifle barked loudly in the close quarters, nearly deafening her. The room filled with so much smoke she was barely able to make out the neat round hole she had blown through the pan.

"You goddamn bastard son of a bitch!" she screamed, then wheeled around and headed out the door.

When she'd unhitched the draft horses from the tree trunk and turned them out in the paddock behind the barn, she saddled her line-back dun and started cross-country for Spernig's Roadhouse. If Gordon wasn't there, someone there probably knew where he'd gone. She needed the old cowboy's help; what's more, she needed to know that he was alive.

Having galloped along the snowless ridges most of the way, she came out on the lip over Spernig's half an hour later, then spurred the dun down the canyon, along an old eroded horse trail cowboys had been carving since Spernig's was just a shanty.

She found Nils in his office at the far back of the building, crouched over his books, a twisted cigarette drooping from his mouth. "Nils, you know where Gordon is?"

He'd heard her boots on the wood floor and was turned to the doorway, his long face with its heavy black brows obscured by a smoke veil. "How in hell would I know where Gordon is?"

"He was in here night before last, wasn't he?"

"I reckon, but—"

"But he hasn't been home since," Jacy finished for him. "You know where he went?"

Nils shrugged and lifted his eyebrows, removing the quirley with the thumb and index finger of his right hand. "Well, he took Mrs. Sanderson home, you know, like he usually does."

Jacy's voice was urgent. "That's all you know? They didn't go off to get hitched or nothin'?"

The barman shrugged again, dropping his jaw. "Well, not that I know . . ."

Jacy slapped the door frame. "Shit!"

"Well, you know, maybe they did go off to get hitched. I reckon if Doreen can find a man who likes her piano playin' as much as Gordon, well, hell—"

"Thanks, Nils."

Jacy turned around and walked back toward the door, wondering what she should do. Her heart drummed irregularly and her breath was short. A voice in the back of her head told her that Gordon was dead, shotgunned by Double X men.

Trying to ignore it, she mounted the dun and started at a gallop toward Big Draw, along the riverside route Gordon would have taken. The recent snow had covered his tracks, so all Jacy could do was head for Big Draw and hope she found nothing amiss along the way.

It was cold and edging on toward late in the afternoon, and the gray clouds turned the color of dirty rags as the sun waned. Crows cawed in the weeds along the river, and chickadees peeped. Jacy paid little attention. Her mind was on Gordon, but she flashed frequently, with a shudder, on Jack Thom and the thick brown stain on his cabin wall.

When she was about three miles from the roadhouse she saw something lying in the weeds and stones left of the trail. Riding up she found a red wagon wheel with several missing spokes and a badly twisted rim. It did not look like it had been there more than two or three days.

Full of dark thoughts, Jacy dismounted and tied her horse to a plum bush, and looked around. Moving farther off the trail and thrashing around in the snowy brush, she came upon an undercarriage to which two more damaged wheels were connected.

She'd been pushing through the hawthorns for only another two or three minutes when she caught up short and squelched a scream. The body of a woman in a green dress and a long fur coat lay before her, its head resting on a deadfall log, face aimed at Jacy with open, staring eyes.

Taking pains to keep her breath steady and even, Jacy pulled her pistol and looked around. Then she took several slow steps, rustling brush and snapping branches, until she stood about ten feet from the body.

She did not have to get any closer to see that it was Mrs. Sanderson and that wolves had been working on her. Gagging, Jacy stepped around the body, making a wide arc, and continued through the brush.

She came upon the rest of the buggy about fifty yards downstream. The horse that had pulled it was nowhere around. Jacy peered at the wreckage, wondering what had spooked the horse so badly that it had left the road and tore though the brush, throwing Mrs. Sanderson and pulverizing the carriage.

She spent the next half hour scouring the brush for Gordon, finding him nowhere near the buggy or Mrs. Sanderson. Finally she turned and walked upstream along a game trail switchbacking through sawgrass and cattails.

She'd walked a half-mile when she stopped to consider turning back. Letting her eyes wander along the river, she saw something lying next to a clump of cattails and several beaver-gnawed saplings.

Walking slowly over, she saw it was a man. Coming within ten feet of him, she saw through the frozen blood, mauled flesh, and torn clothes that it was Gordon—what the wolves had left of Gordon.

She stared numbly for several seconds. Then her breath came short, her heart hammered, her head grew light, and her knees buckled. She dropped to her knees, twisting her torso so that she faced away from the hideous sight. When she could retch no more she dropped her face to the ground and cried.

Finally she lifted her head and straightened her back, forced herself to look at the body. She wanted to know how they'd killed him.

It wasn't hard to see. There was a big round hole through

his forehead, as though from a hide hunter's gun, and half the back of his skull was missing. A wedge of tightly folded paper shone between his teeth.

After several moments of deliberation, Jacy steeled herself and crawled over on hands and knees. She pinched the paper between her thumb and index finger and withdrew it quickly.

Standing, she unfolded the sheet to a childishly scrawled "Hasta Luego." The paper was the same kind of small notebook leaf that had been nailed to her door.

"Those sons o' bitches," she breathed. She glanced once more at Gordon lying there, disemboweled by wolves, half his head gone, old eyes still glazed with the horror of his killer's face.

"Those rotten sons o' bitches."

Now she knew what had happened. When they'd shot Gordon, they'd spooked the buggy horse, which fled off the trail, throwing Mrs. Sanderson and destroying the buggy. That's why there was such a gap between the bodies. The wolves had no doubt dragged Gordon into the brush by the river.

Wiping the freezing tears from her face with the backs of her mittened hands, Jacy wondered what she should do with the bodies.

The ground was frozen, so burying them was out of the question. If she had time, she could rig a travois and carry them home, but it was getting late. Soon it would be full dark. Besides, she did not have the stomach for retrieving what was left of the wolf-mangled corpses.

That's all they were, anyway, she told herself. Corpses. Gordon and Mrs. Sanderson were gone. They were in a far better place, and Jacy found part of herself yearning for that place herself.

Another part yearned for justice. So she walked stiffly back to the trail, found her horse, mounted up, and headed for Canaan.

NEARLY TWO HOURS later she was walking her horse, half dead from hard riding, down the main street of the little town on the bone-cold flats above the Little Missouri. The night was pitch-black and starless, and a biting wind was blowing.

Jacy took the horse to the livery and told the night hostler to give the gelding all the oats he wanted, to rub him down good and slow, toss a warm blanket over his back, and put him in a stall with plenty of fresh hay.

She didn't have the money for it, but she'd work out something, if she had to clean stalls in the morning. Nothing was too good for her saddlestock.

Weary and so cold her teeth chattered, she walked up the street to the Sundowner. She hadn't even considered looking elsewhere for the sheriff. She figured he'd be half tight by now, but she had to find him, tell him about Gordon and about the note on her door.

Still angry about Mark Talbot's acceptance of Suzanne Magnusson's invitation yesterday, she hadn't even considered going to him for help. In her eyes Talbot was a traitor, and she wouldn't have asked his assistance had he been the last man on the Bench.

Jacy ignored the men turning to look at her as she entered the saloon. She pointed her eyes straight ahead and made for the bar before she collapsed from exhaustion.

"Good Lord, Jacy, what brings you out in weather like this?" Monty Fisk asked.

"The sheriff here?"

The bartender shook his head. He had a dark look. "Nope. He's over to his house. Ain't feelin' too well. What you need him for, Jacy?"

She removed her hat with both hands and set it on the bar. Staring at it, she said stiffly, "Someone killed Gordon and

Mrs. Sanderson on their way home from Spernig's."

Someone close to her shushed the others in the bar, and the room quieted.

"Jesus Christ," Fisk said, looking at Jacy searchingly.

One of the men behind her said, "What's going on, Monty?"

"Shut up, Duke," Fisk said, turning his look back to Jacy. "You look about froze. Your eyebrows are white as the ground outside. Why don't you go sit down by the fire and I'll bring you a cup of coffee?"

"Give me a shot of whiskey right here," Jacy said. "Then I'm gonna go find the sheriff."

"The sheriff ain't in any condition to help you tonight, Jacy." Fisk planted a shot glass on the bar and filled it. "He rode out to Magnusson's and got the hell beat out of him. They tied him to his horse and slapped him home. Couple o' the boys found him out here in front of the hitch rack last night."

Someone grunted a laugh.

Jacy slammed back the whiskey and Fisk refilled the glass. "Why in hell did he ride out there alone?" It contradicted everything she knew about the man.

Fisk shook his head and stepped away to pour refills for a couple of cowpokes.

The cowboy standing next to Jacy said, "That's what we're all tryin' to figure out. First he ain't got no balls at all, then he's got 'em big as a—"

"Al!" Fisk scolded the man.

"Sorry," the cowboy said to Jacy.

Someone behind her said loudly, "Jed Gibbon is a drunken fool. He won't be any help to you, Miss Kincaid."

Jacy turned. Before her, unbelievably, Homer Rinski was coming up from a table circled by Verlyn Thornberg and three of Thornberg's drovers. Rinski blinked his eyes intensely and stared right through her.

He was half shot and as stirred up as a Baptist preacher. Jacy had never seen the man in the Sundowner before. He was far too pious for saloons, or so Jacy had thought.

Rinski stopped a few feet away, the round brim of his black hat sliding shadows across his big, emotional face.

"Jed Gibbon is a cowardly fool," Rinski continued. "If us ranchers are going to remain in the basin and remain alive, we must stand together and stand up for ourselves!"

The room had gone quiet. Someone yelled, "You got that right, Homer!"

Rinski paused dramatically, wide blue eyes probing Jacy's with a rheumy, haunted cast. "That's the only way we'll face-down the devil. That's the only way we can stay here and raise our families and live our lives with God's grace, and not be run out of our homes like a bunch of weak-kneed"—he paused, searching for the right word—"pumpkin-rollers!"

"Tell her, Homer!" someone yelled from over by the door.

Rinski's voice deepened, his face reddened, and his countenance grew more and more grave. Startled by the man, Jacy took an involuntary step backward. Rinski took two steps forward, closing the gap between them. The room was so quiet you could hear the wind breathing in the stove's old chimney.

"King Magnusson is the devil, sure as I'm standin' before you now," Rinski continued. "And the Lord does not mollycoddle those who run from the devil. He grants grace to those who face him down and stare him in the eye and say, 'No, I won't run from you, Lucifer. I'll die before I run from the Beast.' "

Jacy stared at the man, spellbound. She'd never seen the quiet, pious Rinski this animated. Rinski stared back at her. She was aware of the other men watching them both and nodding. The room rumbled dully with muttered curses of agreement.

Shortly, Rinski drowned it out. "So, Miss Kincaid, will you stand with us against the Beast? Will you join our army and help us drag the devil from his lair?"

Rinski's eyes narrowed. He slid his face toward Jacy until she could see the pores in his skin, smell the liquor on his breath. He was waiting for an answer. She looked around, not quite sure what to say.

She cleared her throat. "I . . . I'm not exactly sure what you're sayin', Homer."

Rinski blinked, staring in silence. But for the wheezing of the big stove, the room was silent. Then Verlyn Thornberg scraped his chair back and gained his feet slowly.

Turning to Jacy, he said, "We're gonna hunt down King Magnusson and his men like wild dogs, and make them pay for what they're doin'. You with us?"

Held by Rinski's gaze, Jacy felt her heart beating wildly and sweat popping out on her forehead. She swallowed and licked her lips, thinking.

They were right. Magnusson was the devil, and he deserved to die as horribly as the men he'd killed . . . as horribly as Gordon and Mrs. Sanderson.

Thinking of them lying out there now along the banks of the Little Missouri, their bones gnawed by wolves, Jacy turned her head to look around the room. They were all there, she saw—the six other ranchers on the Bench and their winter riders.

And they were all looking at her . . . waiting for her answer.

She pursed her lips and nodded her head slowly. "Okay," she said. "I'm in."

CHAPTER 16

SUZANNE MAGNUSSON WAS getting dressed for her party. She stood before the freestanding walnut mirror in her big, roomy bedroom with its lace curtains, canopied four-poster bed, and two giant carved armoires her father had shipped up the Missouri River from St. Louis and then hauled by freight wagon to the great mansion he'd built in Dakota. The mansion was a virtual castle. Magnusson had designed it himself after the old fur-company trade houses.

Suzanne had protested the move from the family's original home on the outskirts of St. Louis—a palatial plantation with oak trees, rolling green hills, white board fences, and impressive painted barns and corrals for the family's blooded horses. How her father had even been able to consider leaving such peace and tranquillity still baffled her.

But then it probably hadn't been as tranquil for him as for her. He'd had two brothers to compete with, and an ancient patriarch overseeing the family's main business, a giant brickworks north of the growing city that had become a veritable gold mine since the start of the Western building boom.

So here she was, in northern Dakota, dressing for a party to which a handful of middle-aged businessmen from Big Draw would sit around with their wives and leer at the main attraction whenever her father's back was turned. At least Harrison would be there, Suzanne told herself as she stepped into her lacy blue-silk dress and pulled it up to her waist.

And Mark Talbot would be there, as well, taking her mind off the tawdriness of her present circumstances.

If any man could do that, it was Talbot. They really had a lot in common, she and Mark. Dakota was too small to hold either. Both were well-traveled, schooled in other places and other cultures—in the exotic.

And of course, both were now stuck here for the long winter. Not getting together would be quite mad!

Suzanne arranged the dress's lace so that it fell flat across her opulent bosom, then lifted both hands to her neck and tossed her long dark-brown hair out from her collar. She was thinking of Talbot's broad shoulders, long-muscled arms, and ruddy face with piercingly blue eyes—eyes as blue as the Dakota sky on those rare winter days when the sun shone.

She tipped her head and bit her lip, trying to see herself through his eyes—the long, well-brushed hair cascading down her naked shoulders, ringlets brushing her brows, eyes nearly as blue as his, a fine long neck, a smooth chin, and a generous bosom. She pulled the lace down, revealing a healthy portion of the cleft between her breasts.

Liking what she saw, she pulled the lace even further down. Suzanne wondered what her father's cowboys would give for such a view.

She hadn't had much in the way of bedroom adventure on her last trip. Harrison, recently jilted by a high-ranking British soldier, had dogged her every move, suffocating her with his need, making romance impossible. If Talbot didn't come through for her soon, she'd have to bunk with one of the cowboys.

Horrors! The thought sent a chill up her spine and made her want to jump back in the bathtub.

Someone knocked on the door.

With a start she pulled the dress back up over her bosom. "Yes?"

"It's Father, pet."

Looking down to make sure she was covered, she brushed her hair back from her face, walked to the door, and opened it. "Hello, Papa."

King Magnusson stood there, his six-foot-four-inch frame nearly filling the doorway, a maudlin grin softening his big, rawboned face. Only his daughter could evoke such a look on Magnusson's otherwise severe features. The joke among Magnusson's cowboys, cronies, and eastern partners was that if the old man's wife wanted anything, she went through the daughter.

"Hello, kitten. I just wanted to remind you that the party will begin in about an hour. I didn't want the guest of honor to be late. But I see you're one step ahead of me. Don't you look ravishing!"

She gave a lavish curtsy. "Well, thank you, Papa."

"I also wanted to remind you that this is not going to be the kind of elaborate affair you've gotten used to back east. Mr. Wingate has decided to stay an extra week before heading back to Philadelphia, but I'm afraid the rest of the guests will be . . . well . . . my associates. And your mother and brother, of course."

"And Dr. Long," Suzanne reminded her father with lighthearted censure. The doctor's distinctly effeminate sensibilities, not to mention his fondness for the same sex, had made him an object of Magnusson's private derision.

"Well, yes . . . and that Nancy-boy, of course."

"Oh, Papa, I forgot to tell you—I've invited someone else." She hadn't forgotten; she'd delayed telling him because of what she'd seen her father do to the man who'd visited the ranch three days ago—the man who'd been wearing a sheriff's star.

Magnusson frowned. "Oh?"

"Yes, a Mr. Talbot."

"Talbot?"

"Mark Talbot. He ranches a few miles north of us, I understand. You haven't heard of him?"

Magnusson squinted his eyes and looked beyond his daughter, suddenly thoughtful, not quite sure what to say. He knew that a Talbot had once ranched in the area—on some of the best graze on the Canaan Bench, as a matter of fact—but Magnusson thought he'd run him out of there.

"I . . . don't think I have, no," he said, flustered.

Her eyes were sweetly entreating. "You don't mind, do you, Papa?"

"Mind?"

"That I invited someone else—a nester?"

She smiled indulgently. Suzanne was well aware of her father's hatred for the small ranchers around the Double X; she did not know, however, about the terrorism and murder. That's why his display three days ago had been such a shock to her. She still didn't know what to make of it.

Disregarding her question, he asked one of his own. "How did you meet this Mr. Talbot?"

"Harrison and I met him on the train. He was on his way home from fortune-hunting in Mexico. Isn't that exciting—a real adventurer in our midst! He'll be so interesting."

"Yes . . . interesting," King grumbled.

He could tell that his daughter was quite smitten with this Talbot fellow, and he didn't like it a bit. He'd always envisioned Suzanne marrying someone from her own circle—one of Magnusson's investors' sons, for instance. A gentlemanly type born with a silver spoon and a penchant for fine brandy and horses, not to mention money. Lots of it. That type, he knew from experience, was in short supply in Dakota.

"And not to worry, Papa," Suzanne continued. "Mark is a

clever fellow. I know that if you made him a generous offer for his ranch, he would accept it. He's no rancher—not really—so don't go getting territorial on him."

"What is he, then?"

She shrugged, smiling broadly and tipping her head dreamily. "He's a handsome man of the world."

King tried but was unable to stifle a scowl. But then he thought of something, and he managed a grin and a complete change of tone.

"Well, I certainly am eager to meet this man of the world of yours, Suzanne," he said, putting his big hands on her shoulders and dropping his lantern jaw to look into her eyes. "When is he coming?"

"I hope by six."

"Then for you, my girl, I hope so, too."

"Thank you, Papa."

"Any friend of yours is a friend of mine, pet."

He kissed her on the cheek, too self-absorbed to notice the look of concern in her eyes, and strode down the hall.

When the bedroom door closed behind him, he dropped the phony smile and descended the stairs. In his office he found Randall paging through an English stock journal, his face fixed in that bored, aimless look he always wore.

"Randall, go find Rag and tell him I want to see him."

"What for?"

"Don't ask any of your dull-witted questions now, boy!" Magnusson exploded. He took a deep breath, lowered his voice, and said through gritted teeth, "Go get Rag!"

TALBOT SENSED SOMEONE watching him before he saw movement in a copse of deciduous trees in a low, serpentine swale about a hundred yards to his left.

Whoever was spying on him probably thought they were

invisible against the dark background of trees, and to anyone but Talbot they probably would have been, but over the past seven years he had cultivated an acute sensitivity to danger.

Now as he rode he did not slide a second look toward the swale. If someone was drawing a bead on him, a double take might be all the encouragement he needed to squeeze the trigger.

But he didn't want to make an easy target, either, so as nonchalantly as possible, he spurred his horse into a lope. A half second later he was glad he did. Something whistled in the air about six inches behind him. A rifle cracked. The horse pricked its ears and tossed its head.

The idiot sons of bitches had taken a potshot at him!

Talbot hunched down against the gelding's neck and tossed a look toward the trees. The riders were cantering toward him, yelling curses and hunching forward in their saddles. Both rifles belched fire and smoke, and the lead cut the air with angry sighs. One spanged the ground nearby, and Talbot's horse veered from the trail.

Talbot dug his spurs into the gelding's side, urging the horse into a hell-for-leather gallop. He wanted to buy time to dismount and look for cover.

He'd put about two hundred yards behind him when the trail began climbing a low ridge capped with woods. Until now the trail had been relatively free of snow, the wind having cleared it. But Talbot knew the ridge would be covered and no doubt a bitch to negotiate—even on a horse as stalwart as his speckled gray.

A minute later he saw that what he'd been dreading was true. The trail at the top of the ridge was socked under a hock-high drift that appeared to deepen as it climbed. Talbot cursed and looked around. The woods all along the ridge appeared equally socked in. He had no choice but to push ahead and hope the horse would make it.

It made the first ten yards with little problem. Then, plunging into a knee-high drift, it foundered. Screaming, it fell, and Talbot jumped clear, shucking his rifle.

As the horse thrashed in the snow, complaining loudly, Talbot scrambled clear and checked his backtrail. The two riders had split up to cut him off. One was closing fast, crouched low in the saddle.

Talbot slid his gaze back to the horse and watched helplessly as the animal scrambled out of the drift in a spray of snow, and galloped down the other side of the hill, pitching indignantly, stirrups flapping like undersized wings.

Talbot looked around for a hiding place, then scrambled behind the broad trunk of a lightning-topped cottonwood. He pressed the back of his head against the bark, squeezed his rifle, and winced as the horseman approached in a clatter of hooves.

Finally the horse slowed as it neared the drift, and Talbot wondered if the man had spotted his hiding place. Peeking around the tree, he saw the man leading his horse by the reins, coaxing it through the drift.

Getting an idea, Talbot grabbed his rifle by the barrel. When the man was only a few feet away, Talbot stepped out from the tree and raised his rifle like a club.

"I ain't got all day, horse!" the cowboy yelled, facing his agitated mount.

Just as he'd led the horse through the deepest part of the drift, he turned, and Talbot let him have it with the flat of his rifle stock. The man gave a sharp grunt and fell on his back, instantly unconscious, blood flying from his ruined mouth and nose.

The horse squealed and reared, but before it could gallop off, Talbot grabbed the reins. When he'd gotten the horse settled down, he hurriedly tied it to a branch, then swapped coats and hats with the unconscious cowboy. A moment later, he mounted the man's horse and cantered down the trail.

He spotted the other rider about two hundred yards farther on, approaching from his right. Talbot yanked his hat brim low to hide his face.

"Where in hell is he?" the man yelled when he was about fifty yards away.

Talbot shrugged his shoulders and raised his hands, hoping the man wouldn't realize the impersonation.

"He must have went up in the trees," the man yelled. "You didn't see?"

Again Talbot shrugged his shoulders. The man was getting close enough for Talbot to start delineating facial features, so he turned, giving the man his back and acting as though he were observing the high, wooded country to the north.

As the man neared, he said, "You know, goddamnit, Tex, I could kick your ass for taking that stupid shot back there! How in hell did you expect to hit him from that far away?"

He paused, cantered within ten yards, and stopped. "If you woulda waited, we coulda trailed him into the creek bottom on the other side of the saddle and caught him in a cross fire."

Suddenly Talbot turned. "What in hell would you want to do that for?" he said tightly, laying the flat of his rifle stock against the side of the man's head.

The man gave a loud "Hey!" and toppled from his saddle, hat flying and horse recoiling. On the ground he lay stunned for a moment, then went for his gun.

"Uh-uh," Talbot warned, jacking his rifle.

The man was a big, solid cowboy with gray-brown hair and a savage face. Wrinkling his nose and baring his teeth, he stared at Talbot with all the charity of a wounded grizzly. His hat had fallen off, and blood from his torn ear dribbled down his face. "Why, you . . ."

"Forget about me, friend. Who are you and why were you trying to kill me?"

"I'm Rag Donnelly, foreman of the Double X, and you can go fuck yourself."

Talbot squeezed the trigger and spanged a slug off the flat rock five inches right of the man's head. The man cowered, raising his elbow to shield his face.

"Tough guy, eh?" Talbot said.

"Tough enough," the man grunted.

"Not too tough for bushwhacking, though."

The man said nothing, just stared. Talbot met the cold eyes, feeling his anger grow.

Then the man said, "This is Double X range, and you're trespassin'."

"I was invited."

"Not by King Magnusson, you weren't."

"By his daughter. Doesn't she count?"

"I just follow orders."

"Does Suzanne know about those orders?"

Again the man just stared. Blood trickled from his ear down his neck, and strands of his matted salt-and-pepper hair lifted in the breeze.

"I didn't think so," Talbot said. "Drop your gunbelt and get your horse. You, me, and your friend back there are going to a party."

"You're crazy," the man snarled.

"Yes, I am," Talbot said with a wry smile. "And getting crazier by the minute. Now get your horse."

CHAPTER 17

JED GIBBON'S FACE looked like hamburger, and it felt as bad as it looked. The ankle and knee he'd twisted when Magnusson had pulled him from his saddle throbbed with every beat of his heart.

What hurt worse, though, was his pride. This surprised him some. He hadn't thought anything could damage his self-respect worse than the Old Trouble.

But having ridden out to the Double X all horns and rattles, intent on solving the whole problem in one fell swoop, then getting the shit kicked out of him and sent back to the Sundowner on his horse . . . well, that was just a little too much for even Jed Gibbon to take.

Knowing that riding out to the Double X had been motivated by booze and visions of grandiosity made him feel all the more silly. That's why tonight, while the Double X was gearing up for Suzanne's party, and after two and a half days of lying abed healing up and feeling sorry for himself, Gibbon limped into the Sundowner and ordered a glass of apple juice.

"Apple juice?" Monty Fisk said, wincing at both the request and the sight of Gibbon's battered face.

"Until I've got King Magnusson and his men all locked up together in my little jail, I'm gonna be drinkin' apple juice. So lay in a good supply of it. I'll just pretend it's whiskey."

While Fisk looked around under the counter for apple

juice, Gibbon turned and scanned the room. It was nearly five o'clock, but the only business was a couple of mule skinners and a sour-looking drummer.

"Where in hell is everybody?" Gibbon exclaimed, feeling a twinge of unrest.

Fisk flushed a little and shrugged. He uncorked a stone jug of apple juice and sniffed the lip. "Probably all to home. It's pretty cold out there, you know."

Gibbon narrowed his eyes at the bartender, who did not return the gaze as he filled a glass. "All to home, you think, eh?" Gibbon said indulgently.

Fisk was feigning a casual air. "No doubt."

Gibbon nodded and dropped his gaze to the glass of juice. A fine froth covered the surface of the glass. Bubbles popped and fizzed. "It don't feel any colder than usual to me."

"Well, who knows?" Fisk said, replacing the jug under the counter. His ears were nearly as red as the stove, which had been stoked to glowing.

Gibbon picked up the glass, scrutinized the pulpy fluid, and took a tentative sip. He made a face and spat the juice on the floor. "How long you been aging that stuff? It's liable to get me drunker'n your snakewater."

"Sorry, Jed, I guess that's a pretty old jug. How 'bout some prune juice?"

"Nah, it'll just get me runnin'. Tell ya what you can do instead, though, Monty—you can tell me where all your regulars are."

Unable to meet Gibbon's eye, Fisk lifted his gaze to the dimming windows at the other end of the long room and fashioned a look of exasperation. "I told you—"

"Cut the shit, Monty. They've gathered somewhere, haven't they?"

"I don't know what you're talkin' about, Jed."

"Those stupid bastards are plannin' an attack on the Double X, aren't they?"

Fisk sighed, giving up the ruse.

"Where are they?" Gibbon prodded.

"I'm not supposed to tell you, Jed."

"Tell me, Monty, or I'll arrest you for tryin' to poison a peace officer."

Fisk sighed again. "They're gathering out at the Rinski place, in his barn. They're pretty fired up this time, Jed; I don't see them calling it off."

"Who says I want 'em to call it off?"

Fisk blinked. "What?"

Gibbon drew his pistol and checked the loads. "Hell, no, I just want to make sure they don't get spanked and sent home like I did. I think it's about time we stop playin' make-believe and get organized . . . don't you, Monty?"

Gibbon was high on his newfound pride, a sense of position and duty he'd never had before. Before, he'd been afraid of death. It had made him feel small and alone—a man apart. Now he realized there were things worse than death, and shame was one of them. Odd how he had King Magnusson to thank for this new insight.

Fisk returned Gibbon's smile and shrugged. "Whatever you say, Jed." The barman paused, his face clouding. "Say, you want me to go with you? I could grab my Greener?"

"No, you stay here and watch the town for me. Consider yourself deputized."

The man said nothing. He smiled with relief.

Gibbon left the saloon and stiffly mounted his horse, reining the big gelding around and heading him south out of Canaan on a snowy trace that rose and fell over a series of watersheds.

It was a little-known shortcut, and he hoped it would get him to the Rinski ranch before the ranchers had pulled out for the Double X. Gibbon had been thinking long and hard about an assault on Magnusson, and he thought he'd come up with a good plan. He didn't want the small ranchers going off half-cocked and mucking it up.

When he pulled onto the headquarters of the Rinski ranch, it was full dark. Gibbon saw a light on in the cabin and the silhouette of someone rocking in the window. The sheriff knew it was Rinski's daughter, and the vision of her rocking there, all alone in the dim cabin, gave him a chill beyond anything this winter night could provide.

Hearing voices in the barn and seeing over a dozen horses in the corral, their steamy breath rising toward the stars, Gibbon rode over and dismounted. He tied his reins to the corral and opened the barn door with a grunt.

A crowd of about twenty ranchmen milled in the alley before him. They stood leaning against square-cut posts and sitting on milk stools and hay bales. Two of Thornberg's men sat with their legs dangling off the end of a wagon box. Another was stretched out in the box, head propped on an elbow. Homer Rinski was drawing in the hay-flecked dust with a stick.

Two lanterns hung from posts, spreading weak yellow light against the shadows at the back of the barn.

The men gave a start at the rasp of the door sliding open. Several went for their guns.

"It's too late!" Gibbon yelled. "I'm King Magnusson and you're all deader'n winter roses!"

The men froze, looking sheepish and slowly relaxing. Gibbon walked into the barn, pushed through the crowd, and shuttled his eyes around the group.

"Damn foolish, not postin' a guard," he said. Then, seeing that one of the "men" was Jacy Kincaid: "What in hell are you doin' here, Jacy?"

"What are you doin' here?" Jacy piped back, as disgusted

with the man as any of them. His singling her out because she was female didn't help.

Homer Rinski stood slowly. "She's one of us, Sheriff. She ranches here just like the rest of us, so just like the rest of us, she'll defend her ranch. Lord knows nobody else is gonna do it"—he fed Gibbon a cold gaze—"so we have to."

Gibbon regarded the man with irritation. "Don't get your dander up, Homer. I didn't ride out here to try and quash your rebellion. I rode out here to give you a hand."

The men and Jacy shifted their eyes around, muttering.

"Maybe you better leave this up to us, Gibbon." It was Verlyn Thornberg.

He rose from a hay bale holding a tin cup. The cup wasn't steaming, and Gibbon figured it held something stouter than coffee. Thornberg's eyes were as cold as Rinski's, and his jaw was a straight line beneath the shadow his farm hat slanted across his face.

Gibbon's cheeks warmed. "I deserved that, Verlyn," he said with a slow nod. "I truly did; I understand that. I haven't done one goddamn thing to earn your respect or your trust. But there's something you haven't done to keep me out of your hair, and that's fire me."

Thornberg stepped toward him. "You're fired," he said with a growl.

Gibbon shook his head. "That would take a majority vote of the city council, and"—Gibbon lifted his head to look around—"I see only three or four of you here."

He paused, listening to the angry sighs and muttered curses.

"What's your point?" Thornberg said.

"My point is that we're going to declare war on King Magnusson, but we're going to do it all real legal-like. You're all going to be deputized, and you're going to follow my orders.

I'm in charge. Anybody doesn't like that can go on home and keep out of my way."

He stopped to let this sink in. Glancing around the room at the five or six ranch owners and their dozen or so armed riders, he said, "Any questions?"

Someone said very softly, "Shit."

Homer Rinski just stared at Gibbon, as did Thornberg. Neither said anything. They saw the cold determination in Jed Gibbon's wasted face.

"All right, then," he said, straightening. "Raise your right hands and repeat after me . . ."

CHAPTER 18

TALBOT AND HIS two captives made a silent procession along an old horse trail that rose toward the headquarters of the Double X. The sun had gone down and a few stars were kindling in the east, but the west still glowed with last light. A coyote howled. The horses blew and shook their bridles, hooves grinding snow as they walked with their heads down.

The cowboys rode stirrup to stirrup, hands tied snugly to their saddle horns, ankles shackled with rope. Talbot rode behind them, his rifle aimed at their backs. He knew he'd run into more riders, and sure enough, two cowboys appeared on the trail ahead. In the fading light they were little more than shadows.

Behind them the Magnusson mansion rose on a hill like a Bavarian castle lit up for Christmas. It was still half a mile away, but piano music carried crisply on the frosty air, like sonorous strains from a music box.

"Tell them to back off," Talbot ordered the foreman.

Donnelly said nothing.

"Tell 'em."

"Stay back—he's got a gun on us," Donnelly said.

The two horsemen stopped about twenty yards away. "Rag, Tex . . . that you?"

"Give me some room," Talbot ordered. "I mean no threat

to you or your boss, but these men bushwhacked me, and if you try the same, I'm gonna let 'em have it!"

They said nothing, just sat there wondering what to do.

Talbot peeled back the hammer on his Winchester. The man named Tex must have heard it. "Get the hell back, goddamnit!" he yelled, his shrill voice cracking.

The men sat there for several more seconds. One mumbled something, and they reined their horses off the trail. One rode left, the other right, and stopped about fifty yards away. As Talbot and his captives continued, the outriders paralleled them, keeping their distance. Talbot eyed them warily.

There were two guards at the open front gate, and Talbot had Donnelly order them back. Both men obeyed. One ran into the mansion. The other watched Talbot from a distance, tracking him, an air of defensive caution in his bearing.

Turning, Talbot saw the two outlying riders drift into the compound behind him. They fanned out around him but kept their rifles pointed skyward—for now, anyway.

Talbot and his captives halted at the hitch rack to the left of the mansion's broad wooden steps. The house rose before them—a great peaked shadow with squares of yellow light dulled by curtains. It blocked out the stars. The deep verandah ran the length of the house, its railing decorated with fir boughs and red ribbons. From inside came the smell of roasting beef.

The piano music had stopped. It was replaced by the muffled sounds of angry male voices and boots pounding wood floors. The pounding increased in volume until the front door was thrown open and a tall figure appeared, strode across the verandah, and stopped.

The man loomed over the steps, partially silhouetted by the windows behind him, his face further obscured by a cloud of sweet-smelling cigar smoke.

"Rag, what in the *hell* is going on!"

The foreman's head lowered as he expelled air from his lungs. The man wagged his head slowly but said nothing. The other cowboy simply stared at his horse, shoulders sagging with the pain of his broken nose.

"Just a little misunderstanding, I believe," Talbot said.

"Who the hell are you?"

"The man you ordered bushwhacked. And you must be the great King Magnusson."

Magnusson said nothing.

"I'm a friend of your daughter's. She invited me out to join your little shindig here tonight." Talbot paused, then added with a curled lip, "Just couldn't wait to meet you."

Magnusson cut his eyes at his foreman. "Rag?"

Donnelly shrugged, gave a phlegmy sigh. "He gave us the jump, boss," he confessed.

"For Christ's sake!" Magnusson growled. To the young man who had followed him onto the porch he said, "Cut them loose." Like the rancher, the young man was decked out in a swallowtail coat, winged collar, and tie. The smell of bay rum was nearly as thick as the cigar smoke.

With a caustic snort, the young man moved down the steps, producing a pocketknife, and went to work on Donnelley's ropes.

Magnusson stared at Talbot, sizing him up. Smoke puffed around the stogie between his teeth. Talbot stared back. His eyes were cool.

He said, "If I knew for sure this was all a mistake, I could put my rifle away. In the meantime I think I'll keep it aimed your way . . . just so one of your men don't get trigger happy."

Magnusson said nothing. The smoke drifted to the roof over the verandah and hung suspended in the still air.

Another figure stepped out of the mansion.

"Mark, it *is* you!" Suzanne ran up beside her father, her

head rising to only his shoulder. She looked from Talbot to Magnusson, frowning. "What's going on?"

"I think we just had a little misunderstanding," Magnusson said with an artificial smile. "Wouldn't you say that's what it was, Mr. Talbot?"

"Yeah, just a little misunderstanding," Talbot said dryly.

Donnelly had dismounted and, holding a handkerchief to the bloody side of his head, regarded Talbot with a rancorous scowl. "Listen, asshole, you may have gotten the jump on me back there, but—"

"Rag!" Magnusson hissed, jerking his head at Suzanne.

Hunching her shoulders against the cold and grasping a night cape closed at her throat, Suzanne looked up at her father. She was dressed for the evening, her long chocolate hair in ringlets. "Papa, what is going on here?" she asked with reproach.

"Just a little misunderstanding," Magnusson said, his eyes on Talbot. "Rag and Tex mistook your friend here for trouble, that's all."

"Are you all right, Mark?"

"No problem."

Confident Magnusson wouldn't try anything with his daughter present, Talbot slid his rifle into its boot, dismounted, and tied his horse to the hitch rack. He came up the steps and stopped about three rungs down from her. "You look lovely."

He gave a playful bow and reached for her hand. She laughed and gave it to him. He took it gently, gently kissed it, consciously easing the tension.

Laughing, Suzanne turned to her father. "Papa, I want you to meet the incomparable Mark Talbot."

Magnusson was watching his riders leading their horses off to the stables.

Suzanne cleared her throat. "Papa?"

The rancher jerked his head to Talbot. "Oh, yes, of course. Mr. Talbot, how nice it is to make your acquaintance."

They shook hands.

King said affably, "I'd like to apologize for the trouble. I should have sent someone to inform my outriders you were coming. I hope you can forgive my error."

"I'll work on it," Talbot said.

He and Magnusson shared a look of bemused understanding. The rancher gestured at the door, revealing his long horse teeth in a broad smile. "In the meantime, why don't we all get in out of the cold?"

Talbot followed Suzanne into the house. Magnusson paused with a hand on the door and looked again toward the stables.

Randall Magnusson mounted the steps behind him. "Never seen Rag with so much egg on his face," he said with a self-satisfied chuckle.

King had forgotten he was back there. He glanced at his fleshy-faced progeny, said distractedly, "No . . . me neither," then went inside.

KING CAUGHT UP with Talbot and Suzanne in the foyer, where a crushed velvet settee sat beneath an ornately carved mirror. "I'll take your coat and hat, Mr. Talbot," he said. "And your gunbelt, of course. Don't allow the nasty things in the house."

"Of course not," Talbot said dryly as he started removing his coat, looking into Magnusson's steely eyes with a tight smile.

A maid had appeared, a harried, glassy-eyed girl of no more than sixteen. Magnusson gave her Talbot's coat, hat, and gunbelt, and the girl disappeared down the hall. Talbot watched her go, feeling naked without the gun.

Taking his hand, Suzanne led him through a long, narrow sitting room redolent with pre-dinner cigars, and through a pair of glass doors where a long table covered with snow-white linen and silver stretched between two gargantuan stone fireplaces. The head of a mountain goat was mounted over one mantel, the head of a grizzly over the other.

The cedar logs popped and sparked, tossing shadows this way and that, giving the room a warm, intimate feel. There was no intimacy apparent among the four women and six men gathered at the table, however. Dressed to the hilt in dark suits and bright gowns, and sitting ceremoniously in their high-backed chairs, they looked as festive as Lutheran deacons.

Suzanne made the introductions, and Talbot nodded at each guest in turn. Dr. Long sat beside a Mr. Wingate from Philadelphia, a stuffy little wedge of a man with a bald head and carrot-colored muttonchops connecting beneath his nose.

Harrison appeared bored. Holding a Siamese cat in the crook of his arm, he acknowledged Talbot with a slight dip of the chin and curl of the lip, eyes bright with alcohol. "We meet again, Mr. Talbot!"

"Harrison, I can't believe you're still here."

The doctor shrugged. "To be honest with you, Mr. Talbot, I can't either."

"Why would he leave when our whiskey's free?" Randall Magnusson said with a caustic snort.

He'd retaken his seat next to his father at the head of the table. He was a soft young man with a baby face, a thin dark beard, and chestnut hair hanging over his collar like a beaver tail. Talbot knew now why Rinski suspected Randall and another man of killing Jack Thom and raping Rinski's daughter. Randall had snake written all over him.

A door opened to Talbot's right and a stout, raven-haired

woman in a violet dress appeared looking harried.

Suzanne said, “Mark, I’d like you to meet my mother. Mother, Mark Talbot.”

“My pleasure, ma’am.”

“The pleasure is all mine, Mr. Talbot,” Mrs. Magnusson said with an air of distraction, automatically offering her hand, which Talbot shook very gently. The hand was small and plump, with papery skin and several large rings, including a diamond, reflecting the light from the fire.

The woman’s breath smelled of booze, and a fine sweat glistened above her bright red lips and on her forehead. Her eyes resembled Suzanne’s, but with an additional jaded cast, an oblique pessimism. She appeared both haunted and harried.

Turning to her daughter, Mrs. Magnusson arched her plucked eyebrows. “I wasn’t aware there would be another guest.”

Suzanne frowned. “Didn’t Papa tell you?”

King shrugged guiltily. “I’m sorry, Kendra—I plum forgot.”

Admonishing her father with a look, Suzanne said, “Fortunately I reminded Minnie to set another place.”

Talbot said, “If there’s a problem—”

“Oh, don’t be silly, Mr. Talbot,” Mrs. Magnusson said, breathing heavily and tossing her own reproachful look at King. “The more the merrier! Have a seat.” Turning to the others, she said, “I apologize for the delay with the meat, but Minnie and the girls are utterly baffled by the wine sauce King simply cannot live without.”

Magnusson said, “They’ll make do, Kendra; no point in getting riled.”

Her voice grew as stiff as her smile. “They’re going to burn it, King. I don’t see why we couldn’t—”

King raised his eyebrows and opened his hands palm down.

"Easy, easy, my dear. Let's not bore the guests with our squabbles. Why don't you take a seat and finish your soup before it gets cold?"

Mrs. Magnusson gave her husband a sneering grin, then took a seat at the other end of the table. The guests slurped soup from their spoons, consciously ignoring the tiff.

Suzanne put a hand on her mother's wrist. "Really, Mother, none of us expect a New York meal in Dakota."

Bernard Troutman, the Big Draw banker, said, "Beggars can't be choosers, Kendra. Whatever you put on our plates will be quite sufficient, or we'll go to bed hungry!"

He lowered his chin for emphasis, then looked pompously around for corroboration. The other guests vehemently agreed.

Drunkenly, Harrison said with a theatrical twang, "Give me a ham bone and a bottle o' red-eyed Jim!"

"Oh, Harrison," Suzanne scolded.

"And a bunkhouse full of cowboys," Randall mumbled, dipping his spoon.

Suzanne looked at him angrily. "Randall, I heard that!"

"Not to worry, dear girl," Harrison said. "I think your brother is still struggling with his own . . . *feelings*, shall we say?"

King grinned over his wineglass. Randall aimed his blunt nose at the doctor and opened his mouth to speak.

Mr. Wingate cut him off with a vociferous throat clearing. "So, Mr. Talbot, where do you hail from, may I ask?"

Shrugging, Talbot sipped his soup—cream of onion with butter pooling in the thick, slightly curdled cream. "Here and there. I was raised on the Bench."

"The Bench?"

"My homeplace is about twenty miles northwest of here."

"Oh, I see." Wingate cut his eyes to Troutman, then to

Magnusson. The other businessmen did likewise. The women looked only at each other, growing tense.

King kept his own gaze on his soup. Heartily changing the subject, he said, "I read in the paper just today that Nordstrom and Fontaine bought out McAdams."

There was a ponderous silence. Then King raised his eyebrows at Wingate and the other businessmen.

"No!" one of the Big Draw men exclaimed, catching on.

"Lock, stock, and barrel."

"Well, what on earth will that do to the price of rail shipments?"

"God knows. I'm sending a cable to Stephen Vandemark first thing tomorrow."

The conversation continued similarly throughout the next three courses. No one from King's circle so much as glanced at Talbot. No one, that is, but Randall Magnusson.

Several times Talbot looked up from his venison tenderloin and parsnips, and from his chocolate soufflé with cherries, to see the cherubic-faced young scoundrel considering him darkly. Talbot met the gaze head-on, as if to say, "You murdered my brother, didn't you, you son of a bitch?"

And young Magnusson blinked his eyes coldly, as if to say, "So what if I did?"

Sensing Talbot's agitation, Suzanne put her hand on his thigh. Her flesh warmed him through his trousers, and he suddenly became aroused. It was an obtuse feeling under the circumstances, only vaguely pleasant. Feeling his pants tightening beneath her hand, she looked at him coyly and gave a giggle.

When the dessert was eaten and the maids began clearing the dishes, Magnusson suggested that the men adjourn to the sitting room for sherry and cigars.

Suzanne said, "Oh, Papa, do excuse Mark, please? I want

to show him around the house." Turning to Dr. Long, she said, "Would you like to join us, Harry?"

Feeding a scrap to the Siamese in his lap, Harrison shook his head. "No, you two run along. I'll help the girls and Minnie with the dishes. *They* enjoy my company, don't you, dears?"

Twenty minutes later, when the tour was over, Suzanne led Talbot into a paneled upstairs reading room. There were two deep armchairs covered in floral damask, a mahogany tea table between them, and a brass cuspidor. Against a wall was a serpentine-back sofa with scrolled armrests.

Nearly everywhere Talbot looked were game trophies and marble busts and expensively bound books that appeared to have never been cracked. He wondered how in hell Magnusson had gotten the busts out here without breaking them, and he imagined the poor mule skinners who'd had to haul them from the boat landing at Bismarck. They'd no doubt sweated every gorge and coulee—every knoll!—and kicked up their heels when they'd gotten them on their pedestals in one piece.

"Penny for your thoughts," Suzanne said, lightly poking Talbot in the ribs.

"Oh . . . sorry," he said.

"You've been very quiet. What were you thinking during dinner?"

"Nothing important."

"Liar. You were thinking something dark; I could see it in your eyes."

Silently, she lit two cut-glass lamps, then turned to him with a serious expression. Her long neck—butter colored in the flickering lamplight—looked especially delicate above the low-cut dress that generously exposed the cleft in her opulent bosom.

"I'm sorry about the men who attacked you," she said. "The fault is really mine, not Papa's. I delayed telling him about your coming because . . . well"—her eyes flitted nervously about the room—"because I'm absent-minded." Her eyes came to rest on his and she smiled, perfect lips rising slightly at the corners.

Talbot raised an eyebrow. "Or maybe you were worried he wouldn't allow it."

Her cheeks colored slightly. "That's silly."

"Is it? Those men tried to ambush me, and I don't think it was a case of mistaken identity."

"Mark, please. Why are you being so hostile?"

He looked at her dully. "Someone killed my brother."

Her eyes widened with surprise. "That's awful! When?"

He told her.

She got up and walked to the window but did not look out. "And you think it was Papa?"

He considered telling her about Gordon seeing Randall heading toward the Circle T that day, but decided the water was muddy enough for now. "I don't think he pulled the trigger, but one of his riders did. Amounts to the same thing. He was trying to clean out the Bench for his own herds."

She wheeled around and confronted him, face taut with anger. Gradually her features softened. She raised her eyebrows beseechingly. "Mark, let's please talk about something else."

He tried a smile. There would be little point in torturing her with all this. Besides, it was hard not to acquiesce to a woman like Suzanne Magnusson. She was as willful as she was beautiful. She was also spoiled. It was her least attractive quality, but it somehow added to her power.

Talbot could see how young men could be utterly swept away by her, like a hundred-foot rogue wave flooding the deck while you're hanging in the crow's nest. Young men whose brother had not been murdered by her father, that is.

"Okay," he said.

She wheeled gracefully and collapsed on the sofa, patted the cushion beside her. "Come. Sit with me."

He did as he was told.

"This is my favorite place in the house," she said. "I like to sit here alone and read and dream of faraway places."

"What places?"

"No place in particular. Just anywhere far away—anywhere I haven't been, that is, because when you've been there the romance is gone, don't you think?"

"Dakota's a nice place, in spite of the winter. At least it was."

Suddenly playful, Suzanne sat up and tucked a leg beneath her, then turned to him, folding her hands in her lap.

"Let's play a game." She wrinkled her nose, giggling, and leaned toward him, clasping his hand. "Are you game for a game, Mr. Talbot?"

He shrugged, observing her with puzzled amusement. His murdered brother was the farthest thing from her mind. "Why not?"

"I'll say a noun and you say the first verb that pops into your head."

"Why do you get the nouns and I get the verbs?" he asked, playing along.

"Why, because you're a man of action, of course!"

"Oh."

"Ready?"

He rested his head against the sofa back and nodded.

"Close your eyes. Okay. Stone. Hurry! You have to say the first verb that pops into your head."

"Okay . . . throw!"

"Snake."

"Uh—slither!"

"Horse."

"Ride."

"Cards."

"Gamble."

"Ships."

"Sail."

"Knife."

"Cut."

"Girls."

He opened his eyes. "Girls?"

"Don't think!"

"All right . . . girls . . . uh . . . kiss."

"Kiss?"

He opened his eyes again and gave a laugh. She was looking at him with an expression of wry expectance. "You said to say the first thing that came into my head, and kissing was the first thing that came into my head."

Her eyes flashed slyly. "Have you kissed Jacy Kincaid?"

He laughed again. "What?"

"Have you?"

"No."

"Have you wanted to?"

He thought for a few seconds. "No." It was a lie, but he knew it was what she wanted to hear.

Her expression becoming grave, she lowered her eyes. She spoke quietly, in a throaty, silky voice that reminded him of a gentle breeze combing woods. "Have you wanted to kiss me?"

He stared at her seriously for a moment. "Yes." It was not a lie.

"Why don't you, then?"

He smiled. Unable to help himself, he gently took her face in his hands and kissed her. Her lips were silky. They parted for him slightly.

After a while, she pulled away. "Mark, let's not let any of this trouble my father's involved in come between us, okay?"

"Suzanne—"

"Okay?"

He sighed, gave a nod.

She smiled, said in a throaty, lusty voice, her sweet breath warm on his face, "All right, then, take it away, Mr. Talbot."

His eyes widened. "What? Here?"

"It'll be our secret."

"Suzanne—"

He tried to rise, but she pushed him back against the couch, flattening her breasts against his chest and pressing her full lips to his.

"Suzanne . . ." he said again. But he couldn't help being aroused by her. The feel of her hands in his hair, on his shoulders, on his arms . . . the beguiling taste of her tongue probing his . . . her thighs on his . . . was too much to deny.

She gently bit his upper lip, pushing away. She lowered her head, unbuttoned his shirt, and kissed his chest, murmuring, "You cut a fine manly figure, Mark Talbot. It's been so long since . . ."

He reached into her hair, ran the strands through his fingers. Her head went lower. Her fingers were on his fly.

She whispered, "My God, Mr. Talbot."

"Suzanne . . ."

It wasn't long before he was arching his back and tearing at the sofa with his fists.

It took all his power not to yell.

Somewhere in another realm, boots pounded, shaking the floor. It took Talbot several seconds to realize that someone was climbing the stairs.

"Suzanne!" It was King Magnusson.

Talbot could tell by the increased volume of the pounding boots that the man was within twenty feet and closing.

Talbot tried to push her off him but could not unclench his hands from the cushions. Finally, at the last second, she lifted her head, ran the back of her hand across her mouth, and smiled with devilish delight.

"Now you're in trouble, buster!" she laughed.

CHAPTER 19

THE TALL, BLOND, barrel-chested visage of King Magnusson burst through the open glass doors like a bull through a chute. He was puffing a stogie and holding a delicate sherry glass in each ham-sized hand.

Talbot was happy to see he didn't have a pistol and wondered vaguely about his own.

Stentorian voice booming, Magnusson said, "Suzanne, your guests are starting to wonder where the birthday girl has drifted off to, and Dr. Long is growing tiresome. Maybe you should make an appearance?"

Suzanne scowled. She'd just thrown herself onto the sofa, a prudent, ladylike distance from her guest, and brushed the hair back from her face, on which she'd managed an impossible expression of cool innocence.

"But they're all so dull compared to Mr. Talbot," she protested, folding her arms like an overly indulged twelve-year-old.

"Suzanne," King scolded.

"Oh, all right." She gazed at Talbot and smiled. "We'll continue this conversation a little later . . . all right, Mr. Talbot?"

He cleared the frog in his throat, gaining his tongue. "Of course." He wondered if he'd gotten all his fly buttons closed.

Suzanne stood and kissed her father's cheek. "Be good," she whispered in King's ear.

She turned a parting smile to Talbot, who'd risen from the couch, then left the room in a swish of skirts.

Magnusson watched her, smiling. When she was gone, he gave Talbot a sherry and closed the door. He gestured at the couch. Talbot sat down and regained his composure.

He didn't say anything. He wanted Magnusson to make the first move.

Unbuttoning his coat, Magnusson sat across from him in one of the damask-covered chairs. He stretched his long legs across an ottoman and crossed his calfskin boots at the ankles. Rolling his shoulders and wiggling his butt to get comfortable, he spat into the cuspidor at his left, then rubbed his bushy mustaches down with his thumb and forefinger.

"That girl is my pride and joy."

"I can see why," Talbot said with more exuberance than intended. "She's reason enough to have a man killed, I suppose. Was she the reason you tried to have *me* killed?"

Ignoring the question, Magnusson dug around in his coat for a cigarillo, offered it to Talbot. "Cigar?"

"No thanks."

"Addicted to the damn things," Magnusson said, staring at the coal of the one he was smoking. He lifted his chin and offered a stiff smile. "So we're neighbors."

"I guess you could say that."

"You won't be offended if I ask what your intentions are, will you?"

"Regarding . . . ?"

"Let's start with Suzanne."

Talbot planted an elbow on the arm of the couch and rubbed his lower lip with his index finger, pondering. "What if I said they were serious?"

"Then I'd have to tell you that anything more than friendship is simply out of the question."

"Why?"

Magnusson kept his eyes on Talbot, trying to be as direct as possible. As threatening as possible, too, Talbot thought, without actually drawing a pistol. "Because my daughter belongs to a certain . . . class, shall we say? She is accustomed to certain amenities, creature comforts a man of your station couldn't possibly provide." He grinned coldly and added without a trace of sincerity, "I'm sorry to be so blunt, but if you were a father, you'd understand."

Talbot said nothing.

Magnusson surveyed him critically. At length he squinted and inclined his head, genuinely puzzled. "Have I misjudged you, Talbot?"

"What do you mean?"

"Everyone I run into wants something from me—my daughter, my money, or both. But in you I sense"—he scowled, shook his head—"I don't know; I sense something else."

Talbot stood, shoved his hands in his pockets, and walked to the end of the room. He turned slowly around. He studied Magnusson coolly, then smiled sarcastically. "You're right. I do want something else from you, Magnusson. I want to know who killed my brother."

"Brother?"

Talbot nodded. "I went off to fight in the Apache wars about seven years ago, left my older brother, Dave, home to ranch by himself. About a year ago I decided to start making my way back to Dakota. Decided it was time to settle down, help out on the ranch. Well, I got back last week and learned my brother was dead."

Magnusson dropped his eyes, studied his boots. "Sorry to hear that."

"He was shot twice in the back of the head."

Magnusson kept his eyes on his boots.

Talbot said, "Someone apparently wanted him off the Bench—wanted our land for theirs—so they killed him. You have any idea who would do such a thing?"

King lifted his head slowly, arched an eyebrow. "You've been listening to the nesters around Canaan."

"Who started the bloodshed?"

Magnusson shrugged. "Who fired the first shot at Fort Sumter?" He looked at Talbot as if awaiting an answer. He got none. "They were stealing cattle."

"Before or after you started stealing their land?"

"I'm not going to argue about land rights. I have the law on my side."

"Legally?"

"Does it matter?"

Talbot sat on the sofa and cut to the chase. "The day my brother was killed, your son and another rider were seen heading toward our headquarters."

A muscle beneath Magnusson's right eye twitched. "Did anyone see Randall kill your brother?"

Talbot said nothing.

"Did anyone see Randall kill your brother?" Magnusson repeated, more forcefully this time, as though reproaching a dim-witted schoolboy.

Talbot stared into Magnusson's eyes, his own eyes dark with fury.

Satisfied he'd gotten his answer, Magnusson nodded. He struggled out of his chair and strode about the room glancing at book spines and straightening picture frames. Finally he turned on his heel, adjusted his paper collar and tie, and regarded Talbot with a look of ceremonial gravity.

"I am sorry about your brother. I offered him good money

for his land and he turned me down, but I did not kill him. Nor did I order him killed."

"Maybe your son and a Mr. Shelby Green are doing some independent work out on the range. Homer Rinski thinks it was they who killed his hired man and raped his daughter."

"Nonsense."

Talbot shrugged. "They have quite the reputation for shenanigans, those two."

"An unearned reputation, I assure you. They're . . . boys." Something in his eyes told Talbot the old man wasn't giving his son the credit he deserved.

When Talbot said nothing in reply, Magnusson went back to his chair and sat down. He planted his elbows on his knees, took his sherry in his hands, and regarded Talbot directly. "What do you say we forget about the past? Come to work for me."

Talbot gave a caustic laugh. "What?"

"I'll buy you out. Give you top dollar for your ranch and two hundred dollars a month for your work."

"What kind of work?"

Magnusson sat back in his chair, eyes furtive. "I saw what you did to Donnelly. No one does that to Donnelly. Consider his job yours."

Talbot laughed again. "What makes you think I'd accept such an offer?"

"Because you can't run your own beef on the Bench. I won't allow it."

"If you can't beat 'em, join 'em—that it?"

"Makes sense."

"Go fuck yourself, King."

Magnusson's face fell like a wet sheet. His ears turned red. His voice came tight and even. "You just made the biggest mistake of your life."

Talbot matched the rancher's composure. "And you made

the biggest mistake of yours when you declared war on the Bench and killed my brother."

"Get out."

"My pleasure. But we'll meet again—you, me, and your son."

Magnusson looked at the doors. "Rag!"

Rag Donnelly walked in carrying Talbot's coat, hat, gunbelt, and a rifle. There was a bloodstained bandage over the ear Talbot had smashed. Donnelly studied Talbot with cool malevolence—a big, hard-looking man in an old sheepskin coat and a curled Stetson, strategically tipped away from the injured ear.

"Escort Mr. Talbot out the back," Magnusson ordered.

"My pleasure, Mr. Magnusson."

"I don't want him shot—unless he provokes it, that is."

"Yes, sir."

"I know there's a debt to be paid, Rag, but I don't want any trouble tonight."

Donnelly nodded reluctantly, his cold eyes on Talbot.

"Very well, then," Magnusson said.

Talbot had slipped into his coat and hat, buckled the gunbelt around his waist.

"Don't worry—there ain't no loads in your iron," Donnelly told him. "So don't embarrass yourself."

" 'Preciate the advice," Talbot said. Turning to Magnusson, he asked, "What are you going to tell your daughter?"

Glancing at Donnelly, Magnusson said with a shrug, "The truth. That you were using her to finagle a job out of me—Rag's job. When I turned you down, you threatened to join the other small ranchers in rustling me blind." He smiled. "So I had you thrown out."

Talbot returned the smile, said dryly, "Thanks for the lovely evening."

"Until we meet again, Talbot."

Talbot nodded and walked out the door. Donnelly followed him with his Winchester aimed at his spine.

They went down the back stairs and out the back door. From the sting in his cheeks, Talbot guessed the temperature had dropped ten degrees. The sky was very clear, hard white stars scattering in all directions. A faint luminosity shone in the east, where the moon was about to rise.

"Your horse is in the corral," Donnelly growled. He jabbed the rifle in Talbot's back. "Get movin', slick."

"How's your ear? It looks sore," Talbot said.

"Fuck you."

Inside the corral, Talbot untied his horse's reins from a slat and prepared to mount up. "Well, thanks for everything, Rag."

"Oh, there's just one more thing," Donnelly said.

Talbot had sensed it coming long before he saw the shadow on the snow. He ducked, heard the smack of the rifle butt against his saddle. The horse started and jumped sideways.

Before Donnelly knew what had happened, Talbot had his revolver out. He flipped it, clutched the barrel, and swung the butt hard against Donnelly's bandaged ear.

"God-*damn*," the foreman said in a pinched, breathy voice. Both legs buckled and he dropped to his knees, then to his hands. In the light cast by the distant mansion, Talbot saw the bandage turn dark.

"Fuck," the foreman cursed again.

Talbot reached under Donnelly's coat for his pistol and tossed it over the corral. Then he picked up the rifle and jacked it empty, tossed it down. He grabbed his reins and mounted his horse.

Surveying Donnelly, who was fighting to stay conscious, Talbot said, "Sorry again, Rag. But like you said, you'll have another chance to even things up. Real soon."

Then he spurred the speckled gray and galloped off into the night.

CHAPTER 20

IT WAS NEARLY midnight and spine-splitting cold, and Gibbon knew the temperature would continue dropping for several more hours. He'd had the smarts to don fur boots—he'd vowed not to wear his stovepipes again until May—but his toes still ached and he felt the cold creeping up his legs like death.

He considered halting the posse and dismounting to stomp some feeling back in his feet, but he'd ordered the last stop only half an hour ago, and he didn't want to look like a sissy in front of Verlyn Thornberg. What he wouldn't give for a snort to dull the pain in his battered body and to cook out the cold!

When the procession had descended a broad hogback crowned by a lightning-split cedar and a low stone pillar, Gibbon raised a hand and halted his horse. He stared ahead, listening.

"This the place?" Rinski said.

"Yes. Keep your voice down."

"How do you know this is the place?"

Thornberg gave a dry chuckle. "If there's one thing Jed knows, it's where the roadhouses are, don't you, Jed?"

"Speak up, Verlyn—they can't hear you in Mandan," Gibbon said.

He handed his reins to Jacy Kincaid, who'd been riding

directly behind him. He was pleased now that she'd come along; her presence seemed to keep Thornberg's riders peaceable if not sober.

"I still say we go on to the Double X," Thornberg said. "Deal with the head honcho right up and straight away."

"Drag the devil from his lair," Rinski agreed.

Gibbon shook his head. "That's exactly what he'd want us to do. No, we'll take out a few of his men now, a few later, and force old Magnusson to come to us shorthanded."

"Makes sense to me," Jacy said. "Besides, they're probably all drunker'n skunks down there."

"If they're down there," Flint Skully said. He and his hired man, a big Pole with a smallpox-ravaged face, were sitting their horses back in the pack a ways.

"They'll be there," one of Thornberg's riders said, holding a flask. "There's always a half dozen of 'em down there, poking Gutzman's Injun whore."

"What did I tell you boys about drinkin' on the job?" Gibbon snarled.

The cowboy shrugged and passed the flask to the rider next to him. He gave an insolent smile. "Sorry, Sheriff."

Gibbon snorted angrily and shucked his Winchester. He limped up the trail and stopped just below the ridge so the moon did not outline him against the sky, and cast a look at the saucer-shaped valley below.

The trail snaked down between a low-slung cabin and two hitch-and-rail corrals and a barn that leaned slightly northward. The slough flanking the roadhouse was frozen and moonlit and surrounded by marsh grass and cattails. Low buttes climbed beyond, their knobby, snowless crests showing clearly in the moonlight.

The cabin was well lit, and there were at least a dozen horses in the paddocks.

Gibbon turned and walked back to the posse and said in a

low voice, "I'm gonna go down and make sure it's only Magnusson's men down there. I don't want to see innocent people killed here tonight."

"On that ankle?" Jacy said.

"I'll make it."

"No, you won't. I'll go."

Gibbon shook his head. "Not a chance."

Thornberg said, "She's fleet o' foot, Gibbon. You're about as graceful as a bear on snowshoes."

Gibbon thought for a moment. He nodded. To Jacy he said, "Hurry, and stay low. The moon is behind you. Whatever you do, don't let them see you."

"You gotta gun?" Verlyn Thornberg asked her paternally.

Jacy dismounted, handed her reins to Gibbon, and said with a grunt to Thornberg, "Do *I* have a gun? Do *you* have a gun, Verlyn?"

She shucked her Henry with a snort and started down the trail.

Behind her, one of Thornberg's men said, chuckling, "Guess she told you, boss," and lifted the flask to his lips.

THE HILL WAS studded with several low shrubs, rocks, and crusty snowdrifts, and Jacy wove around them carefully, keeping her eyes on the door of the roadhouse below.

Frozen grass crunched under her boots, and the smell of willow smoke issuing from the chimney was sharp in her nose.

Approaching the cabin, she held her breath and pressed her back against the west wall, then moved to a frosty window. The sound of voices grew. She could feel heat escaping through the loose chinking between the logs and around the window.

She looked inside through the frost, swept her eyes across the room. Five men sat at a table about six feet from the glass.

Another six men occupied a second table on the other side of the iron stove. She could tell they were Double X men by the way they carried themselves, by the smug looks on their faces, and by the oiled holsters tied down low on their thighs.

The only one not directly associated with Magnusson was the proprietor, a big, bearded German named Gutzman who bought Indian girls for whiskey, and put them to work in the lean-to addition at the back of the roadhouse. He stood stoking the fire, swaying drunkenly, his back to the window.

He paused, laughing, and lifted a smile at the second table. "Yah, you cun bet Verna vos surprised to see him!" he yelled, his guttural voice rattling the window. "He said he vos going to shoot dem bot, so Verna skedaddled off da Mexcan, grabbed da Mexcan's gun, and let him haf it six times tru da heart, hah, hah, hah! And dat vos de end off Dieter Ross—hah, hah, hah!"

One of the other cowboys, looking up from his cards and ignoring the German, frowned at a deer hide door at the back of the room. "Come on, Chet! Save some for me, old hoss!"

"Kiss my ass, Shorty!" came the reply.

Gutzman said to the door, "No, no hogging da girl. Your fifteen minutes is up, Chit." Turning to the other men, he said with a big, red-faced grin, "I can't help it if dat's all you got up. Hah! Hah! Hah!"

Jacy crept around the corner of the cabin and peered in the window of the lean-to. A bald man and an Indian girl moved together on the bed, under a ratty buffalo blanket.

The man was on top, pumping furiously, propped on his outstretched arms. He'd arched his back and lifted his head until his face was parallel with the wall, eyes shut tight with concentration. His bald head was a mass of hideous red scar tissue, marking him as an old Indian fighter whose scalp probably decorated the mansion of some aging Sioux warrior.

The Indian girl beneath him lay with her head turned to

the window; her large coffee eyes stared unseeing. Her head moved with the force of the man's thrusting hips.

Jacy could hear the man's frustrated grunts and groans, the singing of the bedsprings, and the scraping of the iron headboard against the wall. But it was the Indian girl's tenantless eyes that haunted her. She'd never seen anyone look so empty.

It took Jacy several seconds to tear her eyes from the Indian girl's. Then she moved to the other side of the cabin and peered into the one remaining room—the kitchen—and found it empty. She headed out across the front yard toward the posse on the hill. When a latch scraped and hinges squeaked, she dropped, hitting the ground on her chest.

Shit!

She jerked a look at the cabin. The front door opened, angling light across the verandah. A shadow moved and a silhouette appeared. Boots scraped.

"Shut the goddamn door!" someone yelled.

The door closed, snuffing out the light. The light from the two windows, one on each side of the door, remained.

Jacy held her breath, silently cursing herself for a fool. She should have gone back the way she'd come.

A man gave a sigh. The shadow moved out from under the awning to stand at the edge of the step.

Silence.

Oh, shit, oh, shit!

Then the man sighed again and water puddled onto the snow. Jacy tried to make herself as small as possible, hoping that if the man saw her, forty feet away, he'd mistake her for a snowdrift or a feed sack fallen from a wagon.

Either the man had a bison-sized bladder or he'd been holding his whiskey for hours; the tinny stream seemed to trickle on forever. Jacy pressed her face against the cold snow and fought the urge to lift her rifle and shoot the son of a bitch.

Finally the flow ebbed to spurts. The man grunted, shuffling his feet. When the spurts finally ceased, he gave another sigh and turned back to the roadhouse. He threw open the door.

"Shut the goddamn door!" came a yell from within.

The door closed. Jacy scrambled to her feet and hightailed it up the hill.

"You should have come back the way you went," Verlyn Thornberg scolded when she walked up to the posse milling in the hollow.

"Shut up, Verlyn," Gibbon snapped. "She's no less schooled at this than you or me or any of us." Turning his eyes to Jacy, he said, "You think that cowboy saw you?"

Jacy was standing by her horse, bent over with her hands on her knees, trying to catch her breath. It had been a hell of a run up the hill. She was as afraid as she was exhausted. This was turning out to be a bigger deal than she'd expected. Lying back there waiting for the drunk cowboy to finish draining the dragon, she'd realized she might actually get shot. Or worse. . . .

With a bunch of sleezy hammerheads like the ones down there, she could end up like Mattie Rinski and the Indian girl.

She sucked in a deep breath, straightened, and shook her head. "If he'd seen me they'd be shooting by now."

Thornberg said, "Or they're playin' dumb and waiting for us to make the first move. Hell, they could be slipping out the back and surrounding us right now—as we speak!"

"Keep your voice down," Gibbon said.

"They didn't see me, Verlyn," Jacy said.

"How many are in there?" Gibbon asked her.

"Fourteen. Twelve in the main room, one in the back with

an Indian girl." Her voice was tight. "Looks like they're taking turns."

One of Thornberg's men said, "That'd be Gutzman's whore." There was humor in his voice.

Jacy didn't like it. She told the man so with a hard look. He stared back, but the lines in his round face flattened out.

"All right, all right," Gibbon intervened. "We're here to fight *them*, not each other." He paused, looking around the posse.

Thornberg stood holding his reins. Homer Rinski sat his mount to Thornberg's right and a little behind. He hadn't moved since they'd stopped in the hollow. His face was dark under the round brim of his hat, but Gibbon sensed his eyes blazing as he looked off toward the ridge and the roadhouse below.

Two of the other ranch owners were standing and smoking cigarettes with an air of desperation, as though they'd be the last cigarettes they'd ever smoke. The rest of the men remained mounted, heads hunched and shoulders pulled in against the cold, breath jetting from their mouths and noses.

Thornberg's five riders were the only ones who did not seem afraid. They'd had too much liquor to be afraid of anything. This was just a game. A game with higher stakes than their usual winter-evening rounds of high five or blackjack, but a game just the same.

That knowledge chilled Gibbon to his soul, but they'd come too far to turn back now.

He gave a deep sigh, let it out slow. "Okay," he said. "Let's assume they didn't see Jacy and take up the positions I talked about back in the barn. Remember, no smoking once we're off the ridge, and nobody shoots before I do."

CHAPTER 21

GIBBON HAD NEVER swapped lead with more than two men at a time before, and he'd had to do it only once, when a couple of scatterbrained grub-liners got tired of stealing chickens for supper and held up the Landmark National Bank in Canaan.

Neither man had a good working pistol, and Gibbon and his deputy at the time—Lon Donner, who literally lost his head during the Old Trouble—plugged one in the wrist. Gibbon shot the other in the neck though he was aiming for the man's shoulder.

That had been a mild skirmish—four boys playing cowboys and Indians—compared to how this was likely to pan out. Twelve drunk Double X men and a half-assed posse from Canaan with at least five drunks of its own. Gibbon didn't know how wasted Thornberg was, but he'd smelled booze on his breath, and even Homer Rinski reeked of the bottle. What the hell was the world coming to, when Bible-slapping Christians turned to guns and alcohol?

Gibbon only hoped that the Double X men were as tight as they normally would be this time of night and that his men would be able to take out a *few* of Magnusson's men before the Double X crew filled them all with lead. That would be something, anyway.

Now he and Rinski crept down the trail in the dark as the

others fanned out to take their own positions at various points around the roadhouse. Gibbon crouched low and was irritated to see that Rinski was not doing likewise. The old soulburner was strolling down the trail as though en route to a Saturday-night prayer meeting, the only difference being the double-barrel side-by-side he carried under his arm.

Gibbon approached the corral, where a dozen saddled horses milled, turning their heads to watch the strangers and to sniff the air. The men were spooky but not spooky enough to warrant the commotion of driving them off.

"Easy now, easy," Gibbon whispered, crawling between the slats.

When he and Rinski had hunkered down behind the corral and a feed trough filled with green-smelling hay, with a good view of the cabin, Rinski rumbled darkly, "What are we waiting for, Sheriff?"

Gibbon frowned. The wrath of the righteous. "I'm waiting for everyone to get settled. Keep your shirt on, Homer."

Hawk nose aimed at the cabin, from which the sound of table slaps and occasional hoots rose. Rinski said, "I don't want them to be so drunk they don't know what's happening to them, that they don't know what they're payin' for."

Gibbon observed the man sharply, trying to restrain his anger. "Just remember," he said, "I'm giving them a chance to give themselves up. Nobody shoots until I've done that."

Rinski's voice rumbled up out of his chest like distant thunder. "Those who ignore the law do not deserve its protection."

"I couldn't agree with you more, Homer, but we're not out here to draft an amendment to the Constitution."

"I don't care about man's law; I care about God's law," Rinski said. He stared at the cabin like a dog fixes on a treed cat. Gibbon laughed ruefully and shook his head.

When he thought the rest of the posse had had enough

time to gain their positions, he took a deep breath and released it. "All right, I'm gonna call 'em out."

"Hold on," Rinski growled, and nodded at the cabin.

The door squeaked open and two men in sheepskin coats and wool collars stepped onto the porch, descended the steps, and walked into the road, unbuttoning their flies. One was tall and broad-shouldered; the other was of average height, and thin.

The shorter man said, "Just one more jack and I could be pokin' some *real* pussy in Milestown."

"It's always one more card with you, Chris," the tall man said. "One more card and you're sitting on top of the world."

"Oh, you didn't see my hand, man. You didn't see it."

As the tinny sound of urine hitting the hard ground rose on the still night, the door opened again, and another man stepped out. A big round figure in a buffalo coat, he took a single step, turned to the right, and opened his pants, keeping his head down.

"What you two doin' way out there—playin' grabby-pants?" he said when he'd gotten a steady stream going.

The tall man said in a throaty voice, languorous with alcohol, "We're enjoyin' the stars."

"Shit," said the man by the door.

"You stole my jack, Cobb," the man called Chris said.

Cobb gave a soft, high-pitched hoot.

"It's gonna be payback time, ya sorry son of a bitch," Chris said.

"Not for me," Cobb replied. "I'm throwin' in and spendin' the rest of the night with the whore."

"No way, amigo."

"Si, si, señor. I paid Gutzman off that pile I just cleared from you boys." He gave another hoot, louder this time.

"Come on, Cobb. I was close, man. I was really close."

"Shut up," the tall man said. He was staring straight out

at the corral. "Somethin's got the horses riled."

The short man watched and listened for five seconds then said, "Coyotes."

"Prob'ly," the tall man said. His voice was flat.

He took a step toward the corral. The short man stayed in the road. Cobb was still urinating off the porch, but his head was turned toward the corral.

Gibbon sighed with a grunt in it, and stood. "Hold it right there."

The tall man and the short man, Chris, stiffened. Their hands jerked toward the pistols on their hips but stopped before they got there.

The tall man in the road said, "Who the fuck are you?"

Gibbon was about to answer the man's question when out of the corner of his eye he saw Homer Rinski straighten his long frame and lift his shotgun to his shoulder. "Your executioner!"

Rising and arcing across the yard, like the voice of God, Rinski's proclamation was followed by the glass-shattering boom of his bird gun.

Thrown high by the blast, the tall man hit the ground on his back and wailed like an animal.

Gibbon yelled, "Goddamnit, Homer!"

The short man palmed his revolver and Rinski gave him the second barrel, driving him into the air and back about six feet. When he hit the ground he turned on his side, gave a shake, and lay still.

"What the hell's goin' on!" someone yelled from inside the cabin.

The man on the porch squeezed off three quick pistol rounds, fumbling for the door. Before he could get it open, Gibbon shot him twice in the chest. The door opened and Cobb fell into the cabin.

Hurdling the dead man in the doorway, two other men ran

out of the cabin and ducked behind the water trough.

"We're the law, and you're all under arrest!" Gibbon shouted, his heart pounding now, his mouth dry and coppery with excitement and fear.

He heard the sporadic bursts of gunfire as the posse began slinging lead. Thornberg's men, no doubt—the stupid sons of bitches. But he knew they were just following Rinski's lead.

"The hell you say!" one of the Double X men yelled. "What's the charge?"

"Rustlin' and murder," Gibbon replied. He cupped his hands around his mouth and yelled to the posse, "Hold your fire! Hold your fire!"

The shooting thinned, but someone was still slinging a few rounds at the back. Probably Thornberg himself.

Gibbon exploded, "I said hold your *fire*!"

The words had barely left his mouth when one of the Double X men by the water trough lifted his revolver and raked off two quick rounds, one of which thunked into the corral about six inches from Gibbon. The other plugged a horse in the corral and set it to screaming. All the horses were running circles around the corral now, knocking against the rails, so on top of everything else, Gibbon had to worry about getting trampled.

He ducked. "You're surrounded, you stupid son of a bitch!"

"Go diddle yourself!"

Rinski blasted the water trough with buckshot. Gibbon was about to yell at him when another man appeared in the doorway. He could tell from the German accent it was Gutzman.

"Holt your fire, holt your fire!" Gutzman bellowed. "Vot's dis?"

"This is Jed Gibbon from Canaan, Gutz. We're here for the Double X men. They come peaceful, no one gets hurt."

"Ve are all just haffing a goot time here tonight," Gutzman

said sorrowfully, as if defending a passel of good-natured schoolboys.

"Tell 'em to come out, Gutz, with their hands up."

Gutzman turned his head and said something. He stood there, listening to the reply. Then he turned his face back to Gibbon. "I haf girl," he said, his voice low and dark. "An innocent girl."

"Send her out."

He turned away from the door and returned to it, clutching a girl by an arm. He pulled her in front of him and they stepped onto the porch together. Gibbon could tell that she was barefoot and wrapped in nothing but a blanket. The temperature was falling below zero, and she had to be chilled to the bone, but she gave no indication, no struggle.

"Put some clothes on the girl, Gutz. Then you and her come on out."

The big German stood behind the girl, his hands on her shoulders—her head came only halfway up his chest—and glanced uneasily into the cabin and at the two men crouched behind the water trough. Apparently, he didn't like what he saw.

"N-nein," he muttered fearfully. "Ve come now."

He pushed the girl down the steps and into the wagonyard, steering her with his hands.

Gibbon cursed. "Come on, Gutzman. She's gonna freeze to death out here."

Gutzman ignored him. He pushed the girl into the road, jerking his head around and giving a little skip as he hurried toward the corral. The girl moved stiffly before him, half running as Gutzman pushed her along.

Suddenly another figure appeared in the cabin door swaying as though drunk. The man was holding a shotgun or a carbine—Gibbon couldn't tell which. The sheriff's throat ached and his heart skipped a beat. Gutzman and the girl were between him and the cabin, in the line of fire.

"Get down!" Gibbon yelled.

He started bringing his Winchester to his shoulder when the man in the doorway said thickly, "This is for interruptin' our card game, ya sumbitch, Gibbon!"

The gun in the man's arms—a shotgun—boomed and flashed, and Gibbon jerked with a start. Gutzman grunted and fell headfirst into a pile of horse apples, knocking the girl to her knees.

Turning to see behind her, she gave a clipped scream as the shotgun exploded again. She flew back, arms flung above her head, releasing the blanket, her naked body skidding on the frozen ground and rolling against a corral post.

Feeling several pellets tear his coat and sting his cheek, Gibbon raised his rifle and fired, and the man in the doorway flew backward into the cabin, shotgun leaping from his arms.

The men behind the water trough lifted their heads and raised their pistols. They'd squeezed off only one shot apiece before Gibbon and Rinski brought their weapons to bear, stood the men up and flung them back against the cabin—dead.

That was all the encouragement the rest of the posse needed to resume shooting. The night exploded with the cracking of rifles and six-guns and the regular blasts of Rinski's shotgun.

Smoke swirled like fog in the moonlight and the air was redolent with gunpowder. The horses screamed as the bullets from their own riders tore into the corral. Finally the saddled mounts bolted through the rails and off behind the barn.

Between the darkness and the fog, Gibbon couldn't make out the individuals in the cabin; he keyed instead on the orange flames leaping from their guns and on the moonlit puffs of smoke. It seemed to work. Three times he heard a grunt or a curse following the bark of his Winchester.

It was fairly easy pickings. With the Double X men pinned down in the cabin, with no means of escape, it was just a matter of time before the posse did them in. Gibbon knew that if he hadn't had the element of surprise—and, he had to admit, the trigger-happy Rinski—things could have gone very differently.

Now they were going like he'd wanted them to, but he didn't feel good about any of it. It wasn't just Gutzman and the dead whore, either. It was the thunder of the gunfire and the yells and screams from the cabin and the wails of the dying horses in the corral behind him: the whole bloody mess.

He'd wanted to feel redeemed. Instead, he just felt dirty.

The shooting from the cabin petered out about twenty minutes into the fight. Ten minutes later it stopped altogether.

Gibbon knew the Double X men were dead. They hadn't had a chance in such tight quarters. If they hadn't been so drunk they might have tried running for it—slipping out the windows and scattering. But the booze had made them clumsy and disoriented and incapable of coming up with any kind of defensive strategy.

So they ran around like rats in a cage as the bullets flying through the windows and through the chinking between the logs turned them into hamburger.

Gibbon put his rifle down, but the rest of the posse kept shooting. No one was returning fire, but they kept shooting just the same, with as much vigor as they'd started with. Gibbon knew they wouldn't stop until they ran out of bullets.

He shook his head, slumped down behind the feed trough, rolled a cigarette, and smoked it down to a half-inch nub.

The shooting thinned. The posse was running out of bullets. Gibbon took a deep drag from his quirley, burning his fingers, and glanced over his shoulder at the cabin. There was an orange glow in the windows.

Fire, he knew. A spark from one of the bullets had ignited kerosene.

Well, that should do it. He could go home now, wait for Magnusson to make the next move.

Out of the corner of his eye he saw a figure crouch down before the corral. Turning his gaze, he saw Jacy Kincaid approach the Indian girl.

Gibbon bent his weary body between the corral slats with a grunt. Flames from the cabin spread quickly. They were licking through the windows, spreading a burnt-orange glow on the ground around the roadhouse.

The gunfire had ceased and men were whooping and hollering, probably passing the flask again. Gibbon could see their silhouettes as they moved in to admire their handiwork.

Gibbon turned to Jacy. She was kneeling over the Indian girl, rifle across her knees. She stared at the girl but kept her hands on her rifle. Her hat was tipped, covering her face.

Finally she lifted her eyes to Gibbon. Neither of them said anything. Finally Jacy stood and walked up the road toward the horses. Gibbon watched her go.

"God has been served here tonight."

Gibbon turned. Homer Rinski stood behind him, looking at the cabin, the orange flames reflected in the hard plains of his face.

"Say what?"

"God has been served here tonight," Rinski repeated.

Gibbon turned to watch the cabin burn, sighed fatefully. "Well, let's see what the devil has to say about that."

Then he turned and followed Jacy up the trail.

CHAPTER 22

IN THE MAGNUSSON mansion, Charles Franklin Wingate III grinned in his sleep. King Magnusson's primary eastern investor was dreaming of Suzanne. The lovely girl was asking him to remain at the ranch for another week.

She was clad in only a sheer chemise that clearly outlined her breasts. Her hair hung loose about her shoulders and her eyes were smoky with lust.

"Oh, *please* stay, Charles," she begged. "I know you don't want to be disloyal to Abigail, but I feel we're just starting to get to know each other."

She smelled of lilac-scented orris soap, and he didn't know which aroused him more—her face, which fairly glowed with unadulterated beauty, or the swollen orbs of her breasts, which poked at him wantonly, prodding him from his characteristic reserve.

"Really, Suzanne, I *must* go."

"Oh, *please*, Charles. There are so few men like you in Dakota . . . sensitive yet virulent."

She ran her hands over the thick head of hair he'd lost fifteen years ago, pressed her warm lips to his. As she ground her hips against him, wrapping a bare leg around his waist, he engulfed her in his arms and fairly moaned with desire.

Someone pounded on the door. "Chuck!" It was King Magnusson.

Wingate's heart did a somersault. He pushed the girl away as the door opened and Magnusson's big, ruddy face appeared beneath his cherry-blond mane. The blue eyes flashed.

"King!" Wingate cried.

"In the flesh, old chap. Up and at 'em—let's pound some grub and get ready to ride!" Magnusson studied the easterner. "Remember? We're going hunting this morning. I'll send Minnie up with your bath."

He turned away and turned back. "Oh, uh . . . sorry to interrupt."

"Huh?"

"Sounded like you were having quite the dream. Anyone I know?"

Wingate must have looked as stricken as he felt, because King said in a hurry, "Don't worry, I enjoy a hot fancy now and then myself."

Leaning forward he added conspiratorially, "Tides me over between business trips." He winked and pulled his head back. The door closed, and his boots pounded away down the hall.

Sitting up in the bed, the tail of his nightcap wrapped around his neck, Wingate stared at the door and tried to quell the pounding of his heart. He ran a hand absently over his red muttonchops.

"Oh," he said weakly, swallowing. "Oh, my goodness . . . it was just a dream."

As he looked around the room, getting his bearings, his relief was replaced by bitter disappointment. The girl had not visited his room with her lovely breasts; she hadn't wrapped her legs around his waist and pressed her warm lips to his.

He lifted a hand to his head. His hair hadn't grown back, either.

"Goodness me," he grumbled, and swung his old legs to the floor. Among Magnusson's associates, King was infamous for throwing his eastern visitors into potentially humiliating "western" situations. It was a sort of game, Wingate knew, and he supposed it was his turn to shrink from a charging grizzly or miss a preposterously easy shot at an elk or some other four-legged beast.

Slouched there on the edge of the bed, waiting for his bath and staring out the frosty gray window—not a tree in sight—Wingate wished he were home. In New York he was not tormented by bored western ranchers and their buxom daughters.

"Hunting, for Christ's sake. In this weather? That man's going to be the death of me yet."

A half hour later he was bathed and dressed, but he still hadn't worked up any enthusiasm for Magnusson's hunt. Oh, well, give the sadistic bastard another story to tell at the Cheyenne Club, he thought as he headed for the dining room.

"Where you going, Charles?" the devil himself hailed as he passed his office.

Wingate walked back to the trophy-laden study. King was standing in the middle of the room decked out in a buffalo coat and a fur hat. He was smoking a fat cigar and holding a rifle, caressing its glistening walnut stock with a white rag. Another, similar weapon stood against his desk. A hot fire popped in the hearth.

Wingate frowned. "Am I too late for breakfast?" he asked meekly.

"Oh, not at all," Magnusson said. "I thought we'd go out to the bunkhouse for breakfast. I like to rub elbows with my men now and then. Keeps me in touch. Besides, the cook out there can whip together the best chuck you'll ever taste in your life. A real treat."

"You don't say," Wingate said, crestfallen. He'd been looking forward to prunes stewed in French wine, cheese croissants, and Minnie McDougal's wonderfully airy omelets.

Magnusson rubbed the rag down the stock of his rifle and

nodded at the other gun leaning against his desk. "There's your rifle, Charles. Fetch it up and treat it like a baby. It might just save your life today." He looked at Wingate and grinned wolfishly.

When Wingate had decked himself out in a borrowed coat and hat like Magnusson's, he hefted the heavy beast of a rifle—it must have weighed fifty pounds!—and followed the rancher outside. The dour and brooding Randall Magnusson brought up the rear.

They moved down the slope behind the corrals toward the bunkhouse—a long, narrow building of logs, with two brick chimneys sprouting thick gray smoke smelling like bacon.

Magnusson knocked and opened the door.

"Boss," Rag Donnelly said as though startled. He was sitting at the table nearest the door and the first of the two stoves, drinking coffee and smoking a cigarette. His hat was off, exposing the fresh bandage on his ear.

There were seven or eight other men in various stages of dressing and washing, crowding around the farthest stove. They regarded their visitors from the Big House with subtle suspicion, cutting their eyes at Rag.

A big, gray-haired man with a bushy mustache and deep-sunk eyes stirred a pan of potatoes sizzling in bacon grease. A cigarette drooped from his lips, a grimy towel was thrown over his shoulder, and the thick gray hair on his chest grew out of his long johns.

"Have a seat, boss—just about to throw some vittles on the table," he said with too much exuberance, his eyes on Rag.

"Just thought we'd come out and see how badly you're poisoning my men, Lute," King said, throwing his mittens on the table beside Donnelly. "Hope we haven't interrupted anything." His gaze circled the room, and he realized what was wrong. Men were missing—more than should be out on the line at this hour.

"Where is everybody, Rag?"

"Who's that, boss?"

"You know who." Magnusson's voice became tight, his eyes hard. "The men you're paid forty dollars a month to keep track of."

Donnelly looked at the other members of his crew. He was in a bad position. To keep his men's respect he couldn't go tattling on their every indiscretion. Some things had to stay between him and them. He had no choice now, however. If they couldn't see that, fuck 'em.

He gave a sigh and looked at Magnusson. "They ain't come back from the roadhouse yet."

"They ain't come back from the roadhouse yet," Magnusson mimicked, lowering his eyes to his foreman's chest and giving several short, thoughtful nods. He lifted his cold eyes again to Donnelly's, and it was odd how the foreman had never before noticed the reptilian cast in those unblinking eyes. "How many went?"

"Twelve."

"You know I never allow more than half a dozen men off the ranch at one time."

"I know that, Mr. Magnusson, but they must've slipped off while I was up at the house last night. When I got back, they were gone and there was nothin' I could do about it. I figured . . . well, I figured they'd be back long before now. Hell, long before sunup! They know they get their pay docked for this kind of horseshit."

Magnusson's eyes were on the table now, and he was pursing his lips. His earlobes poking out from under his beaver hat were bright red. His face was mottled white.

"Swell. Just swell," he said woodenly. Then his head jerked

up. His face twisted savagely and he shouted, "*Send someone out to fetch them, goddamnit!*"

Donnelly remained calm, though his face blanched. It wasn't the first time he'd taken both barrels of Magnusson's fury.

He spread his hands apart, opening them, smoke from his cigarette curling and uncurling above the table. "I did that, Mr. Magnusson. I sent Press Johnson out. They should all be back in about an hour or so."

Magnusson pursed his lips and exhaled through his nose. "Very well. Make sure they know they're due a visit from me this evening, as well as a very substantial dock in pay."

"I will, sir. They're good men, sir."

Magnusson laughed scornfully and regarded the cook, who'd been standing there watching and listening to the conversation with his cigarette dangling from his mouth while the potatoes burned. As if throwing a switch, Magnusson returned to his old offensively ebullient self.

"Well, Lute, serve up the grub. We don't have all day, ya know. Mr. Wingate here has talked me into taking him hunting, haven't you, Charles?"

CHAPTER 23

FATHER AND SON Magnusson each shot one whitetail and one mule deer respectively by ten o'clock in the morning. They left both animals to the wolves, however. It was too early to start packing meat. They wouldn't start retrieving what they shot until they were ready to head home. Until then, they'd hone their aim on moving targets.

"Plenty of game in Dakota, Charles," King intoned as they traversed a nearly featureless prairie. "Plenty to shoot for sport, plenty to shoot for food. Besides, what we don't kill the damn Indians will."

"Indians around here?" Wingate asked, glancing around cautiously and squinting his nearsighted eyes, tiny dark marbles buried in the heavy, florid flesh of his face. He sat his high-stepping Arabian stiffly, chilled to his soul in spite of the buffalo robe that reached his calves.

"Not as many as there used to be, praise the Lord. We had to run off a whole damn village when I first came. Greasy beggars kept stealing cattle. They'd shoot 'em, butcher 'em, and devour them—all on my land! Can you believe such arrogance?"

Randall offered his two cents' worth. "When an Indian butchers an animal, he don't leave nothin' but the hoofs, and sometimes he even takes those. Those people eat *everything*," he added with disgust.

"Are they dangerous?" Wingate asked.

"Can be when they're sober," Magnusson replied.

"I've never see one, just read about them."

Magnusson took several puffs from his cigar. "Well, if we see one, I'll have Randall shoot him, and you can tell your New York friends how you got to see an Indian up close."

"Only good Injun's a dead Injun," Randall said. "Ain't that right, Pa?"

They passed a few derelict sodbuster shacks—Magnusson had had nothing to do with running the yokels off, he laughed; the weather and the tough prairie sod had done that for free!—and followed a game trail into a ravine through which a frozen creek snaked.

They followed the creek south. Randall brought down two more deer but missed two coyotes bounding up the opposite ridge. Frustrated, he shot a porcupine from a tree.

Wingate took a couple of shots, but the game was practically out of sight by the time he'd snugged the heavy gun to his cheek. The kick of the big rifle nearly threw him from his saddle. King and Randall turned away, but he could feel them grimacing.

"Where are we heading now, King?" he asked as they cantered single file along the creek. He was ready for a nap followed by a brandy and a soft chair by a hot fire.

"While we're in the area I thought we'd pay a little visit to a . . . a friend of mine."

"Wouldn't be that greaser friend of yours, would it, Pa?" Randall asked, grinning.

"Mexican, Randall," Magnusson corrected facetiously. "*Greaser* isn't nice."

Randall laughed. "After last night, I had a feeling we might run into that gre—I mean Mexican—today."

Wingate had no idea what they were talking about, but he'd become so inured of their double-talk and intrigue, playing him for the mindless dandy, that he didn't insist on an explanation. He distracted himself with fantasies of a sparking fire, Spanish brandy, and a naked Suzanne sprawled on a damask-covered couch until a small gray shack and an outhouse appeared around a bend in the creek. A tarpaulin weather cover fronting the shack afforded shelter to a single black stallion.

Smoke lifted from the chimney, and as they rode closer, Wingate saw there was a man outside in front of the cabin, his back to the approaching visitors. He was scraping a very large hide nailed to the cabin, right of the door.

A thick, sickening odor hung in the air like an invisible curtain. It emanated from the chimney, Wingate could tell, and he found himself yearning for a strong wind to blow it all away before he puked.

They rode up to within ten feet of the man. Still he didn't turn, but continued working on the hide, giving little grunts as he scraped.

Magnusson leaned forward, hands on his saddle horn. "Mighty trusting for a man of your profession, aren't you Del Toro?"

The Mexican snickered and kept working. "You announced your arrival an hour ago, amigo. All your shooting. No one shoots as much as you and your boy, señor. It got so annoying I felt like doing some shooting of my own, in your direction."

Magnusson ignored the comment, regarding the hide nailed to the cabin through its four spread paws, large as dinner plates. "What do you have there, a griz?"

"Sí—old man *oso*. He came calling on me last night as I slept, so I let him in." Del Toro snickered again. There was no voice to it—just air trapped and released by his tongue. It sounded like a noise a self-satisfied reptile might make.

"Pity the bear that comes calling on you, José," Magnusson said, impressed by the image he was conjuring.

"Or men, uh?"

Del Toro turned for the first time, giving the visitors the full impression of his lean, grinning face, small teeth glinting like nailheads within the wild mustaches drooping around his mouth, blue coyote eyes flashing. He wore his wolf coat with its big silver buttons and his black hat, snugged over a home-made wolfskin liner with ear flaps tied under his chin. The flaps were in the shape of a wolf's paws.

If it weren't for the startling blue eyes and cold-blooded grin, he could have been a preposterously displaced hony-onker from Old Mexico, Wingate thought. He associated the sickly sweet smell with the gunman, with killing, and he had to swallow hard to keep his breakfast down.

Still grinning, Del Toro held up his wide-bladed skinning knife, examined it, then wiped the blood and tallow on his breeches and stuck the knife in his belt sheath.

Pulling a cigarillo from his coat pocket, he said, looking at Randall, "One of you gentlemen has a light?" He stuck the cigar between his teeth and grinned, his eyes on Randall.

Magnusson and Wingate turned to see how Randall was taking it. Not well. It was obvious by the lad's flat eyes and slightly curled upper lip that he did not like Mexicans, and this one least of all. His mouse-brown gelding bobbed its head and lifted a foot, but Randall held the gunman's gaze. His face turned slowly red.

Del Toro said, "Uh, you got light for this greaser, amigo?"

"Plum out o' phosphors," Randall said tightly.

"Give the man a light, Randall," Magnusson said as though chiding an ill-mannered youngster.

"Why should I?"

"Because I told you to," King said.

Wingate could tell he was enjoying his son's discomfort and wondered if there was anyone's discomfort King would not enjoy—except Suzanne's.

Finally Randall dug around in a coat pocket for a box of matches. Del Toro stepped forward and allowed the young man to light his cigar, the gunman taking his time about it, puffing smoke.

Looking around at the stark gray cabin and outhouse fronting the creek, Magnusson said, "I sure am sorry to keep you holed up out here in this old trapper's cabin, Del Toro, but it's probably best for both of us if we're not seen together."

Still puffing, trying to get a good draw, Del Toro turned away from Randall's match. "How good of you to be concerned for *both* of us. But it's really not so lonely. You know—this may be hard to believe and you probably think José drinks too much out here by himself—but a man and a very beautiful girl pass this way on horseback just about every day."

He pointed to the buttes behind the visitors. "They ride along the ridge there. Just riding for the thrill, I think. The girl always waves real big and smiles. Muy bonita. I think if it weren't for the man, she would even come and visit me in my cabin."

He took the cigar from his lips and smiled.

Magnusson did not return it. His face had grown dark. A muscle in his cheek twitched. "That's my daughter," he said, voice taut as razor wire.

"I thought she looked familiar."

"She's off-limits."

"Sí, you told me, señor. Maybe you better tell her that. I think she finds me . . . curious. Your daughter looks to me like a very curious girl."

Magnusson just stared at him, wide-eyed with outrage.

"Yes, very curious," Del Toro prodded some more.

Randall turned to his father and said with disgust, "Pa, this man here is—"

"Shut up, Randall," Magnusson said. To the gunman he said, "I've hired you to do a job. See that you do it"—his lips curled back revealing his big yellow teeth—"and get the hell out of here, you insolent bastard. Get the hell back where you came from!"

Magnusson was light-headed with fury. He was thinking, "If he so much as touches a hair on her head . . ." The thought was as repellent as the stench of the Mexican's cooking.

"Easy, señor. Hey, easy. I was just making conversation. Telling you I don't mind being housed out here like a wild dog in this goddamn gringo winter. That's what you wanted to hear—that I am keeping warm and fed and reasonably happy while you and your friends are singing and dancing in your big house."

Del Toro gave an exaggerated shrug. "You are worried about me. I tell you not to worry. That's all, you see? Comprende? I am an easy man to get along with."

Magnusson's fury was a confused, slippery thing that threatened to get away from him, turn him into a babbling idiot. He felt as though he'd been cut down at the knees. He felt an instinctive, repulsive fear of this man. He wasn't sure how to counter it. Nothing he could say would make him feel better, would give him back the advantage, and you didn't try to kill a man like this without plenty of help.

He stammered, hating the hesitant trill in his voice. "Just do your job," he finally managed, thoroughly flushed.

"Sí, señor. Is that what you rode out here to tell me?"

Magnusson had been thrown so far afield that he had to expel considerable energy in recalling the original intention of his visit. Then he remembered last night, Suzanne's birthday party, and the insolent *white* bastard who had threatened him in his own house.

All of this was getting too goddamn close to home.

To Suzanne.

"I've got a name to add to your list. To the *top* of your list. You'll be compensated appropriately—don't worry."

Del Toro studied him expectantly, like a hawk perched in a dead tree waiting for another mouse to happen by.

"Mark Talbot," Magnusson said. "You'll find him on the Circle T ranch on Crow Creek. When you've killed him, dispose of the body somewhere it won't be found." He was thinking of Suzanne and decided right then and there to send her away again until deep summer.

Del Toro smiled with his eyes.

"The sooner the better," Magnusson added. To the others he said, "Let's go," and reined his horse around.

Randall had already turned around, facing back the way they had come. "Pa," he said with an ominous air, looking off.

Following his son's gaze, Magnusson picked out a man in a sheepskin coat and tan hat riding furiously along the creek, giving his horse the quirt and spurs. It was Rag Donnelly on a buckskin.

"Mr. Magnusson!" he yelled as he approached the tarpaulin shelter, slowing to a canter, his exhausted mount blowing and snorting.

"Rag, what the hell?" Magnusson yelled.

When the horse came to a sloppy-gaited walk, Donnelly lowered his head to take a deep breath, then tipped his head back, his big, rugged face thoroughly flushed. He regarded Magnusson for several seconds while he caught his breath. He swallowed hard.

"W-would've sent a rider but I wanted to come and tell you myself."

"Tell me what?" Magnusson said impatiently.

"It's the men—the ones that didn't come home last night."

"What about them!"

"They're dead."

Magnusson mouthed the word silently before saying it out loud. "What are you talking about?"

Donnelly shook his head. "Every single one of 'em. Press Johnson found Gutzman's roadhouse burned to the ground and the men along with it."

"Burned?" Magnusson said, the force of the exclamation throwing him forward in his saddle.

As if following Magnusson's thought process, Donnelly shook his head. "It weren't no accident. Press said what's left of the logs is riddled with lead, and several of our men and Gutzman are layin' outside, shredded like they been hit by a hayrake. There's shell casings galore."

He paused to let this sink in. His boss watched him owl-like, blinking at regular intervals. Randall sighed and released it through his lips, whistling.

"My god," Wingate muttered.

Magnusson swept the ground with his eyes, as though he'd lost something. "Who . . . who—"

A thought struck him. His eyes ceased their restless quest and rose to Donnelly's. The foreman had a knowing look. He'd had time to put it all together, was one page ahead of his boss.

"Gibbon," Magnusson said flintily, with a savage curl of his lip. "And Thornberg, no doubt. Hell, it was probably all the nesters on the Bench."

"Includin' Talbot," Donnelly added with a growl.

"You think?"

"Sure. Hell, they prob'ly sent him up to the house last night to keep us occupied while the others rode over to Gutzman's.

He prob'ly joined their little ambush party after he left here."

Magnusson's eyes were searching the horizon now, thoughts, plans, strategies snapping this way and that. Finally, adrenaline-pumped, he swallowed hard and said to his foreman, voice shaking with controlled rage, "You and Del Toro take care of Talbot. We three will ride back to the ranch, organize the rest of the men, and head for town. We'll see you back at the house."

Randall said, "I'll go with them, Pa."

"No, you stay—"

"Come on, Pa. *Please?*"

Magnusson saw the kill lust in his son's eyes. He thought a confrontation with a man like Talbot might be just what the lad needed to scrape some green off his horns, teach him that this was not just a game of cowboys and Indians. This was the real thing. This was the Magnusson name they were fighting for.

Behind him, Del Toro said calmly, "I work alone, señor."

Magnusson turned. The Mexican had already retrieved his Big Fifty and his saddle, and stood in the cabin doorway looking rough and ready, holding the saddle by the horn in one hand, the rifle by the other.

He said, "But since I haven't scouted this Talbot yet, your foreman and boy can be my scouts—as long as they don't mind taking orders from a bean-eater."

Randall's lip curled at being called a boy.

The gunman strode past Magnusson and Donnelly, lugging his saddle and rifle and heading for the shelter and his black stallion. He shuttled Donnelly a bland glance and added, "But they stay out of my way, uh? Or I shoot their ears off."

Donnelly snarled as Del Toro walked away, "Why, you fuckin'—"

"Easy, Rag," Magnusson cut in. "Remember your ear, and save the hostility for Talbot." He spurred his horse savagely and yelled, "I'm saving mine for Gibbon!"

CHAPTER 24

WHEN TALBOT LEFT the Double X the night before, he rode back to the Circle T, stabled the speckle-gray in the barn with fresh hay, and spent most of the night pacing the hollow shell of a cabin and feeding split cottonwood logs to the fire in the living room.

He fairly fumed with anger at Magnusson's arrogance and nonchalance regarding Dave's murder. If it hadn't been for Randall Magnusson, Talbot and Dave would be laughing and playing cards and making plans for expanding their holdings, maybe building a big clapboard house on a hillock over Crow Creek.

Instead, Talbot was here alone in a derelict cabin, crushing frozen mouse turds under his boots, filling with hate, and hip-deep in another damn war.

Finally exhausted, he spread his saddle blanket and stretched out on the cold wood floor, near the breathy, popping fire, and propped his head on his saddle. He came awake with a start several hours later, reaching for his rifle and jacking a shell in the breech.

He'd heard something.

He got up, stiff with cold, and moved to a window and looked out. It was dawn; the eastern sky was scalloped pink and salmon. Just beyond the barn a horse and rider cantered around a hillock, disappeared behind another, then came out again on the trail curling through cottonwoods.

As the rider passed between the pumphouse and barn, Talbot saw from the hair bouncing on her shoulders it was Suzanne.

She rode the black thoroughbred like a true equestrian, back straight, mittened hands holding the reins up near her breasts. In spite of the store-bought fur coat hanging to her calves, she looked characteristically lithe.

Talbot went out to the porch, holding the rifle in his right hand, barrel down, ready to bring it up if he needed to. You never know; someone could have followed her out from the Double X intending to use her as a decoy while laying a bead on him. Her brother or Rag. Maybe Magnusson himself.

"You're up early," he said conversationally.

She stopped her horse a few feet away. Her features were grim. "Is it true?" Her voice was hard and distant.

"Is what true?" he asked, though he knew what she meant.

"That you used me to get a job out of my father?"

He gazed at her silently.

Suddenly her eyes softened and she shook her head. "Mark, please tell me it's not true."

"Would your father lie to you?" he said, feeling his anger grow at her complete acceptance of everything her father said and did. "The noble King Magnusson?"

She studied him suspiciously, trying to read him. Finally he decided to make it easy for her to ride away and forget about him. "Why not? If you had a chance of working for Verlyn Thornberg or the great King Magnusson, which would you choose?"

She scowled. "So what—now you're going to work for Thornberg? You're going to *cowboy* for Thornberg?"

"Why not?"

The thoroughbred danced in a circle, wanting to keep going. Suzanne clutched her thighs to its ribs and held the reins taut. "Stop, damn you!" she cried. Returning her eyes to Talbot, she said, "So you'll be riding against my father."

"He killed my brother," Talbot reminded her.

"Oh, Mark, don't tell me you still believe that?" She said it like he was sharpening his horns over a mere insult or an unfortunate poker hand.

Talbot clutched a porch post, trying to subdue his anger. None of this was her fault. She was an innocent albeit spoiled coquette raised by a charming albeit evil man. "Go home, Suzanne. Pack your bags and hop the next train out of here. I don't want to see you hurt."

"My father is a peaceful man, Mark."

He gave a deep sigh and looked at her with frustration mixed with sympathy. "You believe what you want, Suzanne. But your father has to be stopped."

"If he really were doing what you say, wouldn't stopping him be up to the law?"

"You know there's no law out here. We have to police ourselves. Besides, he killed my brother. It's personal."

She stared at him, the hate growing in her eyes. "You bastard," she said tightly. "You're just like the others on the Bench—jealous of my father's money and power and spoiling for a fight."

Talbot just looked at her. His eyes were flat.

Her own eyes sparked with outrage. "You simple bastard, you could have had me."

Talbot laughed ruefully. "For a week maybe, until you got bored and went looking for some other stud to grease your wheels."

She was outraged. The horse could sense it and danced around, agitated. "Most men . . . most men would give their eyeteeth to spend just *one night* in my good graces, you"—she pursed her lips and shook her head—"*fool!*"

"For your own good, Suzanne, get out of here. Stay out of the way."

She gave an angry, frustrated cry, reined the black around, and spurred him back the way she had come. "What they say is true—brains and brawn really *don't* go together!"

Talbot watched the horse pass through the cottonwoods and turn on the road behind the barn. She gave it the quirt and spurs and galloped away through the hogbacks.

Talbot swore and went back inside the cabin. He stomped around until he realized the fire had gone out. Then he went out behind the cabin, retrieved an armful of cottonwood logs, and got the fire going again. He'd forgotten how physically tiring the cold could be.

He sat brooding before the fire for another quarter of an hour. The rumbling in his stomach told him he needed to eat, so he scoured the kitchen for food. All he came up with was a can of peaches and a coffeepot with a small pouch of Arbuckle's beans tucked inside.

He ground the beans with the butt of his revolver, filled the percolator with snow, dumped in the ground coffee, and set it on a grate in the fireplace. Later, drinking the coffee and eating the peaches with his fingers, it became clear to him that before he could go after Magnusson, he'd need to fill his larder. And because there were only about three or four more cottonwood logs left in the woodshed, he'd need to cut wood, as well.

The breaks of the Little Missouri would be the best place for getting wood *and* food. The only problem was he had no wagon with which to haul it all back to the ranch.

Maybe Jacy would lend him a wagon . . .

Thinking of her shoved back some of the hate he felt for Magnusson. She was the single bright spot in his returning home, and he felt a deep hankering to see her again. He knew, though, that his visit to the Double X had made him a villain in her eyes, and it was going to take some explaining to get himself back in her good graces.

When he finished the peaches and a second cup of coffee, he went out to the barn and saddled his speckle-gray, shoving the loaded Winchester into the saddle boot. A half hour later the corrals and outbuildings of Jacy's Bar MK ranch rose from the frozen prairie a hundred yards ahead.

THE SUN PEEKED through high, thin clouds, spreading a washed-out, tawny glow over the hogbacks and hay stubble half covered in crusty snow. Ahead, the cabin was a black smudge beneath the blue mesa looming behind it.

From the corral, several horses watched Talbot approach, hanging their heads over the top rail and twitching their ears. Their manes hung limp; the lack of wind today was an unexpected treat. It was cold, but not the penetrating, stinging cold the wind whipped against your face like sand.

A rifle cracked, the squeaky bark rising in pitch as it echoed. Talbot flinched and brought his horse to a halt. Looking ahead, he saw a figure standing outside the cabin door. It was Jacy in her green mackinaw holding a rifle in her arms.

"Who are ya and what the hell you want!" she yelled, more than a touch of anger in her voice.

Talbot waved. "It's me, Jacy. Mark Talbot."

She said nothing, just looked at him with the rifle in her arms. Talbot was too far away to see the expression on her face, but the rest of her told him there wasn't one. He was about to say something when she turned and walked back inside the cabin and closed the door.

Talbot spurred his horse ahead, dismounted, and looped the reins over the tie rail, then mounted the narrow porch and knocked on the door. She didn't answer the knock.

"Can I come in?" he said, turning his head to hear through the door.

Nothing. He turned the knob. The door opened, and he stepped inside.

"What the hell do you want?" she said.

She was sitting at the kitchen table fronted by a whiskey bottle and a half-filled water glass. The rifle stood within easy reach to her right, propped against the table. Her tawny hair was mussed and her face was flushed.

"Looks like I'm late for the party," he said, closing the door behind him. "Must've been a beaut."

Thickly she said, "Nope. Drinkin' alone today."

"What's the occasion?"

"Life."

"I see. In that case, mind if I join you?"

"Yes, as a matter of fact."

"Then I suppose lending me a wagon for a couple days is out of the question."

Frowning, she turned her head to look at him. "What for?"

"Need to haul firewood and game. It appears someone made off with all Dave's implements."

"Figured you'd be gone by now. Little Miss Queen of England entice you into staying?"

"No, her father did." Remembering that he hadn't seen smoke lifting from the bunkhouse chimney and hadn't seen the old cowboy working outside, he asked where Gordon was. "Didn't he ever show up?"

Jacy took a slug from her glass. "Yeah, he showed up. What was left of him."

Talbot slid a chair out from the table and sat down next to her. "What happened?" he asked darkly.

She told him about finding Gordon and Mrs. Sanderson dead along the Little Missouri. Then she told him about joining Gibbon's posse and the attack on the roadhouse. She'd barely finished the story when she convulsed in a sob, cupped her mouth in her hands, and lowered her head in tears.

"Jesus Christ," Talbot muttered, absorbing the information. "Do you realize what this means? Magnusson's going to pull out all the stops. He's going to hunt each member of that posse down and hang him, or worse."

"I know," she said weakly.

Talbot's mind was racing, trying to come up with a plan. "You need to lay low for a while. Visit your mother in Mandan. I'll cable you when the dust settles."

Jacy lifted her head and shook it defiantly. "It was a major fuck-up," she said. "Innocent people died. We never should have done it. But I'm not running from it." She added after a pause, "That poor Indian girl. Her life was hell, and then she died like hell. They all died like hell, like nothing means a goddamn thing."

Talbot nodded. "Nothing means anything when it comes to war," he said. "And that's what we have here—a war."

"We?"

"You heard me."

"What about little Miss Queen of England?"

"You underestimate me, Jacy."

Pursing her lips, she nodded. "Sorry. I won't do it again."

"How 'bout that wagon?"

"You're going *hunting*?"

He shrugged. "First things first. Without food and heat, I'm helpless."

She pinned him with her green eyes. "Stay here."

He thought about it and shook his head. "I don't want that son of a bitch burning the Circle T, and that's what he'll do if he comes looking for me and I'm not there to stop him. The cabin has to be my base. Besides, he won't harm you if you're alone. Magnusson's a bastard, but he's a proper bastard. Just the same, you better cork that bottle. If he comes here, you'll want to be ready for him."

She wrinkled her nose. "What makes you think you can boss me? You haven't even gotten in my pants yet." She tipped back the last of the whiskey and slammed the glass on the table. "You'll find a buckboard where they're usually kept—in the wagon shed."

He splashed a finger of whiskey into her glass and slammed it back. "Much obliged," he said, and headed for the door.

"Mark?"

Her voice stopped him.

She said, "Will you stop again on your way back from the river?"

He looked at her thoughtfully, then smiled. "Be my pleasure."

"Good luck hunting," she said.

He touched his hat brim in a mock salute and left.

CHAPTER 25

AFTER TALBOT LEFT her cabin, Jacy lost her taste for the whiskey. His appearance had somehow quelled her loneliness and fear, and she no longer felt the need to numb herself.

Having found most men querulous and undependable at best, she didn't like feeling dependent, but she sensed in Talbot a maturity based on a wry melancholy that went deeper than Dave's death. No doubt his experiences in the War and his wandering in Mexico had seasoned him, and Jacy thought that, given time, she would find a sensitive, passionate man.

Regretting that she'd jumped the gun about his relationship with Suzanne Magnusson, she yearned to have his masculine arms around her now, to curl her naked body against his and sleep for a million years.

Lost in reverie, she'd scrubbed two iron skillets and several plates before it dawned on her that horses were nickering outside. She jumped, startled, splashing soapy water on the floor, and reached for her rifle. She moved quickly to the window and saw a man creeping along the barn, holding a rifle out before him.

She ran to the front door and opened it.

"*Oh!*" she screamed.

Another, bigger man stood before her, nearly filling the doorway. He wore a sheepskin coat and a tan hat, and was holding a rifle level with her belly. When Jacy tried to bring her own carbine up to shoot him, he grabbed it.

She fought but his power was too great, and finally he jerked the rifle from her hands, throwing her to the floor. She jumped to her feet and went at him with her fists, but she could have been punching a brick wall for all the damage she did.

Casually, the man pushed her back into the kitchen. It wasn't much of a shove, but there was enough force in the man's arm that she fell backward, bouncing her head off the floor.

"Son of a *bitch!*" Jacy lay there a moment, stunned, then rose to her elbows.

The man took two steps into the cabin. He had a big slab of a face with cold eyes and an anvil jaw, the deep lines above his cheeks epitomizing belligerence. He had a pure, raw, gladiatorial demeanor, and Jacy knew she was face-to-face with one of Magnusson's firebrands.

"Where's Talbot?" he said with a growl.

"Who?" She'd been so certain they'd be coming for her, to extract payment for the part she'd played in the roadhouse debacle, that she wasn't sure she'd heard him correctly.

"Mark Talbot," he repeated, louder this time. "We know he's been here. We tracked him from his cabin."

Jacy climbed to her feet and put her hands on the counter behind her, cutting her eyes around for a weapon—a knife, a fork, anything.

"Don't even think about it," he said, reading her mind. "You don't think I'd shoot a woman?"

"What do you want with Mark?"

A smaller, baby-faced man stepped into the cabin behind the big man. He had to take a long step to get around the big man's muscle-bound girth. When he did, Jacy saw the grinning, pendulous-lipped features of Randall Magnusson, whom she'd seen occasionally before—in dry-goods stores and roadhouses. Once he'd pulled his horse up to hers as she stopped for water at Big John Creek. Openly staring at her breasts, he'd asked if she wanted to go to a dance sometime and she'd told him to go diddle himself.

"Well, lookee here—if ain't Miss Smart Mouth herself," he said, giving her the twice-over with his shiny blue eyes.

"You two can just get the *fuck* out of my cabin," Jacy said, hating the fear that made her voice tremble.

Randall turned his head to look around the cabin, then slid his cold eyes back to Jacy, the infuriating grin still there. "You all alone here, Miss Smart Mouth?"

"What's it look like?" the big man answered for her. To Jacy he said again, "Where'd Talbot go?"

"What's it to you?"

Randall laughed. He was standing between the big man and Jacy, sweeping Jacy with his eyes. "Ol' Rag here's got a score with Talbot. See that ear of his—the one with the bandage on it? That's Talbot's work." Randall laughed. "Yes, sir, he sure did show Rag and my pa what was what and who was who up at the big house last night." He laughed some more. There was no real mirth in it, but not for his lack of trying.

"Shut up," the big man, Rag, said. To Jacy again: "Twelve of my men were ambushed last night, and I think he was part of it. Where is he?"

"He wasn't part of it," Jacy said defiantly. "*I* was part of it."

Rag studied her cynically through slitted eyes. "Very funny. Where is he?"

"How should I know?"

"I just told you, we tracked him here, and from here, his tracks lead south. Now where's he going? You tell me, you sassy little bitch, or so help me—"

"Rag," Randall chided, his eyes remaining on Jacy. "That's no way to talk to a girl. You have to charm a woman into giving up her secrets."

"You're a real lady's man, Randall. Stay out of this," Rag ordered, taking a step toward Jacy.

Eyes afire, Randall wheeled and lifted his heels to bark into the big man's face, "Shut up! Just shut up, you hear? The great King Magnusson is not here, so I'm giving the orders, you understand? *I'm* in charge!"

Jacy turned her fearful, angry gaze to young Magnusson. Trying to steady her voice she said, "Be a man, Randall, and get out of here."

"I don't like how the girls around here talk to men. I'm thinkin' you need to be taught a lesson, like that Rinski bitch."

Jacy studied him, her anger growing keen. She inhaled sharply and swallowed. "You're the one . . . you're the little *boy* who shot Jack Thom in his bed and savaged Mattie."

Randall laughed, then said good-naturedly, "There goes that mouth of yours again." His voice turned hard and his grin faded. "I don't like being talked to like that."

He reached out suddenly and grabbed her by the hair. Jacy cursed and lifted her arms to defend herself. Randall jerked her around by the hair, thrust her against the big man called Rag.

"Hold her good and tight, Rag. I'm gonna teach Miss Smart Mouth to show some respect to her gentleman callers."

"We don't have time for this, Randall," Rag said without heat.

He was enjoying taunting the girl, watching the fear and anger in her eyes, feeling her tremble in his arms. It aroused him. He knew they needed to catch up with Talbot, but he couldn't tear himself away. He wondered what Randall was going to do, how far he would go.

Randall produced a butcher knife from a shelf. He held it up before his face, inspecting it, tested his thumb on the edge. "Ouch," he said. "Sharp. Look at that." He held up his hand to show Jacy the bead of blood on his thumb.

Jacy struggled but could not free her arms from the big man's grasp. Randall stepped forward, thrusting the knife to within four inches of her face. Heart pounding, Jacy turned her head to the side, recoiling against the big man's chest.

"Where did Talbot go?" Randall asked calmly.

Her voice was small but fervid. "Go fuck yourself."

Randall lowered the blade to Jacy's neck, held the blade against her throat. He lifted his eyes to hers, smiled. "Where's Talbot?"

Jacy swallowed, fighting the urge to beg for her life. She was not going to beg these savages for anything. She'd rather die.

Still, she felt as though her heart would explode from the fear. She kept seeing Mattie Rinski in the rocking chair. "I told you to go fuck yourself," she said, breathless.

Randall lowered the blade to her chest, pressed it flatly against her breasts, and with a sudden flick of his wrist sliced a button from her cotton shirt. "Anytime you're ready to tell us where Talbot went, I'll stop," he said matter-of-factly.

He flicked another button from her shirt, then another. Jacy heard the big man breathing in her ear, felt his hands grow warm and sweaty against her wrists. She cursed. Another button hit the floor. Then two more and the shirt fell open, exposing her undershirt and a fair amount of cleavage.

Randall stepped back and inspected her breasts straining the thin, washworn fabric. He pressed the knife point against her left nipple. Jacy sobbed again. Tears rolled down her face.

"Are you going to tell us where Talbot went now, or do I have to keep going?"

"Go fuck . . . go fuck . . ." she said through the sobs that came freely now. She hung limp in the big man's hands, her head hanging to her chest, hair down around her face.

Randall grabbed the neck of her undershirt and began cutting and tearing.

"No!" Jacy screamed, feeling something give way within her. *"No!"*

Just then a floorboard squeaked and another man appeared in the open doorway—a tall, thin man with a casual air. He had a long, angular face and thin lips between which a long black cigar poked. His features were distinctly Latin, but his eyes were impossibly blue.

The eyes held Jacy's for a moment, and it was like having your gaze held and the air sucked out of your lungs by the sudden appearance of the devil himself.

"Come hither, my gringo amigos," he said. "We don't have time to play with little girls. Talbot's tracks are clear."

Then he turned away, giving his back to the kitchen. He stood on the porch, puffing his cigar, and looking across the ranchyard.

Randall cursed, staring at Jacy with animalistic desire. "This one on your list, José?"

"What, the girl? No. Just her hired man. I don't shoot girls, I fuck them. But I don't have time to fuck that one, so let's go, amigos, before you piss me off."

"This one's being smart. She won't tell us where Talbot went."

"I know where Talbot went," the Mexican said casually. He left the porch, and Jacy watched him walk across the ranchyard, mount a tall, black horse, and rein it south out of the yard.

Rag opened his hands and Jacy slumped to the floor, pulling her shirt closed, bringing her knees to her chest.

"Come on," Rag said, turning for the door.

Randall cursed. He prodded Jacy with his boot. "Hey?" he said. "We'll be back for more."

Jacy turned her head and stared at the floor, crying softly and holding her arms over her breasts.

The big man turned on the porch and said, "If we happen to miss Talbot and he circles back, let him know we burned his cabin." He laughed fiercely. "That should slow him down."

CHAPTER 26

JED GIBBON SAT in the Sundowner playing solitaire with a rifle across his thighs.

Occasionally he looked up at the three men sitting across the room, in the shadows on the other side of the ticking stove—Thornberg's men—to make sure they weren't drunk. They were drinking beer instead of whiskey, and they were only sipping the beer, not guzzling it like they'd guzzled whiskey last night.

Like Gibbon, they kept glancing out the window, and whenever a wagon or horseback rider appeared in the street, one or two of them would jump, then cover it with a cough or with a curse at the cards in their hands.

Like Gibbon, they were nervous. Like Gibbon, they had a bad feeling about today.

Today was a long way from last night. They knew that Magnusson was on their trail. He could show up outside the window any second now, with a posse of his own, and turn the tables a full hundred and eighty degrees in his favor.

Gibbon laid a jack of diamonds on a queen of spades and gave a start at the clatter of a buckboard. He looked out the window to see a farmer in an immigrant hat bounce down the street behind two broad-backed draft horses.

When the man was gone, Gibbon sipped his tepid coffee and peeled a three of hearts from the coffee-stained deck in his hand. He gave a slow sigh, pooching out his lips as he released it. By now Magnusson had to know about the roadhouse killings, and Gibbon would have bet a bottle of good Tennessee whiskey that he was on his way to town right now.

But you never knew. Maybe the rancher was going to wait until Gibbon's defenses were down, until he'd grown heavy and slack with anticipation and worry, then ride to town in the dark of night and confront the sheriff when Thornberg's men weren't around to back him up.

That's what Gibbon would have done. But he was hoping Magnusson would act on impulse. He was hoping the big blond Scandahoovian would be so angered at what had transpired at Gutzman's roadhouse that he'd head for town pronto, careless with rage.

Turning his head to glance out the window again, Gibbon saw two more of Thornberg's riders, sitting on the roof of the livery barn across the street. They were hunkered down beneath the peak, backs to the wind, smoking cigarettes. Gibbon knew there was one more man inside the barn, and several more stationed at other locations around the saloon.

Thornberg himself was inside Delmonico's Café, three doors down on the other side of the street, waiting by a window, out of the cold. He'd sent several of his men home to man the ranch in the unlikely event Magnusson went there first, to burn him out.

He and his six other men had ridden with Gibbon to town. Like Gibbon, Thornberg figured Magnusson would come here first, aimed at killing the sheriff before he lit out across the Bench tearing down barns and turning up sod.

All the other ranchers in Gibbon's posse had returned to their ranches. Homer Rinski had wanted to join Gibbon and Thornberg in town, but Gibbon had talked him into returning to his ranch and his daughter. It hadn't been easy convincing the old Bible thumper that his duty now lay at home, and Gibbon half expected to see Rinski ride into town with his Greener in his lap, those cold eyes fairly glowing.

The door of the saloon suddenly burst open, and Gibbon dropped his cards and swung the carbine out from under the table. The farmer who had just passed in the street entered, his little round spectacles frosted over so thickly he couldn't see. His face was red and his scruffy beard was nearly white. The stoop-shouldered little man carefully closed the door then turned to regard the room.

Gibbon sighed with relief. "Good Lord, Asa," he said, "why in hell did you have to pick today of all days to come to town? You haven't been off the farm since August!"

Peering blindly through his frosty spectacles, the farmer said, in a heavy German accent, "Yah, vot's going on? Vhere is everbody? It's Sunday?"

"I've shut down main street 'cause I'm expectin' trouble. Turn your team around and go back home, Asa. We'll see you in May."

"I need supplies."

"Not today, Asa," Gibbon said.

The farmer shook his head stubbornly. "No, I need supplies. That's vy I come all da vay to town."

"Sheriff," one of Thornberg's men said.

Gibbon looked beyond Asa Mueller to the street beyond the window and said, "Shit."

Nearly a dozen men had ridden up. Most were typical Magnusson riders in sheepskin coats, Stetsons, and scarves, rifles in their gloved hands. They were a hard-faced, belligerent-looking bunch that looked none too pleased with what had transpired at Gutzman's roadhouse.

In their midst was Magnusson wearing a fur coat and a fur hat, the mustaches above his grim mouth frosted white. Beside Magnusson rode the stout little man with red muttonchops who had been at Magnusson's place when Gibbon had gotten the shit kicked out of him. He was the only one who did not look like he'd been chomping at the bit to come to town. In fact, he looked like he'd rather be anywhere *but* town.

All the rest more than made up for his reluctance. Magnusson himself looked like he was about to collect the proceeds from a million-dollar bet. "Come on out here, Gibbon!"

"Go out the back, Asa," Gibbon said tightly.

The farmer had turned to look out the window. He was mumbling something under his breath, but Gibbon ignored him as he gained his feet and jacked a shell in his rifle breech. He stood and pulled on his coat, taking his time with the buttons.

Lifting his collar, he walked to the window and looked out. Magnusson stared at him through the glass, his face expressionless. Only his eyes showed a faint amusement.

"Okay, boys," Gibbon said.

Thornberg's riders had put down their cards, picked up their rifles, and now followed Gibbon onto the porch. They stood in a line, facing Magnusson and his riders.

"Mornin'," Gibbon said casually. "Or is it afternoon now?"

Magnusson said nothing. He sat his big Arabian and scowled.

Gibbon shrugged. "Well, what brings you to Caanan, Magnusson? I thought the Double X did all its business in Big Draw."

"You know why I'm here, you pathetic old bastard. You bushwhacked my men."

"They were resistin' arrest."

"What's the charge?"

"Suspicion of murder and cattle rustlin'."

Magnusson laughed without mirth. The smile faded. Glancing at Thornberg's men, he said, "Hired you some deputies, eh? Must have been expecting me."

"Take a look behind you."

Magnusson twisted around in his saddle, peering at the other riflemen on the roofs behind him. Gibbon heard a door open. Looking right, he watched Thornberg step out of the café and come down the boardwalk holding a rifle across his chest.

Thornberg tipped his hat and said, "Good day to you, King. I have a feeling you're gonna lose that sappy grin of yours in about thirty seconds." He jacked a shell and scowled.

"Mighty sure of yourself, aren't you, Verlyn? How many men you packing today?"

"Ten, same as you, King. I'd say that's a pretty fair fight."

Gibbon said, "Doesn't have to be a fight, Magnusson. All you have to do is throw your guns down, order your men to do likewise, and follow me over to the jail."

"What are you talking about?" Magnusson scoffed. "You actually think you have any legal jurisdiction in this matter, Gibbon?"

"No," Gibbon said. His face turned to stone. "I was just bein' polite."

He and Magnusson locked eyes.

Finally, a low growl rumbled up from the rancher's chest, his lips fluttered, and his face reddened. He drew the silver-plated Bisley strapped over his coat, but he was too steamed to shoot straight. The bullet whistled past Gibbon's ear and shattered the window behind him.

Gibbon lifted his Winchester and shot Magnusson in the shoulder just as the rancher's horse swung around, spooked by the sudden gunfire. Magnusson yelled and clutched the wound with one hand while trying to control his mount with the other.

Magnusson's riders lowered their rifles and Gibbon swung

his own carbine around, dislodging one man and wounding another in the thigh. He gave a shriek and fell from the saddle of his bucking pinto.

Beside Gibbon, two of Thornberg's riders went down in the hail of bullets flung by Magnusson's crew. The other jumped off the porch and ducked behind a watering trough and commenced firing.

Thornberg and the rest of his men were opening up across the street, dislodging several of Magnusson's men from their saddles and scattering the others in a thunder of clomping hooves and high-pitched whinnies.

Gibbon had just taken down another man when Magnusson, who'd pinned Thornberg behind a hay wagon, swung back around and emptied his carbine at Gibbon.

The sheriff, who'd dropped to one knee behind the hitch rack, felt one of the slugs tear meat from his side, just above his belt, but he kept firing until the hammer of his Winchester clicked. He dropped the carbine and ran back into the saloon, clumsily pulling his revolver from the holster beneath his coat.

A cat-like moan sounded behind him. Swinging a look, he saw Asa Mueller curled up under a table with his arms over his head.

"Just stay there 'til I tell you to come out, Asa," Gibbon said.

With the gun in his hand, he stepped up to the window and was about to cut loose when he saw that the street had cleared and most of the shooting was now happening between and behind the buildings across the street. Two horses and six of Magnusson's riders lay dead. The three men that had followed Gibbon onto the porch were dead as well, spilling blood on the boardwalk. There was no sign of Thornberg.

Magnusson was retreating up the boardwalk on the other side of the street, stumbling and clutching his shoulder. Gibbon yelled, "The fight's back here, Magnusson!" and snapped off an errant round.

The rancher stopped, pressed his back to the livery barn, and squeezed off a feeble shot. Then he pushed himself away from the barn and ran up the street, toward his horse that stood twitching its ears at the gunfire.

Gibbon ran after him, keeping to his side of the street. He stopped when Magnusson tried to mount the jittery Arabian, and fired two shots in the air over the horse's head. The horse bucked and ran kicking down the street.

Magnusson tried to hold on, but his left foot slipped from the stirrup and he landed in a pile, cursing and raging at the disobedient mount.

Gibbon walked up behind him as Magnusson tried to gain his feet. "Stay down there," Gibbon said. "Throw down your weapon and hold your hands above your head." He noted that the gunfire was dying away behind him and he wondered vaguely if anyone was still alive.

He got his answer a second later, when a shaky voice rose behind him. "H-hold it r-right there, Sheriff."

Gibbon froze. He'd been so preoccupied with stopping Magnusson that he hadn't thought to watch his back. Turning slowly, he confronted the man behind him. The stocky little easterner with the red muttonchops and rosy red cheeks held a revolver in both his shaking hands, the barrel aimed at Gibbon's chest.

Swallowing, the man looked beyond Gibbon to Magnusson. "K-k-k-king, what should I d-do?"

Gibbon didn't give Magnusson a chance to answer. He shot the little man in the chest, then brought his gun back around to Magnusson, who had turned but was not holding his revolver. Gibbon saw the Bisley lying about ten feet from the rancher, where he must have dropped it when the horse threw him.

Gibbon felt a grin shaping his mouth. He heard a gun crack and felt a bullet tear through his middle. As though clubbed with a two-by-four, he fell forward on his knees, struggling to keep his gun up.

Turning, he saw the little man lying on his side, still aiming his revolver at Gibbon. Smoke curled from the barrel. As the man thumbed back the hammer to fire again, Gibbon shot him through the forehead.

The easterner's head jerked back with the force of the slug, then came forward and hit the ground. The shoulders quivered for only a moment.

Hearing footsteps, Gibbon turned his head forward. Magnusson was reaching for his Bisley. Gibbon squeezed off a shot but missed cleanly. His hand was shaking; he was going into shock. He thumbed back the hammer and squeezed the trigger again, but the hammer slapped the firing pin without igniting a shell.

He felt a heavy darkness brush over him like warm, wet tar. He was out of shells and out of luck. He gave an involuntary groan against the pain in his middle as he watched Magnusson straighten with the silver-plated pistol in his hand.

His lower jaw jutted angrily out from his face and his nostrils flared like a rabid dog's.

"You bastard," Gibbon muttered, his breath growing short. He felt drunk, and he chuckled silently at the thought. Here he was on his last leg, shot in the back by a chicken-hearted little tinhorn, and sober as a Lutheran preacher.

Magnusson walked stiffly toward him, holding the Bisley out from his chest. Blood glistened on the right shoulder of his coat. He stopped near Gibbon and pressed the barrel to the sheriff's forehead.

"You're finished, Gibbon," Magnusson growled.

"So are you, King," Gibbon said before the gun barked.

CHAPTER 27

MARK TALBOT HAD just started tracking a whitetail buck when he sensed he was being followed.

He halted his horse on the buttes over a creek and turned his head in a slow circle squinting his eyes. He saw little but snow-dusted hogbacks and small, isolated cottonwood copses, a distant line of skeletal trees tracing the course of another creek. In the far distance, wind-sculpted sandstone monuments stood sentinel over the vast canvas of colorless winter landscape.

It was getting late in the afternoon and the high, dense clouds were turning sooty. The sun was an opalescent wash edging down the western sky.

Talbot appeared to be alone. Still, the hair on the back of his neck was standing straight up, and heeding such a warning had saved his life more times in the past than he cared to remember. He clucked to the horse and continued following the impressions the buck had left in the hard ground, periodically cutting his eyes around for trouble.

Having lost the tracks, he stopped by a flat boulder to try to recover them. He squinted his eyes at the tufts of frozen grass and lowered his head for a closer look.

Something shredded the air near his ear, whistling softly with a guttural edge. He felt the wind on his neck and recognized the sound of a lead ball ripping air.

A long gun boomed in the distance. Talbot had heard the reports of enough large-caliber rifles to know instantly, without having to ponder it, that this was a Big Fifty, accurate up to seven hundred yards.

He was out of the saddle and reaching for his carbine before the echo of the boom had died. He slapped the horse and ran for the ridge over the creek, found cover behind a boulder wedged precariously atop the steep grade.

Behind and below him the frozen creek curled in its brush-lined bed. Talbot considered it momentarily before returning his gaze to the open benches, from where he knew the Big Fifty had been fired.

More rifles popped thinly in the distance. They were carbines, like Talbot's Winchester, and well out of range. It was the Big Fifty Talbot was worried about. Whoever had pulled its trigger had had enough time to reload the single-shot rifle and was no doubt worrying a bead on Talbot's head at this very moment.

As if to confirm his suspicion, a ball shattered against the rock, spraying rock and lead in the grass like heavy rain. The boom followed half a second later. More rifles popped, and the popping was growing louder.

Talbot jerked a look around the rock and saw a man riding along the ridge to his right. Swinging around, he saw another man coming from the left. They were about a hundred yards away and closing. No doubt the man with the Big Fifty was straight out in the prairie somewhere, hunkered down behind a hogback.

Talbot jacked a shell in his Winchester, brought the rifle to his shoulder and squeezed off a shot at the man on his left, then turned and squeezed off another at the man on his right. One rider gave a yell and halted his horse to dismount and look for cover, but the other—a far bigger man—kept coming.

Talbot considered holding his ground and shooting it out, but he knew he'd be caught in a cross fire. With no time to spare—he could hear hooves beating the hard earth—he scrambled down the ridge to the brush along the creek, running hard. Tiny silvery birds rose from the brambles, screaming and wheeling toward the opposite ridge. Rifles cracked and lead ripped the air.

He ran deep into the cattails, sending the cotton billowing in all directions. He knew his attackers would be able to hear him thrashing in the weeds if he kept moving, so he stopped at the trunk of a dead cottonwood and hunkered down to scan the ridge behind him.

Three men sat three horses near the rock he'd used for cover. Talbot was too far away to make out distinguishing features, but he could tell from body shape and size that two of the men were Rag Donnelly and Randall Magnusson. He didn't recognize the other man, the man sporting the Big Fifty.

What he did recognize was the fact that all three men were riding for King Magnusson, and they had no doubt tracked Talbot here from his cabin. Which meant they'd tracked him to Jacy's. Talbot felt a sudden, desperate urge to return to her ranch to make sure she hadn't been harmed.

But first he had to deal with these three uglies.

He was trying to figure out how to do that when two of the riders rode down the ridge, leaving the third man—the man with the Big Fifty—alone on the ridgetop. Apparently Donnelly and young Magnusson were coming after him while the third man covered them from the ridge.

Talbot turned and headed up the creek through the heavy brush. Soon the man on the ridge started cutting loose with the big Sharps—one heavy blast after another. He couldn't see Talbot in the weeds but that didn't keep him from probing the creek bed with intermittent lead balls, making sure

Talbot didn't get too comfortable down there while the other two beat the brush for him.

After fifty tough yards, Talbot turned to watch and listen. He couldn't see much but sky and the ridges on either side of the creek, rising above the bending weed tips, but he could hear the heavy boom of the Sharps and voices.

The occasional cries and calls lifted behind him about seventy-five yards, and they seemed to be spread apart by several dozen yards. There was the rustle and crack of heavy animals moving through brush, and Talbot knew Magnusson and Donnelly were beating the creek bed for him the way you'd beat the brush for whitetails or mountain lions.

Meanwhile, the man on the ridge was trying to flush him with the Sharps.

A slug whistled past Talbot's ear and snapped a willow limb behind him. Talbot ducked suddenly and cursed. He shifted his gaze to the ridge. The man with the big gun rose from his prone shooting position and cupped his hands around his mouth. His voice carried on the crisp air.

"He's ahead and left, sixty yards!"

The son of a bitch must have eyes like a hawk, Talbot grumbled to himself, turning and pushing his way through the brush.

Five minutes later the brush thinned and there was the creek—a wide, frozen horseshoe dusted with a thin, crusty layer of snow etched with animal tracks. On the other side stood a beaver house about five feet tall and seven feet long.

Talbot looked behind him. The man on the ridge was still shooting, but apparently he'd lost his target, for none of the recent slugs had landed near. Keeping his head low, Talbot ran out of the brush, slipping and sliding on the icy creek, boots crunching snow, and hunkered down on the far side of the beaver house.

A bullet tore into the house, snapping several of the carefully woven branches, and Talbot knew the man on the ridge had rediscovered him.

That's okay, he thought. Send him over here.

He stood and yelled to the ridge, "Come on—send him over here! Tell 'em to come and get it!" Turning to the brush across the creek he shouted, "Come and get it, Rag! Come and get it, Randall! I'm waiting for you!"

Suddenly a horse burst out of the brush behind him, another whinnied across the creek, and Talbot realized they'd been moving around him and slowly tightening the circle.

"Eeee-ha!" Randall Magnusson yelled as he bore down on Talbot, trying to trample him.

Talbot swung around to shoot, but Magnusson's horse bulled into him, knocking the rifle from his arms. Thrown back against the beaver house, he went for his revolver, but before his hand touched the grips Randall's rifle cracked, belching fire and smoke, and the slug tore into the house a half inch right of Talbot's face. The barrel hung there, only a few inches away, so instead of drawing his revolver, Talbot reached out and grabbed the rifle and pulled.

Randall came with it, landing with a cry on the root-webbed cutbank, his mount shrieking and kicking as it scrambled away.

Talbot crouched behind the beaver house just as Donnelly snapped off a shot. The slug barked into the house. Talbot stood, lifting Randall's Winchester to his shoulder, and returned fire at Donnelly, who was too preoccupied with his prancing mount to take another shot.

The bullet caught the big foreman in the shoulder, pushing him back in the saddle. He gave a yell and fumbled for his reins, but the horse was bucking in earnest, slipping and sliding on the ice, and he fell heavily out of the saddle, cursing.

Turning sharply to his right, Talbot saw that Randall was lying on his back, his head propped against the weeds, a Colt revolver extended in his right hand. The barrel was aimed at Talbot's head, and the trigger was locked back, ready to fire.

Time stopped, and Talbot saw the grim smile etched on the young man's thick-lipped mug. Magnusson's eyes were slits through which the frosty eyes reflected the dull winter light. The muzzle bore down on Talbot like the round, black yawn of eternity.

Randall licked his lips. "Your brother thought he was too good to beg for his life, so we made him kneel down and I shot him in the back of the head like a dog." The smile widened. "Where do you want yours?"

Before Talbot could answer, a round black spot the size of a double eagle appeared on Randall's forehead, just above his eyes. He was only vaguely aware of a rifle crack as the kid's head snapped back and hit the ground with a thud. The Colt dropped from his hand. He gave no cry, no sound whatsoever. One leg spasmed for a few seconds, and that was all.

He'd obviously been shot, but by whom Talbot had no time to ponder, because Rag Donnelly suddenly slammed him to the ground with the full force of his body. Talbot went down hard on his side, Donnelly's weight forcing the air from his lungs in one painful exhalation.

Then Donnelly was slamming his head against the ground and raging incoherently. Talbot kicked himself up with his legs. At the same time he laced his hands together and slammed them down hard on the foreman's head. It wasn't much of a blow, but it gave Talbot time to roll sideways and scramble to his feet.

Donnelly gained his own legs and, breathing heavily, threw off his gloves. His face was swollen and red, his hair atangle. Blood soaked the shoulder of his sheepskin.

"Come on, you son of a bitch!" he shrieked. "I'm gonna take you apart limb by limb and hear you howl like a stuck pig!"

Talbot threw down his own gloves and fisted his hands, crouching. They circled for several seconds, then Donnelly leaned in with a right hook. Talbot ducked and the blow went wild. Before Donnelly could regroup, Talbot landed a left cross, opening a two-inch gash on Donnelly's cheek.

Brushing the back of his hand across the gash and growling like a wounded griz, Donnelly stepped back to consider the blood on his hand. Then he closed in again, swinging his right fist.

Again Talbot ducked, but before he could get his head back up and fade left, Donnelly caught his right brow dead-on with a crushing, ham-sized fist. Talbot staggered backward as the pain tore through his skull, and before he could regain his balance, Donnelly charged, bulling him over backward.

The foreman slammed Talbot's face with three brain-numbing right jabs, then he reached down to his ankle and produced a stiletto. The slender blade came up under Talbot's chin, and following the blade with his eyes, Talbot saw the naked woman etched in the tempered steel.

He reached up and grabbed Donnelly's hand just before the blade pierced the tender skin over his jugular vein, and the naked woman twisted and turned as the two hands struggled for dominance.

Through gritted teeth, his eyes on the naked woman, Talbot grunted, "You always fight this fair, Rag?"

"Fuck you, Talbot . . . you're a dead man."

"Don't . . . count . . . your . . . *chickens* . . ." Talbot funneled a sudden burst of adrenaline into the fist that held Donnelly's, and the naked woman turned suddenly away from him, as though twirled by an invisible partner, and plunged head first into Donnelly's leathery, whisker-bristled throat.

Ruby blood gushed over the hilt and onto the handle, covering Talbot's hand. Donnelly opened his mouth to speak but only blood issued. His body stiffened. As he faded sideways, turning onto his back, he clutched at the blade with both hands. He pressed his back to the frozen ground and struggled feebly with the deep-set blade, kicking his feet, stark terror in his eyes.

Then his hands fell to his chest, his face turned to the side, and the light faded from his gaze.

Talbot pushed himself to his feet carefully, trying to quash the pounding in his head. Sensing someone near, he turned quickly, ready to defend himself once again.

Jacy stood behind the beaver house, where a faint deer trail opened onto the creek. She held a rifle across her chest and she was looking at the body of Randall Magnusson lying several feet away, blood dripping from the black hole in his forehead.

Realizing that she had been the one who'd shot Randall, probably from the ridge behind them, opposite the man with the Big Fifty, Talbot watched her take three stiff steps toward the body, lower the rifle barrel, and blow another hole through young Magnusson's face.

"That son of a bitch," she said.

Talbot didn't know what to say. He just stood there, watching her with Donnelly's gore on his hands.

"Are you all right?" he said finally.

She turned suddenly away from Magnusson's inert body, ran to Talbot, and threw her arms around his neck, sobbing. He couldn't hold her because of the blood on his hands but he pressed his cheek to hers, said in her ear, "I'm so sorry, Jacy. I led them right to your cabin. I just didn't think they'd be after me so soon."

"Those sons of bitches," she sobbed, her face buried in his shoulder. "The one shooting from the ridge . . . he took off when he saw me . . . *he* was the one that shot Gordon and Mrs. Sanderson."

"Oh, Jesus. Are you okay?"

She nodded. "They just roughed me up a little." She lifted her head and looked into his face through slitted, teary eyes. "They burned your cabin," she cried, studying him.

He stared back at her, feeling numb, his heart quickening. "How do you know?"

She indicated Magnusson and Donnelly with a tip of her head. "They said so. I saw smoke that way when I left to find you."

Talbot looked off, setting his jaw so tight that his teeth ached. By now, the ranch would be no more than rubble. Magnusson had left him with little but the shirt on his back. Fuming, he looked at the dead bodies, wishing he could resurrect them and kill them all over again.

Maybe he couldn't work miracles, but he sure as hell could fix the head honcho's flint but good. He'd kill Magnusson—now, today—or die trying.

He knelt down and rubbed his gory hands in the weeds and snow. "Go home and stay there," he said tightly.

"I'm coming with you."

"No."

"I'll get my horse," she said, turning.

"I said no," he called after her.

She turned around sharply, long hair flying. Her green eyes were bright with fire. "You say no because I'm a girl, but you get something straight, mister—Magnusson is into me for as much he's into you, and girl or not, I'm calling his note due. Are you with me?"

He studied her, a tender expression growing on his face. In the vast desert of his loneliness, sorrow, and rage, she was the one bright thing.

He sighed and shook his head fatefully, tried a smile. "I sure as hell wouldn't want to be against you," he said.

Then he watched her turn and stomp off through the weeds, thoroughly in love with her.

CHAPTER 28

IT WAS TOO cold and too late in the day to be this far from home, and Homer Rinski knew better. He just didn't care. What he had on his mind would not be stymied by such earthly concerns as fading light and plummeting temperatures.

He followed a shallow, curving draw along St. Mary's Creek, steam jetting from his and his horse's nostrils, the swaybacked roan appearing as sullen as the stoop-shouldered man astraddle it. The sharp breeze played at the floppy brim of Rinski's black felt hat, tied down with the red wool scarf Mattie had knitted for him last Christmas.

He hadn't had a conscious thought in weeks. It was all impulse—a single, otherworldly drive driven by holy hate.

When he came to an offshooting draw, he followed it through a scattering of burr oaks and junipers, the trail rising gradually until Rinski's head was level with the tableland above. He halted the horse and peered north.

The corrals, hay barns, and bunkhouses of the Double X headquarters sprawled in a coulee below the back of the big house, two hundred yards away. Smoke issued from the mansion and horses milled in the corrals, but smoke curled from the chimney of only one of the outbuildings.

Rinski studied the structure for several seconds, then growled "Giddyup" to the horse.

He slipped the butt of his old bird gun under his right arm and, fingering the paper shells in his right coat pocket, moved out toward the single low-slung cabin issuing smoke from its battered tin chimney. Rinski could tell it was a summer cook shack. There was an abandoned chuckwagon parked haphazardly in front, and two sets of footprints led to the door.

Dismounting and tying his horse to the wagon, Rinski heard voices inside the cabin. He lifted the barrel of his shotgun, stepped resolutely to the plank door, and kicked it open.

"God-*dang*!" came a surprised yell.

Someone screamed. Rinski thought at first it was a girl's scream. Then his eyes adjusted to the cabin's murk. Two men lay on a single cot beneath a papered-over window.

One had a neatly trimmed, carefully waxed mustache, and he looked eastern or British. His naked, porcelain-white legs were carpeted with fine black hair. The second man was a young cowboy with a sparse, sandy mustache and a black felt farmer's hat with a round brim and a bullet-shaped crown. A red neckerchief encircled his scrawny neck. His breeches lay on the floor and his long johns were bunched around his feet and soiled socks.

There was a long silence. The men on the cot stared at Rinski; Rinski stared back.

"Do you *mind?*" the dandy yelled finally.

Rinski ignored him. He stared at the cowboy, fairly shaking with rage. "Did you . . . did you savage my girl, Shelby Green?"

The cowboy raised his hands placatingly. "I-I didn't harm Mattie, Mr. Rinski," he said thinly.

Rinski appeared more taken aback by the declaration than by the boy's exposed member or by the realization of what he'd been using it for. He growled at length, with a slow nod and a speculative squint.

"No! . . . it was Randall. He's the one savaged Mattie. I only . . . I only . . ."

"It was you and Randall."

"No! Like I said—"

"You and Randall savaged my little girl."

The young cowboy's voice was small and thin. "Please, Mr. Rinski. I didn't meant to do it . . . It was Randall . . . He made me!"

"You and Randall Magnusson."

"No!"

"Tell the Lord about your devilish desires, Shelby Green. Maybe he'll have mercy on your soul."

Rinski brought the shotgun to bear. It boomed, sprouting flames. The cowboy's head disappeared in a cloud of bone and blood, basting his hat against the log wall. Limbs akimbo, his headless body flew off the cot and hit the floor with a slap and a thud.

Rinski turned to the dandy.

"Please, no!" the man wailed, covering his head with his arms, bringing his knees to his chest. "I'm a *doctor!*"

"You're filth," Rinski intoned. "May the Lord accept you back from the Beast."

He pressed the barrel to the man's head and tripped the left trigger. He appraised the mess the gun had made, grimly pleased, then turned and left the bloody cabin.

He mounted his horse and rode up the tawny rise to the big house. He dismounted and tied the horse to the hitch rail at the back door.

Rinski hefted the shotgun, tightened his coat collar about his neck, and strolled up the three wooden steps to the sashed door. He was not surprised to find it unlocked—the devil was known for his arrogance—and stepped into the kitchen.

A spidery old woman in a poke bonnet and purple cotton

maid's dress and white apron turned from the range. "What in heaven's name?"

"Get out," Rinski ordered.

Staring at the shotgun held across Rinski's chest, the woman stuttered and stammered, trying to speak.

"Get out!"

She gave a start, wringing her hands, and sidestepped past him on her way out the kitchen door.

Rinski saw a rose lamp on a table with carved legs. He grabbed the lamp, stepped into the dining room, and threw it against the drapes. It shattered when it hit the floor, spilling kerosene.

Rinski stepped up to the pool of the liquid and produced a match from his coat pocket. Scratching the lucifer on the polished mahogany table, which was nearly as long as Rinski's cabin was wide and which shone like a moonlit lake at night, he dropped the flame in the kerosene. It went up with a whoosh. A toothy line of flames curled back agaist the wall, instantly igniting the heavy drapes.

"Oh, my God! Fire! *Fire!*"

Rinski turned to see two women descending the stairs in a hurry. One was young and pretty, with long raven hair bouncing on her shoulders. The other was older, heavy-bosomed, and made up like a nickel whore you'd find in any boom town.

"Save yourselves, charlatans!" Rinski told them, voice raised above the whooshing flames. "You'll no longer find shelter in the devil's lair!"

"That's cashmere, you fool!"

"Mother!" the young woman cried in warning.

"Get the men!"

"They rode away this morning, and I haven't seen Harrison for *hours!*"

The older woman ran to the drapes, screaming, looking

around feebly for something with which to put out the fire. The younger woman ran up behind her, grabbed her arm, and pulled her out the front door.

Rinski found another lantern and walked down the hall on the other side of the rose-carpeted stairs. He lit the lantern and tossed it into a study with a cave-sized stone hearth and a hide-covered desk as large as a wagon bed, then proceeded upstairs—slowly, deliberately, as though walking in his sleep.

He'd just tossed a lantern on a lace-covered, four-poster bed when he heard the girl's voice rise from the yard below. "Oh, look! Oh, Mother, it's the man from the *trapper's* shack!"

Rinski went back down the stairs several minutes later, nearly the whole second story in flames behind him. Through the eye-stinging smoke of the ground floor he saw the silhouette of a tall man in a fur coat filling the open front door, swathed in smoke. He was holding a long-barreled rifle straight up in the air.

When Rinski stopped on the stairs, the man brought the barrel down level with Rinski's chest. The smoke parted enough for Rinski to make out the man's blue, blue eyes and his grin, shaped around the long thin cigar clamped in his teeth.

"You have a light, gringo?" he yelled above the flames.

Rinski didn't even have time to bring his shotgun down. Fire leapt from the barrel of the Big Fifty, blowing a four-inch hole through Rinski's chest. He flew back against the stairs, tripping both barrels of the shotgun and sending buckshot into the flame-engulfed rafters.

He was dead on the landing before he could mutter a final prayer.

"No, I didn't think so," Del Toro said, turning around and heading back toward King Magnusson's lovely daughter standing dumbly with her mother in the yard.

They were looking at him like Jesus Christ had just ridden up on a donkey.

Hee-hee.

KING MAGNUSSON TURNED from Jed Gibbon's body and looked down the street to where all the shooting had taken place.

Dead men and dead horses littered the street between the Sundowner and the livery barn. Wind shepherded a blood-stained hat in Magnusson's direction, bouncing it along the frozen ruts of the street until it caught in the legs of a feed trough before the mercantile.

The bartender poked his head through the saloon's broken front window. Magnusson brought his pistol up reflexively, but, seeing him, the man gave a start and lurched back inside. One of the bodies in the street moved and Magnusson walked toward it.

It was Verlyn Thornberg. He lay grunting and cursing as he tried to stretch his arm out for his pistol, several feet away. There was a gaping, blood-soaked hole where his stomach had been. His coat was spilling viscera.

Magnusson stepped on the pistol and grinned down at the dying man. Thornberg turned his head up sideways, blood washing over his lower lip. He tried to say something but nothing came from his mouth but more blood, as dark and thick as molasses.

"Look what you did to yourself, Verlyn," Magnusson sneered. "Instead of pulling up stakes and moving on, leaving the Bench to me, you're layin' here in the street drowning in your own guts. Tsk, tsk, tsk."

Thornberg's lips curled back from his teeth, and red rage shone in his face for just a second. Then the color faded and the light in his eyes dimmed. His head dipped. It fell in a puddle of quickly congealing blood. Thornberg sighed, and he was dead.

Magnusson gave a self-satisfied chuff.

He had to admit, though, the rancher and Gibbon had given him a run for his money. And they'd hurt him beyond the bullet in his shoulder.

But he'd be back in action in no time. He'd start sending notices for gun-savvy riders as far north as Calgary and as far south as Amarillo.

He'd have the Bench to himself in no time.

After all, he was almost there. He might have lost most of his men—all but Rag and Del Toro, that is (you couldn't really call Randall a man)—but he still had his herds.

He still had his headquarters . . .

Thinking of that gave him a funny feeling in his gut, a bitter taste at the roof of his mouth, and he felt a sudden compulsion to get home as fast as he could. It was an irrational fear, he knew. Donnelly and Del Toro would have taken care of Talbot, and there was no one left on the Bench with balls enough to threaten the house.

Still . . .

He looked up and down the street for a horse to ride and didn't see a one—standing, that is. His silver-gray, always a little gun-shy for some reason, was long gone. Turning to the livery barn, Magnusson saw that the horses in the paddock had knocked the rails down and lit a shuck out of there after the shooting had started.

Then, as if answering his silent plea, he heard a knicker behind him. Turning, he saw a horse poke its head out between the drugstore and the feed store. Its reins dangled as it turned its head and twitched its ears nervously, looking around for its rider.

Magnusson started slowly toward it, holding his hands out

in a gesture of goodwill. "Whoa, boy," he cooed. "Whoa, now. That's it."

The horse shook its head and backed up a few steps, but it didn't start turning to flee until Magnusson had grabbed the reins and was halfway in the leather.

"Hah! Haaah!" he shouted, giving the horse the spurs and reining westward out of town.

He'd ridden hard for nearly an hour when he saw the smoke.

CHAPTER 29

"WELL, I'LL BE goddamned," Talbot mumbled, bringing his horse to a sudden halt and lifting his eyes to the column of smoke rising beyond the second ridge north.

Jacy reined in, too, and looked where Talbot was looking. "What do you make of that?"

"I don't know, but there's only one way to find out." He touched his spurs to his horse's flanks and started down the slope.

Ten minutes later he and Jacy stopped their mounts on a ridge about four hundred yards from the Magnusson headquarters and watched the burning roof of the grand mansion tumble into the flame-engulfed rubble below. The dragon-like roar carried on the cold air, and the resin in the milled lumber popped like .45s.

The conflagration glowed brightly against the falling night.

Dumbfounded, Talbot and Jacy looked at each other, then at the fire. Someone had torched the house, all right, but where were the men who did it, and where were Magnusson and his riders?

Talbot got half an answer when a horseman galloped in from the west, about a hundred yards away. The man left the creek bottom below Talbot and Jacy and kicked his horse up the ridge beneath the burning house.

The man's large frame and posture bespoke King Magnusson.

Thoroughly perplexed, Talbot told Jacy to keep her head down—he knew from the tracks they'd been following that the hombre with the Big Fifty had come this way, too—and started down the ridge toward the creek.

As they climbed the ridge below the house they spotted a saddled horse foraging in the snow with its reins dangling. Jacy recognized Homer Rinski's brand, and said as much to Talbot.

The furrows in Talbot's brow deepened. He shook his head and rode on, cantering, following Magnusson's trail now and holding his Winchester up high and ready.

He and Jacy halted their horses about fifty yards from the house. Magnusson had dismounted and stood before the house with his back to Talbot and Jacy, his big hands clenched at his sides, shoulders humped, the collar of his long buffalo coat rising like the fur around a cur's neck.

Slowly he lifted his hands to his temples, elbows straight out from his head like horns, and bellowed like a foundering bull, staggering with the force of his emotion.

Through the roar of the fire, Talbot heard him calling Suzanne's name. The thought that she could be in there gave Talbot a jolt, and he spurred his horse forward, feeling the heat.

"Mark!" Jacy cried.

Ignoring her, Talbot brought his mount up even with Magnusson. Seeing him, the rancher's livid eyes grew even keener.

"You!" he cried, lunging toward Talbot's horse. "You did this!"

Talbot turned his horse away from the man, holding his rifle on him. "I didn't burn your damn house!" he yelled. "Did all the women get out?"

Magnusson danced Talbot's horse in a circle, trying to pull its rider out of the saddle. Jacy rode up, yelling, but kept her horse a safe distance from the melee. There was little she could do.

Talbot's horse bucked and rose up on its hind legs, frightened by Magnusson as well as the fire. Holding the reins in one hand and the Winchester in the other, Talbot lost his balance. Magnusson reached up and grabbed him by his coat collar and pulled. Talbot dropped the rifle and came out of the saddle, cursing and hitting the ground hard on his left shoulder.

Pushing himself up on a knee while Magnusson dodged the horse, Talbot said, "You burned *me* out, you son of a bitch!"

"I'll kill you! I'll kill you!" Magnusson roared. He stepped forward and kicked Talbot in the chest. Talbot hit the ground on his back.

Magnusson moved in and was about to kick again when Talbot rolled left and gained his feet, crouched and ready to spring. Sloppy with rage, Magnusson leaned in, hooking with his right fist.

Talbot ducked. He came up jabbing with both hands, pummeling Magnusson's face with satisfying smacks. The rancher staggered back, fear and surprise flashing in his cold eyes. Talbot didn't stop swinging until Magnusson was on the ground in a raging, frothy-lipped heap. Blood poured from the gashes in his face.

Talbot stood before him crouched and ready, his fists held high, feet spread, upper lip curled in anger. "You had enough?"

Magnusson groaned and tried to push himself to his feet, fell back down.

"Now, like I said," Talbot snarled, "I didn't burn your

house, you bastard. Not that I wouldn't have, but someone beat me to it."

Rubbing a jaw, Magnusson climbed to a knee. "Who?"

"I don't know and I don't care."

Magnusson's eyes grew bright with renewed fear as he turned them to the blaze. "Suzanne!" he cried.

"How do you know she didn't make it out?" Talbot asked, anger turning to genuine concern.

A woman's voice rose. *"King!"*

Talbot turned his gaze southward, where two women cloaked in quilts were climbing the bank from the outbuildings in the coulee below. One was Magnusson's wife; the other was the gray-haired maid. Magnusson's wife clung to the older woman for support, her face twisted with anguish.

Magnusson stood unsteadily. "Kendra!"

"King!"

Magnusson ran to her and grabbed her by the shoulders, shaking her. "What happened! Where's Suzanne!"

"Oh, King!" the woman bawled. Her legs turned to jelly and she crumpled in Magnusson's arms.

"Goddamnit, where is she!"

Releasing her, he turned to the other woman, taking Minnie's shoulders in his big hands and nearly lifting her off the ground. "Tell me!"

"Oh, Mr. Magnusson! A man came," she stammered in a thick Scottish accent. "He . . . he . . ."

"What!"

"He come into the house while I was cookin' . . . an' he . . . an' he started throwin' *lanterns* around!"

"Who?"

"An old man . . . old as me."

"Did he take Suzanne?"

"No! It was another man. He come up on a black horse and

shot the first man in the house. It was him . . . a Mexican . . . he took Suzanne! Just grabbed her up on his horse and rode away!"

Magnusson paused, absorbing the information.

"Please, sir, you're hurting my arms," the woman begged.

Magnusson swallowed. "Which way did they go?"

"That way, sir—southeast."

Magnusson released the woman, who gave a scream, clutching her bruised arms. Magnusson turned stiffly, eyes wide and unmoving, and stared south, where the tables rolled away like a rumpled carpet, sooty now with the fading winter light.

The fire grumbled like a distant train, cracking and hissing. A timber fell with a muffled boom, geysering sparks.

The old woman stared at the conflagration, looking stricken. Mrs. Magnusson bawled, her head in her hands. Jacy stood near her horse, about twenty feet away, looking on dispassionately. She had nothing but disdain for these people, and Talbot didn't blame her.

Turning to the rancher, Talbot said, "Who is this man, King? Where's he headed? You have any idea?"

Magnusson started for his horse. "What do you care?"

"It's getting too late to track him. Best to wait till morning."

Magnusson grabbed his reins and climbed into the leather, favoring his right shoulder. "I don't have to track him. I know where that randy son of a bitch is taking my daughter." He looked at the maid. "Harness the sorrels to Mrs. Magnusson's phaeton and drive her to Mr. Troutman's in Big Draw."

He reined his horse around, gouged it with his spurs, and circled the burning rubble of his mansion, heading southeast. Lifting her head to watch him go, Mrs. Magnusson wailed.

Talbot turned to Jacy. "I have to help him."

Jacy laughed caustically. "Are you crazy?"

"He has a bullet in his shoulder. He won't be able to get Suzanne back by himself."

"That's his problem."

Talbot shook his head, not liking the position he was in any better than Jacy did. "I can't just walk away. Suzanne's out there with a lunatic."

"It's Magnusson's problem. He hired the man. Besides, it's not up to you to save the daughter of the man who murdered your brother and burned your ranch."

"Jacy, I have to go."

"Then go, and just keep goin'." She turned, reaching for her saddle horn and shoving her left foot in the stirrup.

Talbot watched her canter the line-back dun down the hill in the early winter dusk. He couldn't blame her for how she felt, not after all that King Magnusson had taken from her. A few years and battles ago, when he was her age, he would have felt the same way.

He mounted up and left the ranchyard by Magnusson's route. There was some light left, and after a mile and a half of hard riding Talbot spotted him. The rancher had slowed to a trot.

"It's Talbot. I'm coming up behind you."

"Get out of here. This is my problem. I'll solve it."

"I'd like nothing better."

Magnusson turned to him. "Then why are you here?"

"It's not Suzanne's fault she's your daughter."

Magnusson laughed derisively. "You fool. I sent that Mex gunman, Rag Donnelley, and my son out to *kill* you!"

"Well, the jokes on you, Magnusson. Donnelley and your son are dead, and in case you forgot, that Mexican has Suzanne."

Magnusson reined his horse to a sudden stop and looked at Talbot with fire in his eyes. Talbot stopped and faced him, reading his mind, seeing his hand edge toward the holster on his hip. He could hear the man take a slow, deep breath through his nose.

Talbot said, "Try it, Magnusson. I'd like nothing better than to settle this right here and now. But think about it—you kill me, you kill your daughter. You can't bring her back alone. Not with that bullet in your shoulder. From the looks of your coat, you're about to bleed dry."

Magnusson studied him for a long moment, lips quivering with restrained emotion. "When this is over . . ." he said tightly, and reined his horse back along the trail.

"You got that right," Talbot agreed.

They rode together in truculent silence. The night came down until there was only a smudge of gray in the west and the breeze had settled. It was cold, but the high, heavy clouds tempered it some.

A single wolf howled in the distance, like the savage soul of the night itself. The horses clopped on the frozen ground. Otherwise, all was silent.

When they came to a ravine, Magnusson dismounted and walked over to the edge. He stood staring down for so long that Talbot finally followed suit.

Below huddled a low-slung cabin in the brushy horseshoe of a frozen creek. The windows cast light on the barren ground, and the stovepipe emitted the tang of river willow and ash. A horse moved under a tarpaulin cover supported by willow poles.

Magnusson took a breath, hefted his rifle, and started down.

"Hold on," Talbot whispered. "He could be layin' for you."

Ignoring him, Magnusson continued down the slope. Talbot cursed, turning back to his horse and shucking his Winchester, then followed the rancher down the hill to the shelter. Magnusson peered around at the cabin, cursed aloud, and jacked a shell in the chamber of his Henry.

Suddenly both hands fell to his sides, and he staggered back against the wall.

"You're getting weak," Talbot said. "Stay here while I take a look."

He glanced at the cabin, then ran to its south wall. Hearing the sound of low, muffled screams, he pressed his back against the weathered cottonwood logs, sidestepped slowly to the small, sashed window, and peered in.

He had to blink several times to clarify the image—a bare-breasted Suzanne straddling the naked gunman on an enormous bear blanket spread on the packed earth floor.

A lantern burned on a table and a fire shone around the doors in the wood-burning stove. On Suzanne's lovely head rested the gunman's round-brimmed, black felt hat.

She was smiling . . . laughing.

Her raven curls bounced on her naked back as she rode the gunman like a horse, and the sounds emitting her parted lips were combinations of screams, groans, high-pitched laughs, and giggles.

"You're my savior, José!" she yelled. "You've *saved* me!"

The gunman's hands kneaded her breasts. His head tipped back, revealing two rows of small white teeth beneath his brushy black mustache. He was wiggling his toes and singing.

Suddenly the door burst open and in stepped King Magnusson, rifle jutting out from his waist. Talbot froze, heart pumping.

"Daddy!" Suzanne screamed.

Silence.

King stood there staring, still as a stone.

Talbot ran around the cabin to the door yelling, "King—*don't!*"

He was too late.

The rifle barked once, twice. As Talbot turned the corner

it barked a third time. Following close on its heels was the crack of a pistol.

Magnusson staggered back out of the cabin. He dropped the rifle and slumped to his knees.

Talbot slammed his back up against the cabin wall and peered through the open doorway, swinging his rifle inside. Crouched low, one hand pressed against the back wall, the other clutching a silver-plated revolver, the naked gunman fired.

The bullet tore splinters from the door frame six inches from Talbot's chin. Talbot fired his Winchester, standing the man up against the wall. The pistol shot into the ceiling. Talbot fired into the gunman three more times, the smoking rifle jumping in his arms. The man rolled along the wall and fell on his back.

Talbot ran into the cabin and knelt next to Suzanne. She lay on the rug with an arm flung across her face, as if shielding her from the light. One of Magnusson's rifle shots had gone through her wrist, breaking it. The other two had gone through her chest.

She was dead.

Talbot sighed and cursed, ran his hand down his face. He hung his head and knelt there for a long time.

He'd never felt so old.

Where would it end?

When would the blood ever end?

Finally he stood and pulled King Magnusson's lifeless body into the cabin, went out, and closed the door behind him.

CHAPTER 30

IT TOOK TALBOT a good three hours to ride to Canaan. When the town's main street closed in around him, as dark as a graveyard, he was chilled to the bone and more tired than he'd ever felt in his life.

He woke the hostler at the livery barn. "Stable my horse and give him a good rubdown, will you?"

"At this hour?"

"You want my business or don't you?"

"It's gonna cost you."

"No, it's gonna cost you. Give me a hundred dollars, and the horse is yours."

The old man blinked. "What? You just bought him last week for two hundred."

"Don't look a gift horse in the mouth," Talbot said. "I won't be needing him any longer. I'm taking the train the hell out of here."

"Thought you were *from* here."

"I am."

Muttering, the man retrieved a key from his desk and opened a small safe sitting under a pile of account books and catalogs. He counted a hundred dollars into Talbot's outstretched hand.

"I reckon I can't blame you," he said. "After what happened here today, just outside those doors, I'm about to pack up and try my luck in Glendive."

"What happened?"

"Didn't you hear? The sheriff was killed just down the street by King Magnusson. Verlyn Thornberg, too, and a handful of his riders. Main Street was like a damn battlefield. We were all day cleaning up and carting the bodies up to the undertaker's."

"So that's where Magnusson got that bullet in his shoulder," Talbot said thoughtfully.

"Say again?"

"You know the old trapper's cabin on Little Wibaux Creek?"

"Sure. Charlie Gallernault used to hole up out there."

"Well, King Magnusson and his daughter are out there now. Dead. Send the undertaker out for the bodies, will you?"

The stableman stood there looking flabergasted. "Holy shit in a handbasket!"

Talbot turned to strip his saddle from his horse. "You'll find Mrs. Magnusson at Bernard Troutman's in Big Draw."

Saddle slung over his shoulder, Talbot walked over to the hotel and pounded on the door. After ten minutes the woman proprietor came to the door in an old duster and nightcap, looking haggard and worried and wielding a shotgun.

"I don't take in customers this time of the night," she said. "Not after what happened here yesterday."

Talbot sighed, genuinely exhausted. "I don't blame you, ma'am, but I'd sure appreciate an exception to the rule. Sleep is all I'm after."

She studied him. She let the heavy gun sink toward the floor and drew the door wide. "A man out this late can be up to little good," she admonished.

Talbot sighed. "Thank you. Much obliged."

When he'd gotten situated in his room, he stripped down to his long johns and crawled under the covers with a groan and a sigh. As tired as he was, he thought he'd fall right to sleep. Instead he lay there, his mind whirling like a windmill in a steady gale.

Coming home to a little peace and quiet. That was a good one. Almost as good as finding his lovely Pilar stretched out in the barn with her throat cut.

Thinking of her made him think of Jacy, and his heart twisted counterclockwise and gave an additional thump. She was the only thing homey about this place, and if he stayed for anyone or anything it would be for her. But that was over now, before it had even gotten started.

It was just as well. He didn't belong here anymore, and he knew Jacy could never belong anywhere else.

He rolled several cigarettes and smoked them down to nubs, lying there in the dark, staring up at the ceiling, his mind torturing him with all the death he'd seen over the past few hours, of Suzanne lying there on the bear rug beside the gunfighter—murdered by her own adoring father.

And it had all started with greed.

Jacy had said it best: "They all died like hell, like nothing means a goddamn thing."

Talbot didn't fall asleep until practically dawn. He woke four hours later to bright winter sunlight filling his room. The light was so merry golden, the sky so cold-scoured blue over the false wooden fronts across the street, he wondered for a moment if the bloody events of yesterday had been a nightmare and all was right with the world.

It was a fleeting notion, gone before he'd buckled his gun around his waist and headed out the door with his saddle on his shoulder.

"Help you, mister?" the depot agent said through the window.

"Yeah, I need a ticket for the next train, whenever that is."

"Due in at twelve-fifteen, just like it says on the chalkboard over yonder. Where you headed?"

"What?"

"Where you headed."

Talbot thought, looking around. "Ah . . . I don't know . . ."

The agent planted his arms on the counter and scrutinized Talbot under his green eyeshade. "Mister, you mean to tell me you want a ticket, but you don't where you're *goin'!*"

Talbot turned sideways and looked around the station some more. "Well, I reckon that's the long and short of it."

"Who you runnin' from?"

Talbot looked at the man. "What's that?"

"Who you runnin' from? The law?"

"No," Talbot said thoughtfully, rubbing a hand over his chin. "No, I'm just runnin'." Irritation creeping into his voice, he said, "Listen, mister, why don't you just give me a ticket for as far as the train goes, and I'll get off somewhere between here and there."

The man raised his hands. "Don't get mad at me. You're the one doesn't know where he's goin'." He sighed and glanced at the schedule chalked on the board. He shook his head. "Just anywhere that looks good, eh, cowboy? Doesn't sound like much of a life to me. Well, let's see . . . that'll be twelve dollars and fifteen cents, payable in cash only."

Talbot paid the man, took his ticket, and picked up his saddle. "Much obliged," he said, and headed out the door.

He had an hour and a half to wait for the train, and he decided the best place to do it was at the saloon. As he stepped up on the boardwalk he saw that the big plate-glass window was gone, replaced by boards.

He shook his head and walked inside and ordered a beer

and a shot. He asked the apron to keep them coming until his train left at twelve-fifteen.

"Where you headed?" the man asked him conversationally.

"None of your goddamn business!" Talbot exploded, and knocked back his shot. "Can't a man get drunk in peace around here?"

He brooded over several drinks, then moseyed over to the train station at noon.

The train was on time. Two drummers, an old lady, and a cowboy got off, and Talbot got on, threw his saddle on one seat and sat in another across the aisle. There were only a handful of people aboard, reading illustrated newspapers and conversing in hushed tones.

Talbot rolled a cigarette and sat waiting for the train to depart. He was halfway through the quirley when something blocked the sun beating through the window to his left.

Turning, he saw Jacy sitting atop a tall brown horse. She looked in at him, squinting her eyes against the reflected light, breath puffing around her face.

Talbot got up and walked outside. Jacy rode over to meet him.

"Figured I'd find you here," she said.

Talbot shrugged. "Yeah, well, I guess it's time to move on."

"What happened?"

"They're all dead."

Jacy nodded. "I'm sorry about Suzanne."

Talbot nodded.

"And I'm sorry about what I said back there at Magnusson's. I was wrong."

Talbot shrugged. "You'd been through a lot. I'd just been through a little more."

"I guess." Jacy looked around. "Well . . ."

"Good-bye, Jacy."

She turned her green eyes to him and nodded. "Be seein' you."

"You bet."

"Good-bye." She tried a smile, reined her horse around, and rode away.

Talbot called after her, "Throw some flowers on Dave's grave in the spring, will you?"

She turned, gave a nod, and turned away, heading down Main.

Talbot stood there for several minutes. When the conductor yelled, "All a-board!" he got back on the train as it chuffed away from the depot.

But when the train was gone, he was standing again on the siding, in the steam the locomotive had left behind. He had his saddle on his shoulder.

He stared across the platform. Jacy sat atop her horse just beyond the station house, looking at him and grinning.

"How in the hell did you know?" Talbot said with mock severity.

Jacy shrugged. "No man in his right mind would leave a woman like me."

Talbot laughed. Shaking his head, he moved toward her.